THE FICTIONALIZER

A NOVEL

Michael Schulze

To Gary —
my friend.
- Michael
2022

Cover design by Michael Thoresen and Gary Koepke.

Cover image by Scy Heidekamp of Seyhan Lee.

Fourth edition, revised, 2022

The writing of this novel was partly supported by grants from the National Endowment for the Arts and ITT (through the Fulbright program). All characters and events in the book are fictionalized.

Published by eBookIt,
publishing@ebookit.com

ISBN-13: 978-1-4566-3847-4 (Paperback)
ISBN-13: 978-1-4566-3908-2 (Hardcover)
ISBN-13: 978-1-4566-3844-3 (Ebook)

Praise for *Love Song*

Michael Schulze's previous novel (available on Kindle):

"To read *Love Song*, a work twenty years in the creation, an audacious and uncompromising descent into the American fascination with violence and the contemporary pornography of horror, is to be abruptly within the terrifying/intriguing sphere of brutal novelty, something 'deep, formless, and profoundly dangerous.' It plays with genres—the horror story, the play-within-a-play, the psychosexual mystery-thriller—in streams of language that test the weight-bearing capacity of the printed page . . . ."

-Joseph Dewey, from the *Review of Contemporary Fiction*, October 2003

"As well as the stylistic qualities, I like the attitude of this book. Not the puling whine of the postmodernist, the cringing minimalist—but good muscular revulsion, a cadenced roar against the nastiness of humanity ...."

-Laura Argiri, author of *The God in Flight*

Customer reviews:

"You'd need bionic nerves to take on this novel. *Young* bionic nerves. The book is drenched in sex and violence. And monsters. And paranoia. It made me feel titillated, repelled, baffled, and indicted all at the same time.

Still, the narrative, at least at the beginning, barrels like a semi rolling downhill, and even at the end, when the text begins to break down into seemingly random words and letters, the momentum holds. How the author does that, I don't know. The observations are acute; the language has a sort of vibrating flatness, like an obscene joke being told with a face so straight you could roll a marble across it ...."

-Sue Cologgi

"*Love Song* is a highly creative, multidimensional effort combining a detective story, subconscious undertones, and a myriad of characters in a fantasy that's surprisingly readable. This is the book Stephen King might write if he were willing to take the time .... It's a fascinating *tour de force* that works on many levels ...."

-Doug Grant

What matters most is how well you walk through the fire.

-Charles Bukowski

Editor's Note

This book is a labor of love. It had to be, because every step of its creation was a screaming nightmare.

I write this to explain the odd structure of this narrative. I've divided it into four parts. The first three alternate between first-person and third-person accounts. The first-person passages are based on parts of a journal kept by Waldo Stanton, a high-technology executive in New York City in the pre-Angelic year 1999. The journal was retrieved from the office of Alpha Security Systems chief James Gate and given to me by Rebirth team members.

Why didn't I just clean up the journal and have it published? Because at the time he was writing, Mr. Stanton was under the influence of a very strong sedative and hypnotic called Duadine. He was typing on an advanced, classified palmtop PC with a small onscreen keyboard. In addition, he frequently made entries under severe duress. The results are evident in his writing, which for the most part is garbled, incoherent and often incomprehensible.

I've done what I can. When journal entries could be mostly understood, I edited them for typos, grammar and style. When entries were insufficient, I relied on the memories of participants in the story to help me write third-person passages. Part IV of this book took place after Mr. Stanton had stopped writing, so it is entirely in third person.

The perceptive reader may notice that the first-person and third-person passages in Parts I-III alternate in a regular pattern. For the most part this is coincidence. But I admit that I took some liberties to reinforce the design, for aesthetic and thematic reasons (please see Dr. Artak Molotov's comments in this regard).

This approach also allowed me to insert some explanatory sections, such as the back story of Amutha Dharmalingam.

As for the switches between present tense and past tense, I did this for the standard editorial reason—to speed up or slow down the action. Or sometimes because I felt like it.

Why did I undertake this effort? Because I was asked to do so by the Federation Emperor himself. He granted me full use of the archives of the Institute for Pre-Angelic Studies, which funded this project throughout its troubled genesis. I thank the institute's staff for their unstinting and generous support.

After three long years of labor on this literary jumble, I must admit that I've lost track of where Waldo Stanton ends and I begin. All I can say is that I leave the rest up to Fate—or whatever constitutes Fate these days.

-Michael Schulze
Years 1-3
Bora Bora Interdimensional Federation

Contents

I. JOEY

10/31/99 My son died today. This is not easy to write. I alternate between periods of icy emptiness and black, convulsive sorrow. But I guess I should start this journal to ease the pain. Or whatever. At least Molotov says I should.

I also feel relief. It's difficult to imagine any fulfilling future for a protoplasmic blob confined to a glass tank filled with saline solution, only one orifice, combination mouth/anus, big purple lips, feeds on fish food.

Still, Joey seemed secure enough in his aquarium. And I was just starting, these past few months, to crack his transmissions—when suddenly, with no warning, he separated into slender strands of slime.

I was in my office monitoring his forebrain activity when the screen erupted. I was mesmerized at first, sensing with a cold metaphysical shudder that I was witnessing a doorway to a higher order. Then, of course, I realized that something was terribly wrong and rushed into the lab and saw the mess.

First, I felt joy at Joey's release, breathing thanks that he'd been freed of his disgusting corporeal prison. I felt guilt for reasons I don't want to go into. And I felt bitter disappointment, cursing the sky that the enigma of my son, after all this work, and at such an untimely moment, should go unsolved.

We'd been so close! His messages lately, suggesting in their repetition of elements an emerging personal code, had filled me with excitement; I'd hoped against hope that my instructions would provide the bridge he needed. He'd been using, more or less, the alphabet I'd fed him, adapting it to those frighteningly intricate designs made of random signs and numbers that he'd transmitted for some time. Perhaps now, I thought, we'd at last be able, or begin to be able, to talk, and I could verify three nagging suspicions:

1) that Joey had possessed one of the most advanced brains ever known,
2) that Amutha's heightened psychic sensitivity since his birth had been a response to our son's own powers, and
3) that he'd wanted desperately to tell us something.

Waldo decided to explore his feelings of guilt. Dr. Artak
Molotov, his psychiatrist at the Ronald Reagan Fulfillment Center
in Manhattan, who first introduced him to the Alphagraph in '95,
had told him that these kinds of playbacks could advance his cure.

During Waldo's initial stay at the Center, subsequent to the first of
his blackout experiences, the Doctor advised Waldo to surrender
himself to "the baptism of the document." "It's the principle
behind confession," Molotov said: "Turn yourself into an image of
yourself. Murder, yes—as many premodern cultures have
perceived—but resurrection, daybreak too; have you heard the
phrase *cruore ejus roseo gustando, vivimus Deo ....*" Molotov
flashed his familiar looney-tunes grin, brushing his scant gray hair
back—a grandiose, oddly effeminate gesture—then his eyes rolled
up and his fingers snapped out a castanet *cha-cha-cha* pattern, as
they often did when he grew excited.

"Transform yourself into fiction, my boy ... the only way to the
one true place ...."

As with many of Molotov's pronouncements, Waldo found this
both exalted and ridiculous. But he took Molotov's advice and
began carrying his Solo Utopia palmtop, a pocket-size PC with a
snap-down protective cover, smaller and lighter than commercial
versions and available only to certain denizens of the military/
industrial complex. He pecked away at it regularly, feeling in the
process a watered-down version of the brain probe the doctor had
administered to him for three months earlier in the year.

The Alphagraph hardware was simple enough—a standard EEG
setup—but the software was phenomenal. The machine acted as a
one-way, subject to administrator, direct-from-cerebrum
communications device. Its sophisticated translation algorithms
turned the standard firings and suppressions of a subject's
neuronal dance into a series of letters, symbols and pictures that
came surprisingly close to making sense, with the elusive but

intimate quality of a dream language. And generally, over time, the quality of the output improved, with linguistic content increasing and spurious signals declining. In Joey's case, the result was similar to an automatic diary of sorts, bypassing most of the censorship functions implicit in, say, the act of writing a sentence.

As with most breakthrough technologies, this one had begun as a defense project—in this case for use in military interrogations. Alpha Inc., which had developed the system under a contract with DARPA, made it available for limited civilian use in 1993. Only with a grant from Alpha (awarded with the help of Molotov—the Center was an Alpha subsidiary) could Waldo afford one for Joey.

At first, Waldo was driven by paternal feelings: What better way to discover the inner thoughts and feelings of this mute, blind catastrophe that Amutha and he had created? What better way to discern and perhaps satisfy Joey's needs … his hopes, if any?

There were certain complications of course—most notably the oozy, viscous quality of the skin covering Joey's ganglial cluster, which made it almost impossible to attach electrodes. After some experimentation, Waldo found that sutures worked best. But then, when he plugged Joey in, the monitors froze; error messages pointed to some sort of overload.

Alpha brought in a technician named Marty, who reported that Waldo's son had unusually high-speed brainwaves. After a few weeks he came back with a customized damper. Waldo and Marty reprogrammed the software, spliced in the damper … and got the intricate designs mentioned above, which immediately knocked Amutha into one of her trances. This surprised them not a little, as Amutha was blind—though it's possible that the designs produced certain resonances that the sightless could register.

Anyhow, Marty grew pretty excited. He'd been into the Alphagraph since soon after its declassification and was an expert at deciphering output. One day he pointed at a particularly dense section that resembled Mayan pictograms.

"Thought we'd get hysteric-schizophrenic patterns here—how else do you deal with that kind of sensory deprivation? But this … I've never seen." Marty gnawed at his lip as his finger drifted over the intriguing passage. "Maybe it's a random signal. But I have a feeling something ectropic is going on. There's a repeated pattern here, a clear expression of order."

He stabbed at the cluster and grinned. "Your boy's growing up fast!"

The trouble was, what was Joey trying to say? And how could they translate it? That was when Marty disappeared again and returned after several weeks with an Alphagraph connected by a tangle of wires to a Cray T3E supercomputer.

The upshot, Marty said, was that he'd figured out a way to *broadcast into* the brain, as opposed to the Alphagraph's read-only mechanism.

So they began trying to teach Joey to read. They started with a first-grade syllabus. When that didn't work, they simplified it. After four months they were down to a routine used to teach a few words to chimps.

No use. Joey seemed to be using letters as design elements only, and there was no evidence he understood their transmissions.

He tried, though. Waldo was certain of it. And now, when he looked back, imagining the agonies Joey must have gone through trying to comprehend—and when Waldo recalled his own fierce ambition, pushing the boy, pushing, though Joey was still so young—Waldo wondered if his input had ultimately caused his son's destruction: whether he, and only he, was responsible for Joey's gruesome self-liquidation, from desperation or despair.

11/3/99 At the funeral, I slipped an agent an unmarked brown envelope. He faded into the crowd. Joey had of course attracted quite an audience: His name had been news since his birth, even more so since we'd modified the Alphagraph. What had begun as a simple scientific inquiry had transformed, for Marty and me, into a full-time business.

We ran the interoffice parts through an Alpha internal, proprietary computer system called the Data Encoder and Transmission Habilitator (DEATH) 2000. You needed specialized hardware to use it, and the system employed a new, highly secure communications technology called a virtual private network (VPN), which piggybacked on the Internet.

"I like the Internet," I told Marty. "Whoever invented it should get a raise."

He gave me one of his patented limpid looks, which I'd long known to be camouflage.

"That depends on your definition of '*whoever*.'"

I decided not to respond to that.

I'm copying this in:

New York Times 7/7/98

COMPUTER CONDITIONING STIRS DEBATE

In a hastily called Senate-House conference, top legislators met today to discuss the implications of a product launch announced last week by Alpha Inc., the international computer, telecommunications, and military hardware and software conglomerate. The new device is called the "Cablemaster" and can reportedly condition minds by computer.

The Cablemaster, invented by computer technician Martin Weinstein and Alpha technical analyst Waldo Stanton, father of "Joey the Blob," the infamous mutant born in 1995, will be manufactured and sold by a new Alpha subsidiary called Master Control Systems.

(Here the article shows Marty and me standing together. In the photo, we look a lot alike—the same sandy hair, broad forehead, and slim build, though Marty is about two inches taller than me.)

Initial indications are that lawmakers are more enthusiastic than not. "This product has enormous potential for breakthroughs in the psychiatric, education, sports, incarceration, and other fields," stated a group of Senate supporters. "And think of what it can do for advertising." Meanwhile, protesters who burst into the conference chanting DEATH TO ALPHA! were dispersed by police, who arrested five.

11/3/99 Returning home, I guided a sobbing Amutha by the elbow. She clutched a white rose she'd salvaged from our ceremony.

Meanwhile I tried to lose our tail in an alley. But as usual he followed us home. I peered out the window, shivering. He stood across the street under a lamppost, wearing a fedora and lighting a cigarette like a thug from a film noir. I phoned Dr. Molotov.

"It's that Waldo again, doctor. He's returned …."

Waldo didn't remember his birth of course, but according to his father he was born only a minute or so before his brother, who resembled Waldo exactly except for the fact that he was dead. A few seconds later, so was his mother.

Dr. Molotov seemed delighted by this. "This explains your obsessive fear of mirrors. You've no doubt experienced the strange fascination/repulsion caused by the sight of one's reflection while under the influence of LSD. I took the stuff once in '67 and saw pink insects with stiff black hairs scuttling from my eye sockets, bathed in soft amber light." One was not always sure whether Dr. Molotov's asides had therapeutic intention. "It's standard *doppelgänger* stuff, my boy, old hat, really, except for this interesting criminal aspect. You've sublimated the Quest/Hate for the Dead Twin into a modern narcissistic/paranoid psychosis." He grew somber. "Bad form, really. Two victims already, more to come probably. If you want to lose your shadow you'll have to embrace him."

"How?"

Molotov wasn't listening. He opened his desk drawer, removed a Havana cigar and fished a matchbook from his shirt pocket. He performed a ritual with cutting, smelling, lighting and vigorous sucking and then settled back in his chair, contemplating the ceiling.

He'd done this a few times before. Waldo wished he wouldn't. Cigars stink.

Molotov pawed through Waldo's file and extracted a photograph.

"Who is this person?"

Waldo could have sworn it was a picture of himself as a boy— though how could he tell, with quality like that? The shot was

21

horribly focused, overexposed, with scratches running through it like on a World War I newsreel.

"Who could say?"

Molotov nodded, bemused. "Who indeed? Who indeed?" and tossed the photo back in the file, giving it a pat.

Waldo expected him to continue, but instead he reached casually behind his patient's ear and produced a vial. Waldo felt a flood of relief. It was part of their routine.

"Keep writing then." His voice was affectionate. "It will help, I promise. And take more"—Molotov tossed him the pills—"of these."

But the sedatives weren't working. Sooner or later, Waldo knew, another person would fall victim to his condition—only after the blackout would he see it wasn't Waldo he'd attacked. And what would happen then? Would Amutha, or Marty, the two people in the world he held most dear, turn against him—especially if it was one of them, god forbid, that he went for? Would Alpha oust him due to mental instability? Would he be committed to an asylum— only to be encabled and zombified by the very machine he'd helped invent?

Mental institutions were among Master Control Systems' biggest customers.

Waldo shrank at the thought of being reduced to a drone ward of the state, leaving Amutha to fend for herself amid the towers, tunnels and shrieking furniture of this labyrinthine city.

Meanwhile, needless to say, none of these developments had helped ease the tension he'd been feeling since enlisting as a spy for his employer's biggest competitor.

11/5/99 My employer. The story starts in 1994, when Amutha and I drifted to New York City, where I found a job with Alpha. I had computer skills of a sort; the company taught me more at an upstate camp, then parceled me out to subsidiaries. It was then that I learned enough about the DEATH system to interest Dr. Drago Dark five years later.

It was also in 1994 (some months before Joey's birth) that I began to have the first of my paranoid visions. Not that I hadn't had fantasies before, but never had they flared with such violence. Perhaps it's the hideous topography of this city, its spaces grafted together with spiky, flower-like day-glo graffiti that only begin to suggest whole words, that sparked the crisis.

Whatever the case, the rest of the story, as related by the *Times* in 1995, tells of a retail executive who, walking home from his office, got his face grated into a subway ventilation system.

"Waldo!" passersby reported me screaming. *"You fuck! You fuck! You fuck!"*

The second incident, involving a female dry cleaner clerk on the Upper East Side, was a depressing replay of the first.

I'd have certainly been incarcerated had not Alpha intervened, pointing to my clear mental disability. Instead I was treated on an outpatient basis at the Ronald Reagan Fulfillment Center. There I came under the care of Dr. Molotov, who, in a then experimental program funded by DARPA, showed me texts written directly by my mind. Reading them often left me shaking—though afterwards, after Waldo had left, I did indeed feel better for it.

According to a recent missive, Dr. Dark was getting irritable; he wanted more information. So he dared be dissatisfied with the reports Waldo was feeding him? Who did he think Waldo was— Mr. Light himself? So far he'd transferred material relative to upcoming super-taser and laser pistols under Pentagon contracts, antigravity in advanced design stages, not to mention work on intangibility and lucid dreaming that made even the levitation stuff look tame—and he was asking for more? Didn't Dark know he could blow this operation if he showed he knew too much? And what about his encryption? How safe was that?

To be sure, the compensation was excellent—a couple of million dollars so far, all stashed in facilities in the Caribbean, the English Channel, Singapore, and other accommodating places—but Waldo was running incredible risks. Each time he probed deeper there was a chance of triggering hidden alarms. Of course as MCS co-founder he had some of this info at his disposal already, but some of the files he'd been surveilling lately resembled goddam videogames. It took every ounce of concentration to finish in the time given to seasoned employees—any longer and a light blinked in L.A. Plus the false data decoys planted to fool the casual user; punch a dummy entry and the system went down howling. The only thing he could do then was get out fast.

This recent request for dirt on "Operation Renaissance," for example—it took two hours to hook up on the sly with a DEATH bank in the Dominican Republic, only to be fed to Kuala Lumpur, then to Berlin, then to New Orleans, then to Beijing, then to Bruges, then to Tel Aviv, then to Prague, then to an Alpha unit in Chicago called Cybersystems, where for only a few seconds he got a design resembling Joey's final pictogram. Waldo was so frozen by déjà vu that he barely bailed out in time. Even so he must have raised some suspicions within the DEATH network.

It didn't make it any easier to find Waldo waiting for him by his apartment. Though he was definitely weaker tonight …. As Waldo approached, a streetlight diffused in his Double's iridescent body.

11/8/99 Molotov insists that he see my journal; I cry no, no, how can I write when I know he'll be reading it? Which is true enough, everything considered; some of this stuff is pretty incriminating. He says the presence of an audience is essential to my cure, but I don't know; the therapy appears to be working anyway. I'm a bit sluggish from the drugs but Waldo seems to be fading out.

"Fading out?"

I nod. He leans forward feverishly. "I hadn't thought so soon. So you've decided to take him on, eh?"

"What?" I play with my hands.

"And your environment lately … any … *intensity* there? Luminosity? Tell me."

I look up sharply.

"And your journal? Is it easier to write? Almost, say— automatic?"

I feel myself flush.

"So. The Waldo you've been sublimating is phasing out of your grasp …."

"I've no idea what you're talking about."

"No need to deny it. Actually I approve of this development." Molotov peers at me intently. "But the consequences of your choice! Have you considered them?"

I don't know what to say. Molotov pauses, thinking—then beams.

"Only way out, though. Meet the Double on its own terms …."

He leans back, claps his hands. "So tell me what you think about Alpha."

"I have to go."

"No you don't. Tell me."

I consider. "Money."

"Anything else?"

"Richard Light."

"Our CEO."

"Yes."

He produces a photograph. "*This* Richard Light?"

I gasp. It's the design from the Operation Renaissance file! I look up, find him taking notes.

"What does this mean?"

He makes a gesture I can't interpret. Impatience? How much does he know? Could he have discovered what I've been doing lately?

"Where did you get that?"

Molotov doesn't respond. His eyes spark. "Soon"—he drums fingers on his desk—"I too shall become part of your storyline. A dangerous move … could be deadly. But I relish the thought. We'll work this out. You and me, my boy."

He grins like a madman.

As Waldo slumped back in bed with a sigh, he considered that there was something to orgasm that made it doubly pleasurable to ejaculate into a blind woman. When he made love to Amutha he felt that he was reaching into some dark secret part of her. And he knew that, in that explosive final moment, something was communicated that doesn't, with most people, normally transfer.

The day before he'd been working in DEATH when the thing went nuts. He'd encountered this phenomenon before—programmers called it "database ventilation." But that didn't mean they understood it. It just so happened that the more advanced a piece of software, the more it seemed to imitate human idiosyncrasies—including, as some people argued, the desire to get high.

Watching the screen, Waldo was stunned by the amount of data hurtling vertiginously past his eyes. (He later found the entire file, purring like a cat, in a server center beneath the Bay of Fundy.) He watched carefully: There was a certain perversity to the choice and arrangement of elements that intrigued him. Marketing reports, advertisements, hieroglyphics, home movies, Hotmails, poems, videos, math equations, cave paintings, software games, academic articles, sex tapes, book excerpts, pop songs, menus, children's drawings, programming manuals … it was as if the machine was striving, somehow, for comprehensiveness. And he was clued by certain blips and long high hysterical squeals to the possibility, yes, that it might even be *enjoying itself.*

(That's why Waldo went to the office when he worked on DEATH at night. He didn't want to wake Amutha, either with security alarms or ventilation.)

In any case … is it possible, Waldo thought, that orgasm is a sort of data shift? Once, as a kid with fever, he had indeed seen his life flash before his eyes …. What exactly did Amutha absorb in bed?

What parts of him, he wondered, moved through her as they both fed into climax?

Later, stretching and smiling lazily, she silenced his fumbled words with a kiss. Amutha was natural about sex, didn't like to talk about it. She curled into his arm, and he settled back, smoking a joint—already lazily anticipating, with fondness and pleasure, those few seconds a few days from now when her blank eyes would go wide once again and those strange guttural sounds she made would once again paint for him those obscure familiar pictures.

11/9/99 **"He gave me** one of his patented limpid looks, which I'd long known to be camouflage." Reading over the last few days' entries, I realize I should explain that.

To begin, I'm not certain there's such a thing as "character." As far as I can judge, the human organism is a waystation of sorts, occupied by a constantly shifting crowd of personalities, with the ego striving mightily to maintain an impression of control— dashing about, suppressing this voice, amplifying that, trying to put a civilized face on things, *hehheh*, pay no attention to that program—a technical difficulty, a fluke!

The ego is merely the voice that yawps the loudest.

Certainly that helps explain my little problem.

So talking about Marty's "character" feels strange—like committing a murder of sorts. Like what Molotov said about images. All I really know is that, out of the sea of souls I've encountered since birth, Marty's is one of the few I've tuned into, immediately and without doubt, as with a homing device.

One outcome of this, I understand, is that I change when I'm around him. I'm brighter, wittier, quicker on the uptake, lord knows why. For some reason the Waldo he experiences is better than the Waldo I usually am.

And maybe the Marty I know is an improved version, and he degrades when I'm away.

All this should be contrasted with the deep cynicism of our business enterprise. At work we put the best spin on it we can: contributions to prison reform, world peace, all that. But deep down we harbor no illusions: We do brainwashing for pay. Maybe that's why we almost never talk about work offsite.

It's a schizoid relationship—and Marty, like me, has a schizoid aspect. He combines the friendly, inquisitive qualities of an innocent with a remote, oddly dispassionate side.

I have no problem with that. Dr. Molotov imparts the same impression, with his bizarre oscillations between half-mad oracularity and teasing kindness. It's reassuring.

Like Marty said: It depends on your definition of *whoever*.

One day Amutha Dharmalingam's eyes roll up and don't roll back.

At dawn Chinese shopkeepers in torn shorts and T-shirts perform tai chi near the shore. Pink, purple light stains the faces of the genuflecting businessmen. Terns and petrels wheel over the beach, complaining.

Amutha bolts down kaya toast with eggs, swigs Milo. She wears white socks and shoes, blue vest over a white short-sleeve shirt, school name on the left breast (SK RIMBA TERJUN). She pecks cheeks: Amma, Appa, Attai. Weighed down by a backpack, she treads along the village's dirt roads, approaching a jungle path.

Fellow schoolgirls join her, all in uniform. Malay, Chinese, Indian. As they enter the murky path, macaques barrage them with junk—sticks, clumps of leaves, coconuts—shrieking and dancing through the canopy. The girls cackle and throw stones back.

Amutha has wide-spaced eyes, high cheekbones, pleasant features. She wears her hair in a pigtail down her back. When she laughs, she covers her mouth to hide her bad teeth. All the girls do.

They climb a hill and emerge onto a broad cleared area. The Strait of Malacca unrolls in the distance behind them. The girls-only school is a two-story cinderblock painted white. They stand on a lawn in rows to listen to the headmaster read the day's business. It's hot. The headmaster, a small, oily, carp-like man, drones on.

Some of the girls faint from the heat and are carted away.

In English class (third period), Amutha takes notes as her fifth grade teacher, Waldo Stanton, explains how to conjugate the verb *to be*. Mr. Stanton, a Peace Corps worker, is a subject of much gossip in Pontian.

There are a half dozen TVs in the village, and in the evenings many of the residents gather in those houses to watch shows like *Combat,* often interrupted by calls to prayer. They also watch advertisements for shiny cars, glittering appliances and other symbols of the purported American good life. Like the other girls, Amutha understands that she'd be very lucky to marry a Mat Salleh (white monkey) and leave this country, with its endless rice paddies, grinding poverty and boring ways.

One of the Malay girls rolls her head back, and her eyes leave their sockets. She emits a strange, high keening noise. Waldo watches in amazement as the other Malay girls in the classroom follow suit. Soon they all sit slumped in their chairs, faces pointed toward the ceiling, warbling.

The Chinese and Indian girls look around, just as surprised as Waldo is.

Waldo lowers his chalk from the blackboard. The keening spreads rapidly through the school.

11/10/99 "One of the most fruitful hypotheses is that schizophrenia is a hereditary disease …. However, it has been difficult to sort out the relative influences of nature and nurture ….

"The idea of studying identical twins to elucidate this problem was suggested as early as 1885 by the English mathematician and geneticist Francis Galton. Today the most widely quoted evidence for a hereditary cause of schizophrenia comes from a study of the disease in identical twins conducted by Franz J. Kallman of the Columbia University College of Physicians and Surgeons. He showed that if one identical twin suffers from schizophrenia, there is an 85 percent chance that the other twin will suffer from the same disorder ….

"In twins, as in other pairs of individuals who are emotionally close, the condition known as *folie à deux* has been commonly observed. The two partners tend to develop shared delusions and symptoms and to become mentally ill at about the same time …."

Article titled *"Folie à Deux"* by Dr. Artak Molotov, in *Frontiers of Psychological Research*, 1996.

I filched the book from Molotov's office when he stepped out.

I wonder if my dead brother was mentally unstable, too.

Every Malay girl in Waldo's classroom is now entranced—along with the Indian girl, Amutha, who sits rapt in the back of the room, eyes rolled up, keening.

Waldo leaves his classroom. He marches to the headmaster's office a few doors away. The headmaster sits at his desk, writing. He seems unaware of the hubbub.

Waldo is twenty-two, self-confident, in your face. "What the fuck is this? You know what this is, don't you?"

The headmaster looks bemused. "Yes."

"Sexual oppression! These Malay girls barely get to see their own bodies! Their brains are twisted by Islam!"

"No. Older than Islam." The headmaster's English is halting but serviceable. "Thousands of years. It happens. We deal."

Waldo gapes. The headmaster's eyes move past him to the doorway, and Waldo turns to see a boy of about 15—Haziq, the school's go-fer, dressed in white shorts and a T-shirt sporting the words *Another Brick in the Wall*.

The headmaster nods; Haziq nods back and prepares to leave. The headmaster stops him and gives Waldo a dreamy look.

"You go, Mr. Stanton. Educational."

Haziq grins and gestures for Waldo to come. Waldo follows the boy to the school's driveway. Below them they survey the jungle and the Strait beyond, dotted with multicolored fishing boats. The buildings of Pontian cluster around a bay.

"Where are we going?"

"You see." The boy takes Waldo's hand and leads him down the hill into the jungle. The noise from the girls slowly recedes.

They reach the village, and Haziq takes him to a familiar place— the butcher shop, managed by Ahmad, about 70. Ahmad, bent and unsteady but fit, is the village's bomoh, a combination elder, shaman, counselor, healer, and peacemaker. Waldo loves his halal goat.

Haziq and Ahmad chat a bit; then Ahmad hobbles into the back of the shop. He emerges with a white five-gallon plastic bucket about half full with what looks like blood. Haziq grabs the bucket, and he and Ahmad leave the place. Waldo follows uncertainly.

He catches up. "Haziq. What's that?"

"Lamb blood. Important."

The three head up through the jungle. As they approach the school, Waldo hears the girls still keening.

They enter the school clearing and proceed to the headmaster's office. When the headmaster sees Ahmad he practically doubles over with fawning gratitude.

Once courtesies are over, Ahmad, Haziq and Waldo move from classroom to classroom. Haziq stands close to Ahmad with the bucket ready. In each room, Ahmad dips his fingers into the blood and paints a runny cross on each Malay girl's forehead. A few seconds afterward, the girl's eyes roll back down and she goes silent.

The girls painted with crosses look around confusedly. No memory.

Amazed, Waldo follows as they come to his classroom. Inside, the Malay girls and Amutha continue their racket. Ahmad performs his ritual, and the girls gradually revive.

Ahmad approaches Amutha, scowling. Clearly it disturbs him to see an Indian girl in this state. Tentatively, he paints a cross on her forehead, and she stops singing. Ahmad and Haziq grin—then grow still.

Amutha sits silent, with nothing but white in her eye sockets.

11/11/99 After work Marty and I met at our favorite wind-down spot, Grand Central Station. From the elevated lounge we surveyed the faceless mash of humanity on the concourse, a single fevered, lumpen, pulsating organism.

After some drinks I saw he wanted to bring something up. I went on alert. He tapped a finger meditatively.

"No insomnia problems I hope," he started.

I tried to smile. "No worries."

He settled back, contemplating me. "How's it going at the Reagan Center?"

"Fine."

He leaned forward, gazing solemnly through a strengthening spectral image of Waldo's face. This often happens when I get nervous.

"I'm worried about you. You're not looking good. You still doing that Duadine?"

Now we were on safer ground. Marty is the last person to criticize someone for substance abuse.

"What if I am?"

"Well, I'm just trying to say that, if you've been having some, ah, recurrences lately, why don't you think about meeting some people I know. I don't trust Molotov—don't think he's doing his best for you."

He grabbed me by the wrists, looking distressed. I felt a stab of shame.

"You know we've got Alpha by the balls. The contract doesn't expire for nine more years. It's in their interests to have you committed—one less thing between them and the Cablemaster. It was routine when they got you out the first time, and when it happened again they were into Joey, thought he might yield something." He paused.

"But now I suspect they might be giving Molotov instructions."

I was no longer in control of my face. I felt like I was talking to Waldo himself. I tried something reassuring.

"Rest easy. I was being tailed for a while but he went away."

"You sure?"

I laughed harshly. "Delete, Marty. Classic paranoia."

"Maybe so."

He reached over and stroked my head. The intimacy made me shudder.

"But look at your hair. Uncombed. Been that way for days. And your new beard …." He grew grave. "Have you been covering the mirrors in your place again?"

I cringed. I couldn't find words. He eyed me dissatisfied—then waved a hand.

"Forget it. But don't say I didn't warn you …."

Deep in my heart I know he's right. But I refuse to believe that Molotov isn't on my side.

And maybe something else. Maybe something in Molotov's weird cryptic statements during our last sessions that keeps me going back, tranquilized and obsessed, to Joey's last designs.

After Marty and I parted, both fairly smashed, I took a cab home. Had dinner with Amutha and napped. Wrote in this journal. A bit later I kissed Amutha's hair from behind as she worked on a canvas.

Surprisingly, Amutha is a superb painter. Mainly domestic images —the edge of a table, a pot in a window. By now her work commands fairly high prices. She submits to interviews as long as her questioner never mentions that she's blind.

"Heading out, sweet."

She nuzzles my hand. "Work hard."

To my astonishment, Amutha trusts me. She's never seemed to doubt my faithfulness. Though she does yell at me occasionally for hallucinating.

In the office. It's an off chance, but I've uploaded some of Joey's final communications.

I reckon five more minutes before I get to Operation Renaissance.

Trying to imagine how it all could have happened. Joey plugged into my computer room via the Alphagraph, later the Cablemaster. The computer room linked to DEATH.

This is insane.

Was Joey even smarter than I imagined? What, I'm thinking, if he gradually worked his way into the computer system, then the VPN

… and his last fantastical design was actually—an instruction set? Sure it's farfetched—but then Joey wasn't your normal boy either.

At least that's the long shot I'm calling now as I tap out the rest of this entry and wait for OR.

Bingo.

Waldo was entering a subway car when a shot rang out; a girl near him slumped to the ground spitting blood. He shifted immediately into slo-mo. He could tell that those around him did too, from their slack, transfixed expressions, the lucid glitter in their eyes. In this brief pre-fight-or-flight phase, the only thing activated is the perceptual apparatus, which gives everything nearby the shimmering, deadly focused quality of a fever dream.

She looked to be in her low twenties, in a black leather jacket and miniskirt, with white thigh-high stockings and stack heels. Blood gushed from her mouth; then her legs jerked violently and she went still. Waldo stood on the platform and watched, calm and remote, understanding that she was already beyond the ministrations of the few who'd broken the spell and were kneeling by her side.

Waldo contemplated a poster pasted akilter on a nearby wall. It depicted a lanky young man in a fetal position, levitating two or three feet above a circular mat with a mandala design ringed with red glyphs. Beneath the image were the words:

REBIRTH. COMING YOUR WAY!

Waldo snapped out of slo-mo and leaned weakly against the train, which hadn't moved. From the frantic gesticulating and barking of figures at the periphery of his vision, he gathered they were looking for the killer. A few threw suspicious glances his way.

Thing was—he looked back at the corpse—was he the intended victim, due to his moonlighting lately? If so, who ordered the hit?

The hideous creeping consciousness of conspiracy made his heart bang convulsively.

Was Alpha onto him? Was Dr. Dark backing out for some reason? Or was he getting caught in a crossfire? Was some nameless Third Party sending a message to Dr. Dark and/or Mr. Light?

Waldo couldn't see how anyone could have detected his incursions. Even if he'd triggered an alarm somewhere, his transfers, reroutings and erasures should have covered his tracks.

Which left one conclusion. If Waldo was indeed to have been assassinated tonight, it was Waldo who'd ordered it done.

Dr. Dark, that is.

But why? Why, for chrissake?

11/12/99 In the dead of night I found Amutha on the living room floor in the grip of one of her trances, clutching something.

She was babbling quietly in that unique language of hers, incomprehensible as ever—though, as with Joey's designs, I've always felt myself on the verge of understanding it … this haunting extraterrestrial music, familiar as a suppressed memory, knowingly intimate.

I found a tape player and pressed RECORD.

What was she holding? I kneeled and slowly rolled her over.

A frozen turkey.

Bought well before Thanksgiving. Amutha always shops the sales.

After a moment's astonishment I found I wasn't all that surprised. I've found her pressing objects to herself in the past—pillows, sofa cushions and the like.

It makes sense. Like what I said about my "character" around Marty. Because as many people know, walk toward a vintage TV with antenna problems and the picture often clears—walk away and it fuzzes out again. The human body is a superb receiver. Which is clearly why Amutha refers to her trances—what she can remember of them—as "programs" …. She channels the data; she's a tuning mechanism.

Think of all the broadcasts feeding through the hapless flesh at unheard-of frequencies. And if my own body is such a miracle of reception, it's occurred to me—what about Joey? The boy was composed for the most part of highly compressed, undifferentiated cells, a raw slab of meat in many ways, with only an oversized ganglial cluster, vestigial sex, and tiny fingers poking from either side to provide a clue to his origin.

How many and what kinds of signals would such an organism attract? And again, was that why Amutha was hugging *meat* to her belly as she channeled?

In any case, whatever she did tonight marked a breakthrough. Because for the first time in my experience, she uttered a phrase in English. I'm convinced it came from elsewhere, for she didn't speak in her own voice—rather, it was the voice of a little boy.

And now, as she lies sleeping on the floor, curled up, her head on a pillow that I fetched, and I listen to the tape over and over again while typing this … I can't stop crying. For it's very clear whose voice came through Amutha tonight, what entity struggled to make contact through the lonely void of nether space.

It spoke only two words.

"Hi ... dad ...."

Waldo enjoyed playing with Amutha's hands. Lying in bed with her, or hanging out on the couch, he'd turn them over and over. Black backs, white palms. Black backs, white palms. She'd smile tolerantly as he played, his eyes glazed.

Now, around 4 a.m., she crept into the bedroom, undressed, got in beside him. He fingered the hairs on the back of her neck, gazing at her round white eyes in the half-light from the hallway.

Amutha was a beautiful woman, but her eyes were like those of most blind people—discomforting, even ugly. It's only on TV that blind people have pleasant-looking eyes. But after all these years with her, Waldo failed to perceive a defect and saw in Amutha only pure unearned kindness. For it didn't take much to conclude that Waldo Stanton, with his sordid profession, creepy psychosis, and seedy undercover activities, was unworthy of this loveliness, this intelligence, this steady affection.

After the episode with the keening girls in Malaysia, Waldo had found that he couldn't get Amutha out of his head. She never recovered her eyesight and was eventually moved to a school for the blind in Johor Bahru. Waldo visited her whenever he could, and then, when his Peace Corps stint was up, offered to adopt her. Her parents, unable to afford proper care for a blind child, agreed after laying down a few ground rules (No. 1: No sex). Waldo, whose motives were pure, had no problem with that.

Back in the States, Waldo took excellent care of Amutha. He enrolled her in school (after having her teeth fixed). When she turned 18, he asked her parents if he might marry her—if she accepted, of course—and they were delighted. When he proposed, Amutha squealed with happiness and wrapped herself around him like a snake. A while later her parents moved the whole family to the United States, where they invested heavily in motels.

For the past year or so, Waldo and Amutha had often spent moments awake in bed talking about the home they hoped to build in the West, where they could finally escape this lousy city with its hideous landscapes like the last fantastic emissions of a dying brain. Unfortunately the mortgage payments on their brownstone apartment were astronomical, and Manhattan sucked away the rest of their earnings. The savings from Waldo's Alpha gig, coupled with those from Amutha's job as a court stenographer, seemed impressive, but the money still wouldn't pay for the house he imagined for her and support them in retirement. At age 44, Waldo needed to be thinking about their future. That's why he'd signed on with Dr. Dark: some extra income to ensure financial security for the rest of their lives.

Now she nuzzled his cheek and kissed him. "I must've had a fit again."

"Yes."

He didn't mention the voice that had come through her—or the girl he'd seen die.

"An amazing thing happened tonight," he said.

She caressed his chest, waited.

"I discovered Joey was intelligent."

She laughed quietly. "I could've told you that."

"I know. But I found proof. He cracked the security code to a classified Alpha project. The last design that he sent to the Cablemaster fit into the block like a key."

She stiffened. "What?"

He nodded, brushing her cheek with his own. "Joey was smarter than me. I can't tell you what it took to get through that block. It was a type of graphic cipher I've never encountered before."

He glanced at her—her empty eyes stared back. Then her expression fractured.

He cursed himself. This wasn't what he'd wanted. He'd wanted her to be pleased—proud ….

"You're saying Joey knew how to get into a DEATH file?" Tears streaked her cheeks.

Waldo searched for an answer.

"Why didn't he talk to *us*, then?" she said miserably.

Waldo trembled.

Hi … dad ….

He held her close. "I don't know. Maybe he was still too different …."

She cried on his shoulder. He felt pathetic.

Gradually she stopped. They said nothing for a while.

"What was he onto?" she murmured.

"I don't know. Something special—reporting to Mr. Light. A project called Operation Renaissance."

Silence again. Then her voice came, small and determined:

"I think we need to know more about this project."

11/12/99 I should mention that documents in the DEATH system are protected in a variety of ways. First, the VPN, which is highly secure. Second, important documents are protected on multiple levels. You have the initial pass-code, called the block, then some ciphers less complicated, which are called checks. Each check releases more information, allowing medium-level personnel access to some but not all of the file. Each check is booby-trapped with special alarm systems.

What makes the Operation Renaissance security system especially intriguing are the following features:

1) the incredible complexity of the block,
2) the paucity of data on the other side of it—just a code number for Light ("1") and a map of the United States, and
3) the fact that the first check consists of some vocables I've never seen: NAH:::AMAANAA:::NAMAANAA

I mention this because today Dr. Dark repeated, in unusually impatient terms, his request for more dirt on OR.

A few hours after work, Waldo visited Marty on the first floor of the brownstone they shared. (Waldo and Amutha occupied the third and fourth floors, while Marty took the bottom two.) Waldo found his partner, as often, watching TV and popping his favorite drug—one of a number of recently engineered substances called Dr. Omega. Tablets lay scattered over the coffee table. Waldo didn't take the stuff very often—he much preferred Molotov's Duadine—but it had the advantage of imparting the strongest contact high Waldo had ever experienced. Being a high-strung individual, Waldo was susceptible to contact highs anyhow, so entering the living room and seeing Marty's strange crooked grin, he immediately broke into a pleasurable spasm of hiccup-like giggles. He drifted to a chair and popped a pill.

What were contact highs? How did they work?

Waldo lowered the TV's volume to break his question. But as he prepared to speak he paused, struck again by the strange lifestyle of his friend. He saw Marty at 44, an expert on Christian iconography (though he was a non-practicing Jew), a computer genius, unmarried, fairly handsome, and here he sat nodding out in a midtown brownstone. Waldo guessed that Marty, like himself, had always preferred to live a secluded life.

Maybe that was one reason they got along: Marty disliked humanity as much as Waldo did.

One thing they both loved was action/adventure movies. *Star Wars, Die Hard,* stories of the Green Berets and other special forces, sword and sorcery, Western shoot-'em-ups, breathless escapes from impossible situations. They also enjoyed David Cronenberg films. When they weren't watching movies they played first-person shooter video games. Their favorite at the moment was a not yet public release of *Unreal Tournament.*

As part of this, Waldo was a gun nut, though he didn't own a gun himself. Earlier in the day, at the office, he'd been browsing *Guns & Ammo* magazine when he came across an article on the semiautomatic Glock 20 (G20) handgun, introduced in 1991. Black and nasty-looking, it held 10mm caliber bullets in 15-round magazines that packed a serious kick. Waldo was also a fan of assault rifles like those used by SWAT teams.

"What's up," Marty said. Standard opener.

Waldo leaned forward. "What do you know about Dr. Dark?"

"Same thing you do, probably. Operates out of Michigan in a town called Brownwater. Company called BioResearch. A subsidiary of Schwarzcorp."

Schwarzcorp. Alpha's nemesis. Headquartered in Germany. Controlled the lion's share of European and Asian markets.

Waldo nodded thoughtfully. Marty frowned, wondering where his partner was headed.

"What's the deal?"

"Nothing really. Feelers."

"Better money from BioResearch?"

Waldo hated lying to his friend, but what the hell.

"Yeah. But before I think about biting, I'm wondering why they want me on the payroll. I mean, why hire an Alpha tech exec for a biotech program? Do they think I know something I don't?"

Marty shrugged uneasily. "Hardly matters … we got such a good thing going here."

Waldo pressed his point: "But BioResearch? Do you know if they're after something special? Something involving a ... Renaissance project?"

Marty gnawed at his lip. Waldo could see he knew nothing. This was a bad idea; he pulled back.

"Renaissance?" Marty said fuzzily.

Thank god for drugs.

"Ah shit," Marty said. "Don't move west. I'd miss you."

"Not to worry."

Waldo plucked two hits of Dr. O from the coffee table. "To us," he said, downing a pill.

Marty grinned and removed the other pill from Waldo's palm.

11/13/99 Can't sleep. Went to the office and knocked through newsletters in DEATH.

Alpha emerged on the international business scene in the early '80s, child of a dozen or so mergers and takeovers dirtied by rumors of political payoffs and possible homicides while U.S. government complicity was claimed by certain journalists who lost their jobs. The current Alpha logo (a sunrise or sunset, one can't be sure) was introduced in '87. HQ in Hollywood.

Schwarzcorp presents a serious threat, though the two companies have a quasi-symbiotic relationship; that is, they design equipment on common gauges so as not to divide the world into two incompatible networks. They also sign tech-trade agreements on occasion.

Schwarzcorp is an outgrowth of European postwar cartel operations, while Alpha seems to have come from nowhere. No one knows exactly how it works. While the CEO is Light, Alpha's complex web of divisions, subsidiaries, partnerships, proxies, powers of attorney, contractors, and shell companies makes it difficult to pin down any real chain of command—all this further complicated by constant mergers, name changes, patent purchases, reshufflings of personnel, sudden divestitures and acquisitions— and above all Light's own stubborn reclusiveness.

In fact—no matter how much I search—I can't find a photo of Light.

Waldo started awake and found Amutha talking in her sleep. At first she spoke gibberish, then:

"Sun … set."

Then:

"Bi … cycle."

She smiled. For a moment she looked beatific, staring blindly at the ceiling as if all the legions of angels and subangels, rotating around a fantastic white rose, were there. Then she sighed and rolled over.

Soon Waldo heard her snoring.

Now he stared at the ceiling.

Sunset.

Odd.

11/13/99 Christ Amutha what happens if I've fucked up

What happens if I'm a dead man

I don't want to lose you

I don't want you to lose me

Somewhere above the shadows of this looming gray burg the sun sent peeping pink darts of new day to land by some miracle of multiple reflection on the face of the building opposite. Despite the cold, Waldo had opened every window in the place, as he couldn't stand the sight of his face in the glass.

He and Marty usually worked on Saturdays, but he'd decided to beg off. From the bedroom window he watched Marty depart in his BMW. A couple of hours later Amutha tapped her way down the street to go shopping.

Computer room again.

11/13/99 I've done an exhaustive search of DEATH and every other tool at my disposal. Nothing surprising. For BioResearch, press releases on minor product launches, solid but unimpressive financials. Dr. Dark, house, Mercedes, wife, three kids. Boards of directors, over-the-hill business friends, golf on weekends. Pretty ugly guy. Beetle-browed, pendulous lower lip, bug-like eyes.

It's midafternoon. By this time I'm convinced my fears are unfounded. There's no reason I can think of for Dr. Dark, or Schwarzcorp, or Alpha, to want me dead. I'm nothing but a low-level corporate spy.

My proximity to the recent murder was a coincidence.

But if that's the case, why did Molotov show me that photo on Monday? The picture of me as a boy—if indeed it was me?

Why show me a photo with my face *rubbed out*?

This may be another of Molotov's cryptic psychoanalytical ploys. I'll pump him about it next session. Meanwhile I continue to work on the check to the OR file—feeding it more of Joey's final designs.

Alarms sound; I back out.

Well, fuck you too, DEATH!

But I'm onto you, you sonofabitch.

Me and my boy.

On a hunch, Waldo walked a few blocks to the New York Public Library and checked the *Physicians' Desk Reference.*

He glanced around furtively, then tore out a page.

DUADINE

Sedative and Hypnotic

Description: Duadine is a white, crystalline, hygroscopic powder, easily soluble in water. Aqueous solutions, however, decompose and should not be kept more than a day or two. Solutions in propylene glycol are stable indefinitely.

Actions: Barbiturate sedatives act principally at the level of the thalamus and the ascending reticular formation by interfering with the transmission of impulses to the cortex.

Indications: As a hypnotic, for short-term management of insomnia. As a sedative, for relief of anxiety, tension, and apprehension.

Contraindications: Hypersensitivity after repeated use.

Warnings: Psychological and physical dependence may occur. Special care should be exercised in the treatment of emotionally unstable patients. Symptoms of chronic intoxication often include dissociation, paranoid behavior and manifestations of schizophrenia. Abrupt cessation of large doses may result in withdrawal symptoms such as tremulousness, weakness, depression, convulsions, delirium and death.

Dosage and Administration: The average daily dose of Duadine for adults is 10-20 mg. The dose should not exceed 40 mg., though somewhat larger doses may occasionally be necessary for persons with status epilepticus and psychoses. The effects of large doses must be closely watched. Dependence may occur after 60 days of regular use.

Shit, Waldo wondered: *Why didn't I do this before?*

Molotov had been feeding him 100 mg. per day for over six months.

11/13/99 Left the building thinking I'd figured it out. A simple scheme—Dr. Dark had nothing to do with it. Alpha planned to get me committed through chemical aggravation.

Molotov had betrayed me.

I was going to buy liquor.

To my surprise—hadn't Marty warned me?—I was crying. Apparently I'd underestimated how much I'd come to depend on that brilliant, manic, elusive, self-obsessed, pushy, manipulative, doublecrossing, probably drug-addled sonofabitch. I'd grown truly attached to Molotov and suspected he felt the same. And even now I was convinced he remained friendly despite his attempt to poison me.

Molotov's motivation was probably straightforward: cash. I can't say I didn't understand, seeing as I myself was in the blood money business.

But still.

Black clouds hung low over the city, and a chill drizzle fell, turning the streets into a wash of nacreous pinks and grays punctuated by dark, hunched shapes slithering past like fugitive submarine creatures. I wiped my cheeks, grateful for the gloom.

A liquor store approached. I peered through the rain-stained glass at stark fluorescent lighting and two clerks gazing in a trance at a small TV. As I reached the door I heard a soft *pop,* felt my right elbow tingle. Then, with something like clinical interest, I watched the door's grimy Plexiglas fracture into an iridescent web.

Without thinking I went into a crouch and threw myself behind a lamppost. I heard another *pop,* then scrambled on all fours toward an alley to the left of the store. As I entered it I heard a *pop,* felt something slap my right shoe, lurched forward and huddled behind a dumpster.

I waited, numbly watching blood ooze from my shoe. There were no more shots; no one approached. I pulled myself together, stumbled behind the store, dragged myself over a chain-link fence and made my way down another alley onto a street I didn't know.

Sobbing, I hobbled west toward the docks.

I've dropped three Duadine. I write this on my palmtop on a wooden bench on a pier.

"Change, mister?"

Reflexively, Waldo used his good foot to kick the man in the groin. As he collapsed with a groan Waldo followed, landing with his knee on the man's throat.

"What did you say?"

He was a dark-haired, lanky, scrofulous type dressed in rags. Waldo felt a metallic tingling in the back of his throat, like with mescaline or LSD, as he peered furiously at the man's stinking, pockmarked face, watching it seem to shift and bend.

"You fuck!"

"Please! Don't hurt me!"

They regarded each other. Gradually the bum's face came back into focus. Waldo's brain cleared; he slumped by the man's side.

The bum eyed him warily. "Your foot's bleeding."

Waldo pulled out a handkerchief and stuffed it in the hole in his shoe.

"From the elbow too."

Waldo regarded the bloody gash on his jacket and decided to ignore it. He wiped his eyes and shoved himself up.

The bum sat motionless on the dock, looking like some odd mosaic, random fragments of reality tossed together. His black eyes glittered through the broken panes of his face. Waldo was seized by the certainty that this person wasn't human, but rather an icy, alien spirit that had occupied this body merely to accomplish this visitation—after which it would abandon it to whatever hell of wet cardboard, beneath a brutal wet blanket, it had stolen it from.

Waldo rose and started to stumble away. But the bum's voice came again, low and intimate, and he froze.

"Maybe I got something you want."

Waldo felt a chill accompanied by an electric current racing down his spine—an impression of *sizzling* he could almost hear. He pressed his palms to his forehead, feeling something turn inside, slow and deliberate.

Waldo turned. In the rain, in the runny glow of the bleared afternoon sun, the bum sat regarding him. He pulled an object from his rags and held it toward Waldo.

"Look at this …."

In a daze, Waldo leaned close.

It was a water pistol designed to look like a Smith & Wesson Penetrating/Equalizing Neuronal Insertion System (PENIS). The real weapon was basically a taser on steroids, but it had no wires. It looked somewhat like a real penis, with two balls at the back, beneath which was a trigger. The balls led to a barrel with a broadened tip.

Working remotely from as far away as twenty feet, the PENIS's wireless darts could knock you unconscious or kill you, depending on the amount of current applied. The weapon was still deep classified, but Waldo had been given a glimpse.

He burst into a spasm of black, awful, semi-hysterical laughter. He heard the bum's voice as from a distance.

"Five bucks?"

11/13/99 Dressed my foot and elbow in the apartment. Every nerve on edge. I felt an urge to do Duadine but wondered if a good alternative might be Dr. Omega.

Eyed the clock: 4:30. Amutha wouldn't come home until 6:30 or so—charity work with a group called Abiding Angels. Marty would probably return soon.

I have his keys, of course.

I entered his place, rummaged about. He'd hidden the O-pills well. My nervousness was intensified by haste and clumsiness; every move I made was inept; I stumbled over furniture, broke a wine glass, cut myself.

A knock sounded. My guts twisted.

The knock came again.

I intended to stand there silently until the person went away. Then it occurred to me that this person had probably just heard something smash.

"Who is it."

"Messenger."

I shoved the glass in a trash basket, cutting myself again.

"Put it by the door."

"Can't do that, sir. For your eyes only."

I started. These days, I heard that phrase in only one other context.

I licked the blood from my hand, stepped toward the door. Each action felt distant and precise, as if remotely controlled.

Dr. Dark prefers to communicate via personal delivery. Sounds odd until you reflect that a man in the computer espionage business would never trust computers. Besides, the discs are heavily encrypted.

I opened the door. A sallow youth faced me. He held an unmarked brown envelope.

"Mr. Weinstein?"

"Yes."

"ID."

I went to the kitchen and opened a drawer where I knew Marty kept old driver's licenses, credit cards and other junk. I pulled out an expired license, returned to the door and handed the ID to the messenger. He examined it, glanced up at me and handed the license back.

He seemed to have concluded that the face on the license was mine.

He gave me the package and departed. I contemplated the envelope, brain screaming.

I felt the disc inside.

I found a newspaper on a couch, removed some pages, lurched toward the trash basket and spread them over the broken glass. I cast a look about the apartment—everything else seemed fine, though I couldn't be certain, as my vision was blurred.

I shut the door, headed upstairs.

"Hey, pal."

I turned toward Marty, face convulsing. Meanwhile I shoved the envelope in the back of my pants.

"You," I whispered irrationally.

He stared at me. "Christ. You look like hell."

"Hell."

He looked uncertain, smiled weakly. Tapped his briefcase.

"Brought some goodies. Dr. O. I ran out."

I didn't respond.

"Why don't you come inside," Marty said carefully, producing keys, "and tell me about it."

"I'm sick. I feel sick."

Ignoring his baffled look, I turned and found the stairs. Entered my place and ripped open the envelope.

The encryption was new to me, but I'm no stranger to ciphers. Within an hour I'd worked it out.

> I've been informed that you've once again failed in your assignment. I don't think you understand the urgency of the situation. Stanton's role with Alpha counterintelligence is clear. The false information he delivered has jeopardized us all. My supervisor insists that Alpha be sent a clear signal. We have no

choice but to attain Stanton in his quarters. We'll see that his wife is called away Tuesday evening.

Shattered by horror, overwhelmed by nonsensical voices in his head:

Whittling ... veranda ... paradise machine

Waldo left his apartment, took a taxi to his office, which was now empty, and threw himself on a couch in the reception area.

He faced himself in a shimmering white room.

He'd had this dream many times. The room was bare—a table, two chairs. But he understood that it contained everything that ever was, is, will be.

He'd sat here like this for billions of years. He'd do so for billions more.

The room pulsed like a heartbeat. The unrelenting white light, the persistent buzzing sound, would never go away.

He contemplated himself.

This was hell. If heaven is pure space without time, hell is pure time without space. This room was pure time.

He contemplated himself. Himself and the Other.

The Other smiled, leaned forward. It opened its mouth. Waldo saw the smooth tube of the throat—saw the tongue begin to emerge ....

He woke up.

Waldo had never made it past the point where the tongue unrolled.

11/13/99 When death comes to "attain" me on Tuesday—if Amutha is indeed called away somehow, if Marty does creep into my apartment—slinking against walls, poking his head around corners, gripping a pistol in two outstretched hands like in some dumb cop show … how many times have I watched this stale paranoid scenario, always anxious, always conned—how will I respond?

But no. I can't picture it. Despite the evidence, I can't conceive of Marty as a killer. Can't imagine what it would take to make him one. Not money.

Not money alone, at any rate.

That old, familiar vertigo … distant mocking laughter, rattle of bones, dance of the dissociated mind ….

I drift to the office window, look out at the city … towers framed against the gritty red sky, black muscles studded with frigid white squares.

Did Marty really try to murder me? Twice? Did he shoot the girl by accident? On purpose? If I stare hard at the message to him, does that make it more real? I've had extended hallucinations before … is this message a hallucination as well? Merely a bulletin from the brain, so many neurons firing? Is this whole sordid scenario a dreary spinoff of the Duadine?

Am I going mad?

Waldo woke early—mind finally clear.

This, he thought, is what had happened:

Alpha, aware of his moonlighting, had been feeding him bad data. Meanwhile, through Molotov's good offices, it had ensured that he remained mentally unhinged, an easy mark. In the short term, Alpha would lead Schwarzcorp astray, gain a competitive edge or two. In the long term, Schwarzcorp would realize the information was poisoned, Waldo would be revealed as a dangerous, out-of-control junky, and Alpha would let Schwarzcorp do what it thought was necessary.

Result: the mole goes down.

Meanwhile, Marty would be sitting pretty under Waldo's cover. Who'd dream of two partners turning spy at once—and separately? When Waldo was out of the picture, Alpha would figure its problem was solved—when actually it had just taken out the decoy. As for Marty, he'd get rich off Dr. Dark, plus the Cablemaster.

The first thing, Waldo supposed, was to look Waldo in the face.

Marty, that is.

He'd call a messenger service, place Marty's disc in an unmarked brown envelope. When the messenger arrived Waldo would give him Marty's address.

He'd tell the messenger to make the delivery tomorrow morning. He'd also instruct him to say: "For your eyes only."

11/14/99 Seized by spasms of guilt, I rush home and find Amutha preparing for mass. (She converted to Catholicism a few years ago. Me, no. I hate formal religion, though I admit to a fascination with crucifixion scenes, which Marty shares.)

I find her standing in the living room in a white skirt and pearl-gray blouse, attaching an earring by feel. She freezes when I enter.

I close the door behind me, gingerly placing the water pistol on the hall table next to a white rose in a jade green vase.

"I'm sorry."

She thinks, debating how to start. "Were you in blackout again?"

I don't know how to answer that. "I'm not sure."

She shakes her head, approaches. I shrink back as she settles in, embracing me.

"God," she whispers. "You've got to get better help. I worry so much …."

A thought comes to me. I push her away gently.

"Do you remember anything about your program the other night?"

She stares off to the right a bit, puzzled.

"Actually, yes."

"What?"

"I thought I heard Joey …."

"You did, I think."

I step to the tape deck and let her hear the recording I'd made of her channeling.

I turn and find her groping about on a coffee table. I bend and hand her a cigarette; she takes it unsteadily. I light it.

She lets the smoke out slowly. "So Joey's visiting us?"

"I think so."

"What's he trying to say?"

"I don't know. But you have to promise me something."

"Sure."

"Be here on Tuesday. After work. Don't let anything keep you away."

"Is something wrong?"

"Yes."

She seems about to ask a question, then backs off.

"OK."

I sag with relief. But immediately she says something that makes me stiffen:

"Do you have a gun?"

I glance at the hall table. How could she …? But it's impossible to equate a real gun with that pathetic toy, however close its resemblance.

"No. Why?"

"Nothing. It's just this morning …."

She stares at me—her gaze so direct, so intense that for a moment I could swear she can see.

"I dreamt you were holding a gun."

Amutha headed toward the shuttle stop where she'd be picked up for church. Waldo watched from the bedroom window. As she blended into the flow of pedestrians he felt mounting nausea, wondering if he'd ever see her again.

He lurched for his Duadine.

First time since yesterday afternoon.

Four hits.

Within a few minutes he felt his shoulders relax, saw the room take on a softer shape. He went to the tape player and pressed PLAY.

The first time through Amutha's babbling he didn't detect anything—only that little boy's voice that made his throat catch. The second time, at the end of a phrase that sounded like a distant Gregorian chant, in an almost inaudible whisper, he heard it.

"Nah ... amaanaah ... namaanaah ...."

By now he was convinced—irrationally, he knew, but convinced —that the OR file held the key to everything that was happening. And he had a feeling—no, was certain—that if he could access that file, it would teach him what he needed to survive the coming attack.

It was clear that the file's first check was related to the vocables Amutha had whispered in trance. Waldo guessed that somewhere in her transmission, Amutha—or his son—had given him a way to pass that check.

But even if the code was hidden somewhere in that Gregorian-like passage, how was he to know where to begin and end writing letters? And even if he got that right, one character off and he was nowhere—or even worse, the system would go on alert, shut down the file, trace the intruder ….

Waldo decided to try. He went to the computer room, accessed OR, broke the block and studied that tantalizing screen: the U.S. map, the vocables NAH:::AMAANAA:::NAMAANAA. He plugged a headset into the tape recorder, rewound to the beginning of Amutha's channeling and transcribed the sounds into what seemed the simplest spelling. Then he overwrote his passage onto the vocables.

Nothing.

He tried again with different spellings. No. Carved the passage into various bits, based on slight pauses in Amutha's speech. No. Alarms sounded; Waldo cursed and pulled out.

He visited the New York Public Library again. Nothing in *Who's Who*, but he found what he wanted in *World Psychologists*.

Molotov, Artak O. b. '44 Ukraine; emig. U.S. '48; m. '75; 2 children; div. '85; PhD. Mass. Inst. Psych. '69, diss. "Pain Threshold Increases and Reconditioning in Mice"; private practice '69-'74, '76-'85; assigned to South Africa Morale Team, U.S. Agency for Third World Development '85; Intercorp '88; Alpha '91; director (!) Ronald Reagan Fulfillment Center (U.S./Alpha psychological reconditioning coop) '92.

Good god, Molotov was no R Center apparatchik—he was head of the whole operation.

Waldo didn't get it. Why would his case get assigned to such a big player?

Another entry. *Dissertation Abstracts* '70. "Contemporary theories of therapy as fusion are rebutted. Fission is viewed as the preferred end of psychotherapeutic technique. Pain is an essential element in the new method. The raising of pain thresholds results in the emergence of a new psychic 'text'—a 'fiction by fire.' 'Our only chance of survival is to invent new—not reproduce old—psychic states. Mice scuttle in perfect circles after forty days of increased psychosis due to electric torture.'"

Waldo closed his eyes.

The Waldo you've been sublimating is phasing out of your grasp

11/15/99 Office. Marty isn't here. Meeting a client, I'm told. I'm relieved, as I can't calm down.

I was cabbing to work when traffic slowed, then stopped. To the right the taxi was partly blocked by a white truck with the letters GOD on the back. Beneath the letters: Guaranteed On-time Delivery.

I looked left and saw, in front of an electronics store window, a group of men in black leather, wearing black helmets with black visors, methodically clubbing someone on the ground.

Pedestrians in a semicircle watched somberly—none moved to stop the beating. The clubs rose and descended like the arms of an iron machine. The victim jerked with each blow, shielding his face with his hands. Then he screamed and rolled toward the street, clutching his stomach.

My breath caught as he stared straight at me.

He regarded me knowingly, grinning through bared teeth—then his eyes rolled up. The knot of paramilitary types closed around him. On each of their backs was a white letter "A."

To the left, a poster in the window. It was off kilter, as if it had been hastily pasted on. It depicted a man in a fetal position, hovering two or three feet above a circular mat with a mandala design.

Beneath the figure:

REBIRTH. IT'S NOT AS HARD AS YOU THINK!

I'm not sure, but I think the man I just saw being beaten was the bum who sold me the squirtgun. He also looked a lot like the man in the Rebirth posters.

Marty arrived. Waldo played it like a normal day. They reviewed current business: potential contracts with Brazil's security agency, the Spanish school system, an American maker of televisions that hoped to add a wired-in headcap. All the while Waldo saw no indication that Marty had received his package that morning. He seemed jovial, in his element.

Around noon they met in Marty's office. He settled into his chair; Waldo sat on a couch behind a glass table littered with marketing collateral.

Marty reached into his desk and pulled out some Dr. O. He popped two pills and tilted the vial Waldo's way; Waldo declined. Marty leaned back and gazed at a framed photograph on the wall —the 10th century *Gero Cross* statue at Cologne Cathedral.

"You know, this image is way older than Christianity."

Waldo knew that but let him continue.

"In many premodern cultures the crucified figure was called the Big Man. The cross spanned the entire universe, and the crucifixion lasted for eternity."

Waldo hadn't known that. They were silent, pondering the significance of the Big Man, whatever He or It was.

Marty changed the subject. "You had me worried when you ran away like that."

"I was mugged."

Marty glanced at him uncertainly. "Are you OK?"

The honesty and helplessness in his voice confirmed everything. Waldo thought: Marty never received the disc.

Waldo made a hapless gesture. "Good as I'll ever be."

Marty studied him blankly. Then he seemed to make a decision and reached into his desk again.

What happened next is hard to describe.

Waldo had experienced this a few times before. You have the impression you're at a crossroads—and for a fleeting moment two alternative futures present themselves simultaneously. Both are equally real; both glitter like a mescaline vision. And then— **CHUNK**—one of the futures slams into place.

Waldo sat detached, watching Marty's face take on an alien, somnolent quality. When his hand came up from the drawer it held a sheaf of papers. At the same time, as if superimposed, it held a Glock 20.

Waldo couldn't breathe.

The atmosphere was dank, dead, lead in his lungs. He was looking through an aqueous solution at Marty's face, but it was also Waldo's face, and that of some dour underground entity … its lips spread back as it raised the weapon with what looked like a pincer, in a scene from some black and white nature show on TV.

The thing fondled the G20. "If I were you, I'd take better care of yourself."

Waldo's teeth chattered. Struggling but unable to emerge from the quasi-dream, he watched the thing's pincer move toward the desk. Time had skipped; they were back at the place where the hand had produced the papers, or the gun.

Waldo looked at Marty's face and understood that he was looking at evil.

Waldo wasn't schizophrenic. Marty was schizophrenic.

The schizophrenic held a G20. Its lips spread back.

"Now," Marty said, leaning forward with an oily grin, "I don't think it's the best idea in the world for a guy in your ... condition ... to pack a weapon. But let's face it, you can't trust anyone these days—it's every man for himself."

Waldo couldn't speak.

"Oh—excuse me, boys."

Their secretary had entered to deposit some printouts. Waldo sprang back into real time.

"Wow," she said. "What's that?"

Marty stayed cool. Nothing strange at all about having a gun in the office.

"My new pistol, Sarah. Want to see?"

She stared at him, then at the pistol. She licked her lips and stepped forward gingerly.

Waldo was glad for the interruption, as a red mist had obscured his vision. But at the same time he felt a stab of tenderness for his former friend. Because he thought he understood why Marty was showing him the gun.

Waldo couldn't deny it anymore: Marty had been ordered to kill him. But maybe he'd missed the first time on purpose. Maybe he'd come closer the second time to make his mission clear. And maybe he was alerting Waldo now because he didn't want to have to shoot at him again.

It occurred to Waldo that Marty was over his head in this thing—didn't know how to escape.

Sarah reached out. "What kind is it?"

"Glock 20."

She held the gun and stroked the barrel with a green fingernail. "I think I've heard of these. Powerful."

Marty nodded, eyes darting in Waldo's direction. In that quick glance Waldo detected a mix of terror, desperation, pleading and awful loneliness.

Marty regarded Sarah but wasn't really looking at her. "Ever thought about carrying one of these?"

She licked her lips again and removed her finger from the gun. "Oh no. Well, actually, yes, I was thinking about it for a while. But I don't think I'd be able to pull the trigger." She delicately placed the pistol on Marty's desk. "And you know, I feel so much safer now with the A-Police."

For some reason Marty looked amused. "Ah—them."

Waldo closed his eyes.

11/15/99 *New York Times*

A-POLICE PASS FIRST TEST

Two photos. One, captioned "James Gate," shows a man with an ugly scar on his chin. The other, uncaptioned, depicts a scuffle; in the middle an elderly man is being dragged away by men in black leather with A's on their backs. The protester's small round rimless glasses are knocked askew.

Text:

An unidentified man attacked a midtown Fifth Avenue office of Alpha Inc. with an assault rifle yesterday afternoon, shouting DEATH TO ALPHA! No one was injured, and the disturbance was quickly quelled by a group that "has been specially formed to deal with these kinds of crises," according to a city spokesman at a subsequent press conference. It was revealed that a new federal/corporate venture called Alpha Security Systems (ASS) has launched a pacification force dubbed the A-Police, with Alpha Inc. providing the lion's share of funding and personnel. At the press conference, ASS chief James Gate pointed to previous examples of government cooperation with the company, including the Ronald Reagan Fulfillment Center unveiled in 1992.

On the same day, several other major American cities announced similar programs. Meanwhile, protesters who burst into the New York press conference chanting DEATH TO ALPHA! were dispersed by A-Police, who arrested thirteen.

Waldo was trembling uncontrollably. He dropped three Duadine.

Following an impulse, he looked up Rebirth on DEATH.

Chain of detox clinics for the rich based in Manhattan. Hard to know for sure, but it seemed to be owned by Alpha through a tangle of health-care subsidiaries.

"Our philosophy is based on a recognition that most people are locked into a reality they hate. Clearly, the answer is to invent a new reality. Using a cutting-edge combination of biofeedback, medication, hypnosis, psychotherapy, and rigorous daily 'scripts' that reinforce the identify to be adopted—based on the ground-breaking transhumanistic work of Dr. Artak Molotov—we give our clients the kind of one-on-one attention they need to reinvent themselves—that is, to be reborn.

"We stop at nothing to make sure you achieve the desired result. When you arrive at Rebirth, you will be assigned your own treatment team that will consist of a medical doctor, psychologist, marriage counselor, chemical dependency counselor, acupuncturist, masseuse, hypnotherapist, spiritual counselor, physical trainer, and aftercare planner. Meanwhile you will live in the lap of luxury, with meals crafted by master chefs, cocktails by our infinity pool, nightly entertainment, saunas, and group gatherings in hot tubs (clothing optional)."

It seemed that Molotov had a hand in everything.

Time to confront that miserable bastard.

11/16/99 Drove to the Fulfillment Center. Molotov started when I barged into his office, then shot a furtive glance at a TV. The screen was dark.

He shooed out a disgruntled patient and turned to me, nonplussed.

I was pacing back and forth, struggling to stay calm, waving my palmtop in the air. Even now I wasn't sure why I was doing this. One voice in my head warned me to stay cool, avoid tipping off Alpha; another shrieked at me to rip Molotov's Judas face off.

He eyed the palmtop, smiling crookedly. "Writing a lot, are we?"

"Can't stop." My teeth chattered. "Like I'm—addicted."

"Good, good … first person becomes third person …." Molotov was approaching slowly and, I realized, nervously; maybe he was afraid I might go for him.

Or maybe he knew he was looking at someone who was about to die.

"Then the third person detaches, you see … becomes a brand new entity …."

"And maybe the whole thing happens a lot faster when you're overdosing on sedative hypnotics," I snarled.

I both regretted this outburst and felt delicious relief. Meanwhile I watched him carefully. But to my surprise, Molotov showed no sign of guilt—rather, his face took on a sort of abstract glee. He snapped his fingers, *cha-cha-cha.*

"So you figured it out, eh?"

I stared at him in a stupor. With deliberate showmanship, he reached behind his ear, produced a vial, removed eight Duadine and downed them with water from a glass on his desk.

"You'll kill yourself," I whispered.

He giggled. "I wouldn't worry about that. Like you, I've been building up slowly … approaching critical mass." He gave me a sly look.

"Keeping up with the Joneses, one might say."

His voice in my head: *I too shall become part of your storyline*

Molotov edged to the other side of the desk. His eyes darted toward the TV again. "Don't jump to conclusions too fast. It's much more complicated than you think—much more interesting." He contemplated me. "You've probably investigated me as well."

I gnawed at my lip, not meeting his eyes.

"Then you know you're a special case." He reached into a drawer, produced a remote control, pointed it at the TV. "And special cases require special methods." He flashed a disarming grin and pressed a button.

"Look at this, Waldo … tell me what you think."

The screen brightened—then filled with something that resembled Joey's final design. I shivered, feeling that same *sizzle* that had swept through me the moment he died—that icy electric bloom in the brain ….

Then all sense of external reality dispersed, and the room took on a glistening, unstable quality, as in an LSD trip. A frightening sound rushed in from nowhere—a high-pitched twittering, like that of bats, combined with a violent whistling wind and a tumultuous undercurrent, like countless voices speaking at once. Meanwhile the design seemed to float from the screen, then dissolve into light and head straight for me—the room bucked and pitched; I smelled burnt ozone; Molotov appeared dimly off to my left; then the light smashed into my forehead and I slumped to my knees.

The next thing I remember is Molotov bending over me, smiling gently. I clutched my legs to my chest.

"Not a good idea to look at that too long," he murmured.

I glanced at the TV. Dark.

"I never do anymore—gives me bad dreams," he continued. "But I keep it around anyway—better than electroshock in some cases."

He helped me sit up. Helplessly, I began to weep. He looked at me askance.

"But you, Waldo! I'd have thought you'd be used to it."

I held my head. "Where'd you get that."

He kneeled and gripped my face, forcing me to look into his eyes. "Don't worry about that. The question is: Did you recognize it?"

I nodded miserably.

He looked satisfied. "So the block is dissolving."

I pulled myself up to a chair, rubbed my face. "I don't know what you mean. Bastard …."

"No need for name calling." He straightened. "Of course you wouldn't. But perhaps you remember it from your dreams, or a moment just before sleep when it—"

"Bullshit. Who hired you for this."

I stared at him venomously. Molotov studied me a moment—then something in his face sagged. He passed a hand before it.

"Hire ...."

He lost the thread. He thought a moment, then gave me a hounded look and shook his head.

"I can't keep up with you."

"Fucking right you can't. Fucking right!" I jerked to my feet. "Neither you nor your employer can. And don't run a beefed-up Joey design past me and expect me to be impressed. I know all about OR and your part in it. So don't try anything fancy."

He seemed bewildered. "Joey ...?"

"Don't try it!" I shouted. "And don't contact them or I'll cut you to ribbons! Got it?"

I yanked the fake PENIS from my coat; Molotov gaped and dove behind his desk. Waldo flickered before my eyes.

"Ribbons!"

"Waldo!" he screamed. "Don't shoot!"

I rushed from the office.

About an hour later Waldo calls Molotov back.

"Waldo—" Then, unbelievably, Molotov breaks into sobs.

Waldo sees his baffled eyes again. "You really don't know anything, do you?"

"Please … I know more than you imagine. But you've got to understand I'm in no one's pocket."

"They're coming to kill me tonight."

Long silence.

"You're not hallucinating?"

"Fairly certain. No thanks to you."

"I was only trying to help."

"Sure you were. Just about helped me into an asylum—or worse."

Molotov doesn't respond. Waldo tries to calm down.

"They decoyed Amutha. Listen."

Amutha had called their landline from her Nokia 3210 cell phone. Waldo also has a Nokia but rarely uses it.

He punches PLAY on their answering machine.

"Honey, dad's had a stroke—a car's coming. I know you didn't want me to leave today, but this is important. When you get this, call me at St. Mary's."

(Hospital in Brooklyn. Waldo had called. Amutha is there; her father is recovering.)

"How do you know it's a setup?"

"I intercepted their plan."

"Good lord ... you're over your head in this. You don't know half the story, not a tenth …. I want to move you to a safe house."

"Safe house?"

"You're an agent ... a sleeper …."

Waldo thinks: This makes a weird kind of sense. He closes his eyes, sees faded mezzotint images zoom past: girl dies, spitting blood ... goons in black ... Marty raises a G20 ... iridescent web ... his shoe spurts blood ….

My son died today

The next words come not from his brain but his gut.

"Rebirth. Coming your way."

"You know about them?"

"I think we've been in touch. A fake bum, I'm pretty sure."

"Whatever—let me protect you."

"I don't think so." Waldo hefts his squirtgun. "Got a date tonight."

"Christ!" Molotov almost shouts. "Don't mess around with this. You're up against something—"

"Tell me tomorrow."

Silence.

"Please," Molotov pleads. "What should I do?"

"Let me handle this."

"OK. Whatever you do. But meet me."

"You'll come clean."

"Yes."

"Where."

"My house."

"When."

"Morning."

Waldo hangs up.

11/16/99 That queer, familiar phenomenon: register something in your brain, see it everywhere. Read a newspaper, come across the name "Bora Bora"—suddenly you hear and read nothing but "Bora Bora." As if the second you thought of a word or words, the universe is recast about you.

I'm walking streets near the office and that poster is everywhere: always the same floating human figure in a fetal position, looking like a typical twenty-something male, but with an unsettling reptilian overlay.

Posters always at an angle. Paste splashed about. The tag line is sometimes familiar, sometimes not.

REBIRTH. THE CHOICE IS YOURS!

REBIRTH. DON'T KNOCK IT TILL YOU'VE TRIED IT!

REBIRTH. HAVE WE GOT A PINA COLADA FOR YOU!

Called Amutha again. "Sweetheart—you OK?"

"Sure … your voice sounds odd."

"How's your dad?"

"Not great. There's some paralysis."

"Staying overnight?"

"I'll find a motel once they kick me out. You should come."

"Sorry, I can't. Really. We're pitching something too big to lose—could be up all night." I pause to simulate guilty internal debate. "I'll be there tomorrow."

"Promise?"

"Promise."

I expect her to say goodbye—but instead I hear her gasp. She breathes quickly—like hyperventilation. I've heard this before: She's moving into trance state.

Her voice comes low, remote, robotic:

"Waldo?"

"Yes?"

"What are you holding?"

"What?"

"What are you *holding*?"

Waldo was holding a pistol—but this time a real one, a Glock 20, which he'd picked up at a black gun market tucked away in a graffiti-smeared warren of abandoned, rubble-filled spaces beneath the Brooklyn Bridge. The store was there because politicians, riding high on a wave of deliberately induced public terror in 1998, had passed the Protect Our Populace Act, which had predictably made the city more dangerous—for example, by gutting the parole system, slashing the police budget, easing money laundering and permitting the short-term existence of stores like this one, in exchange for hefty fees that rarely made their way into city coffers.

This is what Waldo thought would happen tonight:

He'd remove the refrigerator door. Move the dining room table into a corner of the living room, facing the front door. Prop the refrigerator door behind it.

Then he'd wait for Marty.

When Marty entered, Waldo would threaten him with the PENIS. If that didn't work, he'd flash the real goods.

Hopefully Marty would freeze at the sight of a gun—fictional or otherwise. This would allow Waldo to subdue him and confiscate Marty's own G20.

Then he would interrogate the sonofabitch.

11/16/99 Back at the office.

By now I deeply regret cutting Molotov off. Called the Center; he's gone—called his home, no one.

Fucking Duadine—turns you into a different person. Impatient, impulsive—different face, different voice, belligerent spirit poking through.

Evil twin.

Part of me thinks I'm stupid; the other part thinks I have every right to distrust Molotov. Despite my conviction that he's somehow, in a bizarre and convoluted way, on my side, I remind myself that he's been lying to me for years.

Never again. Next time we meet, I'll keep him honest.

But still ….

You're an agent ... a sleeper ....

Safe house

Marty entered the office beaming. Announced that he'd just cut a deal, high six figures—big paramilitary group.

Waldo grew dizzy. Sure enough: the A-Police.

"Don't look so stunned. After all, they're a fellow subsidiary."

Marty strode to a bar in the reception area, poured a generous glass of vodka, downed half. "You know whose day this is? Our Lady of the Gate of Dawn! She just closed a deal for us!" He finished the rest of the drink and slammed the glass down.

Meanwhile Waldo watched his face. Marty was a typical jubilant businessman—pal crowing about a coup to a trusted pal. Waldo couldn't detect any anxiety, hidden thoughts.

"Who clued you to the contract?"

"Mr. Light. Would you believe it—the Invisible Man himself. Left a phone message—you know, in all these years this was the first time I'd heard him speak."

Marty gave Waldo a cool appraising look.

"It was strange—he sounded a lot like you."

Waldo laughed tinnily, feeling his perceptions distort. He felt like he was about to lose it, go for Marty's throat.

He glanced at his watch, made a show of dismay, lurched hastily to his feet.

"Ah, jeez, I'd love to celebrate—but I'm working a prospect."

"You too? Gonna make it a double play?"

"If I can."

"Who's the target?"

Waldo named the CEO of a major multinational. Marty whistled. "Damn, that'd be a catch."

Corny dialog out of a crummy corporate motivational film. How could Marty keep this up?

Fumbling about, Waldo found his briefcase, stepped toward the door—then pretended to have an afterthought.

"Hey—Amutha's at a hospital. Her dad's sick."

Marty didn't blink—not a suggestion of discomfort.

"Is it serious?"

"Not too much. Gives me a free evening is all." Waldo studied him. "Want to get together in a few hours?"

"Sure. I'll bring a video. There's this flic I like—cross-country firefights, all that."

He pulled his G20 from his briefcase and chortled.

"Maybe we can shoot at some scotch bottles."

11/16/99 Made preparations. Built my defensive nest. Checked my Glock. The magazine is full of ammo. I've never shot a pistol, but hopefully I won't have to use this one.

I can't stop shaking.

Moved the tape player into the nest. When Marty talks, I'll record every word.

Called the hospital. Amutha had stepped out. Her father is in stable condition.

I sit behind the refrigerator shield, G20 in my belt and PENIS in my lap.

To kill time I watch the TV without audio. Evening news. Goon squads in black ... A's on their backs ... New York ... Detroit ... Houston ... L.A.

A flash of the face of the man with the scar—James Gate.

Hunched over my palmtop, I wait for Marty to arrive.

Waldo stumbled into the bathroom and sagged against the door. He removed the covering from the mirror, pointed the Glock 20 at it and pulled the trigger. The glass exploded, cutting his hand and face.

He wandered into the living room. Saw a hint of dawn at the window.

In a daze, he dragged the bodies to the bathroom. Sponged the entrance to the apartment. Locked the door.

Head in hands weeping bash his face on wall rip his guts out

11/17/99 Can't remember too well. Everything wavering, uncertain.

Waited for Marty. Around 9:30 pm, heard footsteps—switched off the TV, lights. Pressed RECORD.

Wind rushing up from stomach.

Scrape at the door. Raised the water pistol.

Wind rushing up. Door opens.

Slo-mo dream state: Waldo enters, stands resplendent. A white aura turns to silver around his head. His body is semi-transparent. He eyes me calmly and raises a G20.

"Waldo!" I think I screamed. *"You fuck! You fuck!"*

The room lit up as I pulled the trigger.

Waldo's face took on a look of mild surprise. Then, in slo-mo, he sagged to the floor.

The dream state lifted. Waldo faded away.

Amutha lay on the floor.

I glanced at my gun. It was the Glock.

I ran to her, dropped to my knees. Blood everywhere, jetting from her neck, it wouldn't stop …. I cradled her body, clamped my hand over her neck, but the blood spurted between my fingers and around my hand. She was shivering, moaning. I cried and clutched her to me.

She stiffened—her legs jerked hard, twice. A death rattle came.

"Holy shit," someone said.

I looked up. Marty. He held his G20.

His eyes glazed. "Holy shit."

I stared numbly at Amutha. Gone.

I shrieked, picked up my gun and shot Marty dead.

Michael Schulze

II. MOLOTOV

Michael Schulze

11/17/99 Went downstairs, entered Marty's apartment.

In his kitchen, my cell phone.

Checked my SMS messages. The last one was to Amutha.

Amutha, come home immediately. Please. It's an emergency. A car will pick you up.

Returned to my place, entered the bathroom, tugged the bodies into the tub.

Cleaned the living room once more.

Turned to the tape I'd made. I think I already knew what was on it.

Just before Amutha's death rattle, I heard it and began to cry. It was almost inaudible.

"Nah ... amaanaah ... namaanaah ...."

A colorless morning had broken over New York City, interacting with labyrinthine buildings and towers to form patterns like those in an M.C. Escher print. Waldo drove to the East River and threw the two G20s in. (One or two—his mind grew cloudy at this point.) He also tossed in his Nokia because he now hated it.

He drove to Molotov's house. If need be, he would beat him to get answers.

Outside Katonah. He'd been there once for a party. Gray Colonial on a hill, flanked by other residences of the upper middle class. Waldo passed through a gate and ascended a driveway under arching half-leafless trees.

A black Mercedes approached and sped past. The windows were tinted black.

Waldo's heart began to hammer.

Molotov's Volvo was parked outside his garage. Waldo stopped and dropped four Duadine.

He pressed the doorbell. No answer. He reached for the doorknob; it turned.

He lifted his water pistol and opened the door.

The place had been gone over. Hall mirror smashed—living room couch ripped open.

He came to the den where Molotov worked. Books, papers strewn about, lamps overturned, holes punched in walls where artwork had once hung. On the desk, smoke trickled from a Havana cigar in an ashtray.

Waldo spotted a slip of paper. He picked it up.

A check made out to Molotov from BioResearch—$100,000.

He found Molotov on the floor behind his desk. A pool of blood deepened beneath his head. His eyes had rolled up. Blood seeped from a hole in his left cheek.

"What are you doing," someone said.

Waldo moaned and turned. A lanky man with dark hair eyed him with eerie calm.

Waldo recognized the beaten bum.

"You shouldn't even be standing," he said.

The lanky man looked perplexed. "What?"

Waldo glanced at Molotov. "What did you do to him?"

The man didn't answer.

Police sirens approached.

Waldo lurched past the man through the house and out the front door. He jumped in his car and took off.

11/17/99 Don't know what's real. Don't care.

Grainy newsreel.

The Other smiles, leans forward.

I too shall become part of your storyline

Design dissolving into light.

Her legs jerk.

"Nah ... amaanaah ... namaanaah ...."

Drive about numbly. Radio on. Evangelical rant.

You are approaching a higher order

As I pass beneath bridges I see how close I can get to the abutments. Two feet. One foot. Shriek of metal; the car careens into the left lane.

At some point I'll be wanted for murder.

I turn up the radio.

Can you see it, brother? Can you see how close you are?

Waldo drove to his bank. A poster was pasted akilter on the window.

REBIRTH. YOU CAN GET IT IF YOU REALLY WANT!

Waldo withdrew $5,000, then drove to a drugstore and bought sunglasses and hair dye. He drove to a mall and wandered around in the parking lot until he found a Chrysler with keys in the ignition.

In a gas station bathroom he dyed his hair black.

West on I-80. In Pennsylvania he came to a roadblock. He put on his sunglasses. Off to the right he saw a black van with no lettering, five or six A-Police standing about. They held assault rifles.

To his surprise, a cop waved him through.

He turned on the radio. Artak Molotov, renowned psychologist and psychotherapist, was found murdered in his home this morning. Police report no suspects.

Strange. Waldo must have left fingerprints all over the place.

In a rest stop john north of Akron, he convulsed for ten minutes. He stumbled into the woods and sagged to the ground.

In his delirium, Amutha fell again and again.

He rolled to his back, pressing his squirtgun to his chest, staring at bare trees.

As night approached he neared Detroit. The senseless landscape scrolled past. He tried to ignore his reflection in the windshield.

He was crying again.

He'd thought everything through a thousand times. Couldn't figure it out.

Dark would tell him. Then Waldo would kill himself.

11/18/99 Brownwater, Michigan.

Home to a munitions dump called the Intersection. Guard towers, silos, warehouses. A dead river passes through the town near the dump.

I parked in midtown. Hiked to the river, passed the Intersection, ascended a hill to the BioResearch compound. It was ringed with barbed wire. All windows dark.

A little after midnight.

Returned to town, checked into a motel. Dropped five Duadine.

In a few hours I'll be dead.

They probably used chloroform. Waldo came to in the back seat of a car, hands duct taped in his lap. Two men up front. Black cardboard figures.

His mouth wouldn't work.

"Taking …."

The man in the passenger seat turned. Pear-shaped forehead, big ears, strangely sympathetic expression. He pressed a G20 to Waldo's nose.

"Shut up."

The man settled back in his seat.

They were nearing a sports field.

Waldo thought nothing—felt nothing. Stared at streetlamps drifting by.

The driver slowed for a light. The gunman coughed into his hand. The driver turned on his left blinker. Waldo lunged to his right.

"Fuck!" the driver shouted.

Waldo fumbled at the door. The gunman took aim. Waldo pulled the handle as a bullet shattered the rear window.

He hit asphalt … skidded … pain … slammed against the curb. The car swerved to a halt.

Waldo got to his feet and ran.

A bullet ricocheted off the road near his feet. He was heading for the sports field. Came to a high wire fence. A bullet passed by his head. He lurched to the right, came to a gate with a snapped chain.

The men rushed up. The gunman stopped and aimed. Waldo dashed inside and to the left; another bullet sizzled past. He ran down a cement corridor beneath the bleachers.

Waldo came to an intersecting corridor, turned right, spotted three figures huddled in shadow—then saw the baseball bat.

He came to moaning. Felt his nose and cried out; his hand came away bloody.

The gunman lay next to Waldo on his stomach. Brain tissue glistened in a gap in his skull.

The driver lay nearby, his face caved in. The bloody bat lay next to him.

Waldo fainted.

At some point he was crawling toward the driver. He found the man's keys and used them to saw the tape from his wrists.

Stood unsteadily. Stumbled to the driver's car. An Audi.

Typical, Waldo thought in his delirium. Audi drivers are assholes.

Dawn. He drove the car to the motel. The desk clerk was asleep.

Waldo dabbed at his face with a towel. His nose was broken; he suspected his left cheek was.

He grabbed his pills, squirtgun and palmtop, returned to the Audi and drove around until he found a big box store. He parked in an out-of-the-way place behind the store, dropped three Duadine and slept.

11/18/99 Night. I park outside an entrance to the BioResearch compound. A light glows at the top of a central tower.

Dr. Dark's office?

I drive around the compound. Entrances locked. I circle the compound twice, then go farther afield. Enter a darkened gas station near the Intersection.

Behind it a gate hangs open amid a row of crumpled autos. A gravel path winds up the hill toward the compound.

The path leads to a warehouse. The tower rises behind it.

One of the warehouse doors is unlocked. Inside is a shipping area. I park there and yank the warehouse door shut. Pocket my palmtop and stuff the water pistol in my belt.

I get out, step up steel stairs to a landing, come to a door. Enter a bright white corridor. Windowless doors on both sides, locked. I approach a bank of elevators and press UP.

Rise seven floors to the top. Emerge into a darkened office. A row of cubicles leads to a white door.

Crack of light beneath the door. I grip my PENIS and approach.

A cough.

I swing to the left. Dr. Dark sits in a cubicle, training a pistol on me.

He turns on a desk lamp.

He's uglier than in the photos in the DEATH articles. Looks like a *Time-Life* illustration of a Neanderthal. For the first time I notice his cauliflower ears. He wears a white lab coat, but oddly, he also sports a gold chain and pendant like those favored by wise guys. I glance at his shoes—scruffy loafers.

Then something occurs to me—no Waldo. I should be seeing him by now, but I don't.

Dark's gun is a Glock 20.

He grimaces. "You look terrible."

I nod toward the office. "Thought you were inside."

"When my men failed to check in I decided to wait. Saw you coming on security cameras."

"Your men were mugged."

"Of course," he says, as if this makes sense.

He contemplates me, then shakes his head ruefully. "What are you doing here."

I take a seat in a chair. "I think you might have an idea, Dr. Dark."

He laughs out loud. "You don't need to call me that. I chose the name because it amuses me. My real name is Marvin Gomez. I'm Mexican. I was a boxer, then switched to *lucha libre*. I think I chose the profession because the masks are uglier than I am. I'm not a doctor either. I have an MBA with a major in marketing from Western Michigan University. My wife is American, which is why I get to live here."

"Why Marvin?"

"Don't ask."

He nods toward my gun. "Is that thing even real? I don't recognize the design. And I think I detect peeling paint on the barrel."

I flush and stuff the PENIS back in my belt.

Why is he trying to charm me?

"I've had a terrible week," I confess.

"Yes—we heard the whole thing. Awful."

"You bugged my apartment? Bastard."

"Not so fast. Who else would have disposed of the bodies for you? Only a very good friend. You did a terrible job cleaning up, by the way. Especially the bathroom. We also got rid of your wife's cell phone."

"Someone is trying to kill me. Is it you?"

He laughs again. "Why would I want that? You're my man in Manhattan. I've made millions off your information."

I'm confused. "How did you even get this job?"

He shrugs. "It's who you know. As you might guess, I'm just a sock puppet."

"Who do you report to?"

"No clue. Never seen him—or her. We've never spoken. Couriers bring me encrypted orders on discs. I'm instructed to destroy them, which I do."

I try to hold back a sudden surge of tears.

"Why would someone want Amutha dead? Why would they make me do it?"

He regards me sadly—with true compassion I think. "Maybe that person wants to prompt you to do certain things. Perform a series of actions you might otherwise never consider."

I croak out a bitter laugh. "There's got to be a less complicated way."

"Self-discovery can be a convoluted process."

I don't understand that but let it go.

"Operation Renaissance. What about it interests you so much?"

Dark—Marvin—chooses his words.

"OR could be a real game changer. I mean it could literally change the world. I've heard it called the Paradise Machine."

"I don't get it."

"Me neither. But Mr. Light is onto something big. I need to know what it is. Or rather, my boss does. Me, I don't care so much."

He laughs again, but this time the sound is false, and his eyes flick to his right. I glance left and see two men. I can't make them out well, as they stand in shadow, but I have no doubt about the pistols they're carrying.

"C'mon. Is this necessary?"

He makes a conciliatory gesture. "Who knows. Insurance. We have some pretty important questions about Joey."

"How do you know about Joey?"

"You talk to yourself a lot. Did you know that? Sometimes I don't know if you're talking to yourself or another person."

"Bastard."

"You already called me that."

I whip out my squirtgun and train it on the two men. "Lower your weapons!"

"Wait!" Dark shouts to his men. "It's just a—"

But these guys are working stiffs. Security men who've probably never fought a gun battle in their lives. Before Dark can finish his sentence, one of them advances into the light, gun hand shaking violently. He pulls off a shot.

I throw myself from my chair, then realize the bullet has gone wildly off. I hear Dark cry out in surprise and pain.

Christ, the stiff has shot his own boss.

I look around to see Dark toppling to the floor. He drops his G20 and clutches his chest. I grab his gun and dash for the office door. I hear another shot behind me but feel nothing.

I burst into a corridor and keep running. No one pursues me. The security men are probably attending to Dark, if he's still alive.

Corridors … corridors … I try a door to my right and it opens. I stumble into another office filled with cubicles.

I sit on the floor sobbing.

Time to finish it.

Waldo had the G20 in his mouth when something in the office emitted a bleat.

He checked a cubicle. It was an alarm from the DEATH network. The setup was like his own.

He dashed around the office. Every workstation was wired to DEATH.

Impossible. No way Schwarzcorp could have hacked into Alpha's VPN.

Or could it?

By now many of the workstations were shrieking. Waldo clicked on an icon and saw black vehicles parked outside the building, bubbletop lights spitting red and blue. He pressed a key. Men in black leather with A's on their backs poured through corridors, gripping assault rifles.

Shouts of men approaching. A door somewhere slammed open. Waldo lurched to a door in the office and opened it onto a stairwell.

He took the stairs down three or four at a time. He turned into a lab, then a room full of cages.

In a corner a macaque sat on a small wooden chair, its eyes rolled up. It was strapped to the chair at the wrists and ankles. Wires fed from its skull into a metal plaque on the wall. It quivered violently but made no sound.

Doors banged; men shouted.

Waldo found another stairway and took it down. It brought him to an office where an elderly lady in an apron vacuumed; he rushed past her startled gaze into a bright white corridor. He heard boots and huddled in a mailroom while an A-squad swept past.

He ran down one corridor, then another. The corridors extended forever; this was a bad dream. Somewhere in a bad dream Waldo Stanton was fleeing faceless pursuers.

He found an exit door and took it. Emerged into frigid air, darkness broken by security lights. Sirens in the near distance.

He shoved the G20 in his mouth again.

A Ryder truck screeched to a halt.

"Waldo!" someone shouted.

Waldo pulled the gun out.

"Get in!"

He stepped uneasily into the cab. Then he laughed spastically.

The driver was Molotov.

Both of his cheeks were bandaged. He grinned, exposing missing and broken teeth. "Glad I found you," he lisped. "I was lucky—" He arched his eyebrows comically. "But of course, at this point I suspect there's no such thing as *luck* ...."

He reached behind Waldo's ear, removed a vial of Duadine.

"Ah," he gloated. "I could use some of this."

Waldo began to sob.

"And get rid of that thing, will you? If you start thinking I'm your Double, you might kill me."

Waldo looked down, saw he was clutching Dark's G20. He opened the window and threw it out.

Molotov drove down roads, pulled onto a lawn, rammed through a fence.

Waldo was crying, crying.

11/19/99 Small room with gray steel walls. Steel door. Bunk beds. Metal tip-down table. Hot plate, microwave. Sink with faucet. Pop-up toaster. Blender. Liquor bottles. Digital clock with date indicator. Cupboards. Mini-fridge. Plastic curtain with sunflowers on it, screening a toilet, small sink and mirror.

Circular mat on the floor—about four feet in diameter, intricate mandala design surrounded by red glyphs.

I sat on the bottom bunk. As I finished the last entry a lanky man entered and approached.

I'd last encountered him in Molotov's house.

Mid-twenties. Face smooth as rubbed stone. A kind of transparency to it, like my visions of Waldo. No evidence of the beating he'd received. He smiled thinly, then seemed to flicker out … then appeared again, looking down at me, solicitous but remote, eyes alert and blank.

His gaze flicked away without interest, as if scanning some featureless surface. I understood that I was in the presence of an alien life form, as fantastic as some desert reptile—icy, arctic, abstract, mindless and deliberate as a shark, frightening in his cold disinterest and self-control.

"Who are you."

He sat on a chair and peeled bandages off my nose and left cheek. "John Smith."

"Not good enough."

"It will have to do for now."

He wiped crusted blood away with a washcloth, dabbed at my face with antiseptic.

"Did you shoot Molotov?"

"Of course not." He glanced at the top bunk, where I suspected Molotov lay unconscious. "Why would I shoot him and then save him?"

"Who did?"

"Undoubtedly the same people who set you up."

"Who are they?"

"Hard to tell. We suspect Richard Light, but there's no proof."

"Why were you in his house?"

"I was alerted to … trouble. Unfortunately I arrived late."

"Who alerted you?"

No answer. I changed tack.

"Why do you care about him?"

Silence.

"Where are we?" I tried.

"Someplace safe."

Move you to a safe house

"Looks like a bomb shelter."

"It is."

"Whose?"

No answer. He produced some clean bandages and began to apply them to my face. It hurt.

"Rebirth?" I tried.

His hands slowed, but he showed no reaction. He taped the bandages.

"I'm sorry we clubbed you. One of our members—not a very advanced one I'm afraid—grew excited and swung too soon."

I wasn't sure what he meant by *advanced*.

"You were after those BioResearch goons?"

"We were trying to help you. We've had an eye on BioResearch. We hoped you'd explore it on your own. That didn't work out as planned—though there seem to have been some fruitful results."

I didn't ask him how he knew that.

"Why did you want me to explore BioResearch?"

A pause. "We suspect this company is doing something important."

"What do you mean?"

No answer.

I tried something else. "How did you find me?"

He gave me a cool, searching look. "We have certain tracking tools."

I didn't follow up on that either.

He checked a bandage, then pulled back, satisfied.

"I had a hallucination a few days back," I said.

His expression didn't change. "How's that."

"I imagined you sold me a water pistol."

He paused as if to consider this.

"You have to be careful about what you hallucinate. It could turn into something real."

He rose and left the shelter.

Waldo napped, woke. Drifted around … the door led to a steel tunnel that ended at another door, locked.

He cooked food on the hot plate, drank scotch. Every so often he checked on Molotov.

Splint on the right forearm. Face swollen twice its normal size, heavily bandaged. Hands bandaged. Molotov's chest was a livid composite of purple, black and brown. Behind the recent wounds, Waldo saw pink, puckered scars extending horizontally through each nipple, about six inches long.

Waldo slumped onto his bunk, brought his hands to his face. He found his bruises with his fingers and pressed into them, again and again.

11/19/99 I have nothing but time while Molotov remains insensible. I'll finish the account of our escape from BioResearch.

I remember it happening.

I think it happened.

After we smashed through the fence Molotov backhanded me. I stopped crying.

"Lead me out of here," he said.

His forehead was bleeding; apparently he'd bashed it against the steering wheel. Behind us a klaxon blared; searchlights swept about; to our left a squadron of black vehicles rounded a building and bore toward us, sirens screaming.

I took in our surroundings. Below us was a steep grade covered with saplings, underbrush and industrial waste; beyond that the gas station I'd entered earlier. Beyond that the Intersection.

The A-vehicles were almost upon us. "Gas station," I said.

Molotov nodded and drove down the hill. We were thrown about; the truck mowed down bushes; saplings snapped against the windshield. I picked myself up and found us on a tarmac, barreling toward the gas station. To the right, another squad of A-vehicles howled toward us.

I was tossed against the dash; Molotov had clipped off two pumps and rammed a gas truck, coming to a stop. The engine died; Molotov couldn't restart it. Gas oozed from the smashed pumps. We glanced at each other, stumbled out and jumped into the gas truck, which was facing the Intersection below us. By this time the A-vehicles had squealed to a stop and we were under fire.

There were no keys in the truck.

Fire from an assault rifle took the windshield out.

Molotov forced the gearshift into neutral, rolled down the driver's side window and yanked a matchbook from his shirt pocket. He lit a match and tossed it out the window.

Bullets blasted through the passenger-side window, embedding in the dash; I threw myself to the left.

Molotov lit the whole pack and threw it out.

Nothing. Then we seemed to float forward. The truck rammed through the Intersection fence as a shrieking explosion sounded behind us. I looked at the side-view mirror and saw vehicles spin and burn; then shrapnel pounded the truck. We were heading down the hill toward a corrugated metal warehouse.

I glanced at the mirror again. The back half of the truck was ablaze.

"We're on fire," I reported.

Molotov began to cackle helplessly. Meanwhile we burst through the warehouse wall and slammed into a cement dock. We jumped out and staggered away from the truck. I looked back; the fire had spread to the cab.

An A-car banged through the gap we'd made in the wall, smashed into a metal pole and stalled out. The two cops inside appeared dazed.

We both had the same idea and stumbled toward the car. I took the driver while Molotov took the passenger. We yanked the doors open and pulled the cops onto the pavement. My cop fumbled for his gun, but I stomped on his hand and he groaned.

"Asshole!" he yelled, not too enthusiastically, while I removed the gun from his holster and threw it away. Then Molotov and I jumped into the car and slammed the doors shut. I turned the key —the engine started!—while Molotov wiped blood off the windshield with his wrist.

I backed out of the warehouse, exited the Intersection, drove down one blacktop road, then another, then came to a squad of A-vehicles roaring toward the dump. I pulled to the side, bubbletop lights flashing, rolled down my window and waved them past.

An explosion brightened the sky.

I wrenched the wheel as the A-car pitched forward. A second explosion tossed the car into a ditch. We got out and ran.

We neared an outbuilding of some sort and rounded it. Came upon a metal gate, traffic lights.

A third explosion rocketed debris overhead; we lay still, then rose and ran forward. We seemed to move with agonizing slowness. As we ran a fourth explosion spat a tongue of fire high into the sky; we reached the gate and found it unlocked.

A white sedan stood outside. A man stood by the driver's door. I now know him as John Smith.

I glanced at Molotov, who stared agape at Smith.

"You!"

Smith opened the back door. "Hurry."

I looked behind us. The Intersection was burning.

A big chunk of white-hot shrapnel spiraled through the air and hit Molotov full on, tossing him about ten feet. We dragged him into the sedan and drove away.

Behind us the south of Brownwater was a sheet of flame.

Waldo woke to a sight that somehow didn't surprise him.

John Smith lay in a fetal position on the mandala mat.

Here's where things got confusing. Because the same phenomenon that had gripped Waldo in Marty's office days before was occurring now: He found himself confronting two different futures.

In one future, Smith levitated two or three feet above the mat. In the other, he lay directly on it.

The two futures shimmered and throbbed. At some points they overlapped.

Then … **CHUNK.**

Waldo gazed at Smith lying on the mat.

He fell back asleep.

11/20/99 I had a dream. It came when I found myself unable to move.

I've read about this: sleep paralysis. It's happened to me several times. Generally it occurs when I wake up at night and try to sleep again. Just at the border between waking and sleep I feel myself shunted into a side channel, and a violent electric current overtakes me, producing a sound like the buzzing of a million bees.

At this point various things have happened. Generally some black, featureless, vampiristic thing leaps silently onto my chest, where it threatens to suffocate me with its oozing, crushing darkness until I wrench myself in a panic out of the spell. A few other times I've performed the roll-over that I understand marks the start of an out-of-body experience, but I've never gone far. One time I had a lucid dream that involved walking around a vandalized apartment, terrorized by shadowy, malevolent presences lurking and tittering behind doors that had been slightly opened or wouldn't lock, with their doorknobs almost imperceptibly turning.

This time Amutha came to me, bathed in light.

I'm certain it was her.

I wept with joy, sorrow, regret, and a compassion so deep it felt like compassion for all creatures living and dead, throughout all time, the rise and fall and awful burning sweep of existence. And in the middle of that blooming, unstoppable emotion she came to me, white, rose-white, and touched my face and straddled me naked, a shining dream succubus, white hair falling over her face onto mine.

She took me into her and the electricity was now *sizzling* through; I was suffocating and didn't care; I felt myself rising up, up; I was rising out of my body and into the glittering space where Amutha was; I was dying into her and wanted to die.

She bent her face to mine … murmured a word in my ear.

"See."

I woke with a gasp.

Found a book on my chest: *The Book of Imaginary Beings.*

Jorge Luis Borges, *The Book of Imaginary Beings,* with
Margarita Guerrero, revised, enlarged and translated by Norman
Thomas di Giovanni, E.P. Dutton, 1969.

The book is composed of brief chapters. One was marked with a
paperclip.

FAUNA OF MIRRORS

In one of the volumes of the *Lettres édifiantes et curieuses* that
appeared in Paris during the first half of the eighteenth century,
Father Fontecchio of the Society of Jesus planned a study of the
superstitions and misinformation of the common people of
Canton; in the preliminary outline he noted that the Fish was a
shifting and shining creature that nobody had ever caught but that
many said they had glimpsed in the depths of mirrors. Father
Fontecchio died in 1736, and the work begun by his pen remained
unfinished; some 150 years later Herbert Allen Giles took up the
interrupted task. According to Giles, belief in the Fish is part of a
larger myth that goes back to the legendary times of the Yellow
Emperor.

In those days the world of mirrors and the world of men were not,
as they are now, cut off from each other. They were, besides, quite
different; neither beings nor colors nor shapes were the same.
Both kingdoms, the specular and the human, lived in harmony;
you could come and go through mirrors. One night the mirror
people invaded the earth. Their power was great, but at the end of
bloody warfare the magic arts of the Yellow Emperor prevailed.
He repulsed the invaders, imprisoned them in their mirrors, and
forced on them the task of repeating, as though in a kind of dream,
all the actions of men. He stripped them of their power and of
their forms and reduced them to mere slavish reflections.
Nonetheless, a day will come when the magic spell will be shaken
off.

The first to awaken will be the Fish. Deep in the mirror we will perceive a very faint line and the color of this line will be like no other color. Later on, other shapes will begin to stir. Little by little they will differ from us; little by little they will not imitate us. They will break through the barriers of glass or metal and this time will not be defeated ....

In Yunnan they do not speak of the Fish but of the Tiger of the Mirror. Others believe that in advance of the invasion we will hear from the depths of mirrors the clatter of weapons.

11/21/99 I wake to find Smith sitting at the table. He wears pressed khakis and a blue polo shirt. His right hand holds a Gauloise. A coffee cup sits near his right elbow.

Ever since Amutha's visitation everything has continued to glitter. Colors seem brighter, edges sharper …. Smith, for example, appears extraordinarily vivid, like an image from Rousseau. I find myself studying his cigarette, the slow coils of smoke above it, each tendril clear and close as if seen through a microscope.

I wash down two Duadine and feel my face. Nothing hurts too much.

"Is Molotov still out?"

Smith nods.

"Is it serious?"

"Hard to say. He may be in a coma. I've done what I can."

I pick up the Borges.

"Why did you give this to me?"

"To help me explain something."

I wait vainly for a follow-up. Meanwhile Smith takes a drag on the cigarette.

"Smoking is unhealthy."

"For beings like me, tobacco is like catnip."

I let that slide.

"How's it going at Rebirth? You guys still stealing from the rich?"

He doesn't take the bait. "I'm not very involved in that. My organization has a public layer and a private one. Like the Masons, for example, or the Vatican. Our public layer is a high-end rehab operation."

"You're proud of that?"

"Even advanced beings have to eat. And the money provides needed support for the private layer."

"Why do you call yourself an advanced being?"

He ignores the question. "Paradoxically, the private layer has a mission opposed to that of the public group. I'm the founder and CEO of the public organization, and I appear in our marketing materials—posters and the like. But I also have a double role.

"We in the underground layer broke from Alpha some time ago, when we began to suspect that Richard Light has dangerous ulterior motives. The public Rebirth is cover. No one would dream of us operating out of New Age, tennis and hot-tub halfway houses."

For the first time, Smith permits himself a smile. I suspect that this is his best attempt at humor.

"Why did you sell me the water pistol?"

He takes a while to formulate his response. Finally:

"One has to suit the weapon to its owner, don't you think?"

I ponder this.

"I never should have touched a real gun."

"No. We didn't expect that. But sometimes events follow their own logic."

I don't get it.

"Why are you helping me?"

He gives me a fixed look. He takes a drag and stubs the cigarette out in the coffee cup.

"We need you, Waldo. We need you to help us get to Light."

I see a flicker of fire in his eyes.

"Light and whatever universe-destroying technology he's working on."

Molotov remained unconscious.

Over the next twenty-four hours or so, Smith filled in particulars.

Meanwhile, Waldo grappled with the effects of Duadine overload —the bomb shelter weirdly magnified, with surfaces that warped and breathed, occasionally producing odd fragments of chillingly lucid detail.

What follows is a composite of three or four conversations, most of which, to Waldo, seemed to occur in a quasi-dream.

He didn't know how much of Smith's story to believe. But then, he found it no stranger than anything else that had happened in the past few weeks.

"The underground level of Rebirth," Smith recounted in his dead voice, "is composed of purified souls who desire only to leave this dimension after the one or two lifetimes that remain to us."

"C'mon. I'm not a complete sucker."

Smith ignored him. "We try to serve time in a dignified manner." He frowned a bit. "Though sometimes one gets impatient."

Waldo eyed Molotov's bunk. "So why hook up with him."

Smith gave Waldo a thoughtful glance, pulled a chair close.

"A matter of strategy. Our group was soon joined by older souls who'd been under cover for decades. They confirmed our worst fears. As early as 1954, they'd detected a field disturbance that soon grew to crisis proportions. They realized that Fish was passing through."

"The thing in the mirror?"

"Not exactly. Borges relates a *doppelgänger* myth; we took the name as a convenience. In fact, I doubt this 'thing' can be named. But certain connections between myth and reality are obvious: the notions of banishment, an alternative universe rising up, a showdown with a mirror image ... you may be interested to know that in some versions of the story, Fish and the Yellow Emperor are the same."

The Double on its own terms

Smith stood to pace. "Understand that beings at my level have long lived with the knowledge of conflicts in other dimensions—of battles being fought, territories conquered, each incursion coming closer. Most of us hoped to escape this region before Fish ever neared it, and some have. But a few of us have been caught behind enemy lines, so to speak—which is why I'm forced to deal with you now."

The space between Waldo's eyes began to throb.

"Richard Light is still young," Smith murmured through the pulsing, "only 44, and we believe he isn't quite yet aware of his full powers. But give him another ten or twenty years and he could destroy us."

Smith went on to recount that the older members of Rebirth had been buying and rehabbing underground safe houses since the first solid psychic affirmation of Fish's arrival in 1955. The consensus was that, if they could sense him—or it—it could sense them. The shelters were lined with a lead/aluminum alloy that provided protection from telepathic intrusion (hopefully enough—no one knew for sure).

All this doesn't seem to have accomplished much. Since 1961—the year Light was finally identified as the human host—over a dozen agents had been sent to kill him. Some were intercepted by Alpha security squads and jailed on various pretexts. Others met their ends in ways less direct.

"In the beginning," Smith said, "several of them killed themselves —or were killed—in different ways. One hung himself. One took poison. Two died in car accidents. One jumped off a high-rise building. Light's powers at close range are extraordinary."

He gave Waldo an arch look. "I'm not too concerned about you. Whatever you do here, or fail to do—no matter how often or how badly you screw things up—it can produce only a small interruption in the million or so lives you have left. But imagine our predicament, where even the smallest adjustment in the system could mean another hundred regenerations trying to recuperate if not worse." Smith regarded him coldly. "And need I mention the irreparable damage I've already suffered by dealing with you."

Waldo pressed fingers to his forehead. Smith's eyes followed him, impersonal and alert.

"Light ordered the death of my wife?"

"We think so, yes."

"Why would he do that?

"We aren't sure."

"You want Light dead?"

"That's one way of thinking about it."

They were silent a while. Waldo felt himself nodding off.

"I still don't understand Molotov's role in this."

Smith's face clouded. "Because your friend Molotov has a—let's call it a 'relationship'—with Light. And he seems to think you can help us. Incredibly, some of our members agree with him."

Smith drew back with a grimace. "And I've been given the task of pursuing this miserable possibility."

11/22/99 Molotov seems to be recovering. His eyelids sometimes flutter, but he hasn't spoken yet.

I pick at some chili. Smith meditates on his mat.

"How did Molotov get out of his house?" I ask.

Smith gives me a cold look. He's told me never to bother him while he's meditating. The trouble is he meditates all the time.

He rises and serves himself food. He sits across from me.

I don't know why, but I always find it unnerving to watch Smith eat.

"I didn't see it happen," he says. "I left when I heard sirens. A neighbor may have heard shots. Or police were in the area for some other reason."

I try again with the question I asked before. "Why did you bother? Why go to his house? What's your connection to Molotov?"

Smith focuses on his chili. No answer.

"Molotov recognized you when you rescued us at BioResearch. How?"

Silence except for the sound of chewing.

I press on. "Where did Molotov go?"

"I traced him to a local hospital. He'd driven there."

"With a bullet in his mouth?"

"It passed through the other cheek."

I step to the bunk beds and gaze at Molotov, trying to imagine that drive.

"He'd already left," Smith continued. "Walked out after treatment. Flew to Brownwater."

I return to my seat. "How'd you know he'd be there?"

Smith opens a cupboard and rummages around. He removes a scrap of paper and hands it to me.

I'm going to BioResearch—I believe the Twin is headed there and is in danger

I look up. "Twin?"

"One of your code names."

I blink and hand the note back.

"How'd you know where to pick us up?"

"Once I flew in you both came through strong enough. I visualized where we'd meet."

"That's all you knew?"

"No. We knew Schwarzcorp was employing you; we knew Alpha controls Schwarzcorp."

I sit back stunned. "They're the same?"

"Pretty common ploy. Evades antitrust. Think Coke and Pepsi. Old Navy and Banana Republic."

"Why was Dark"—I still can't call him Marvin—"asking me to investigate Light, then?"

Smith stops eating and lights a Gauloise. I wish he wouldn't do that. Those things aren't as bad as cigars, but they still stink.

"Come on. You know that interdepartmental espionage goes on all the time—especially in governments and big corporations."

"But Light—he knew about everything?"

"Most of it, I'm sure."

Smoke uncoils before Smith's empty face.

"Why do you fear Light so much?"

"It's complicated. Fish doesn't always produce hell. Sometimes it does better than that. The problem is it makes dramatic change. Its favorite technique is an embargo on emigrations. Souls are imprisoned in its worlds. I can't tell you how important it is for us to leave. Our worst fear is that it might marshal us for some new bureaucracy."

"Operation Renaissance."

Smith's eyes flicker, but that's all. He stubs his barely smoked cigarette on a plate and returns to his mat. He assumes the fetal position and closes his eyes.

Smith has many mantras. Today he uses one that's new to me.

"Nah ... amaanaah ... namaanaah," he murmurs.

I jerk to my feet.

"Nah ...."

After a while Smith emerged from meditation. He rose sluggishly and reached for his stubbed-out cigarette.

"Tell me about your mantra," Waldo said. He had dropped two Duadine.

Smith looked confused.

"The one I used today? Something we've been taught. If you pronounce the glyphs on our mats, that's what you get."

"What's the language?"

"Sanskrit I think. I know *ma* means 'to create.' On the other hand, *mana* means 'arrogance.' I'm not really sure what the mantra means."

He thought about it and actually laughed: an arid *"heh-heh-heh."*

"'Creative destruction'?"

He lit the cigarette and settled back in a chair by the table.

"It hardly matters. A mantra can be any kind of cue. A children's song … a phone number … a shopping list …."

Amutha's face … eyes rolled up

Waldo eyed the mandala mat.

"The English transliteration … what does it look like?"

Smith squinted. "Why?"

"Just curious."

Smith examined Waldo a while longer. Then he rose, found a pen and paper and bent over the table.

Na Amānā Namānā

Waldo slapped his forehead.

"Fucking diacritics! Fucking diacritics!"

11/23/99 Sleep paralysis again. But this time Amutha didn't come. The black, featureless thing materialized at my side and leapt onto my chest, an inky shroud of predatory malevolence. I was seized by panic, convinced that it wanted to occupy my body or suck my spirit from it. It approached my face; I struggled against it but couldn't move. I screamed but no sound came.

Then, as I fought, I had a sensation that my body was relaxing, growing more receptive, more malleable. My fear vanished, and I found myself arching up and entering *into* the black thing … which instantly disappeared, leaving me in a place full of odd, resonant gray light.

Three hours later, the gray light persists. The glittering and lucidity have gone, color has drained away, and now the bomb shelter is overlain with a shadowy substance. There's a weight to it, a soft, torpid presence, making my surroundings seem unreal and remote. At the same time, each element of the room seems *conscious* … watchful ….

Smith checks on Molotov.

"I need Duadine," I tell him.

(I'm out. Lately I've been raiding Molotov's stash.)

Smith regards me without expression. Then—reluctantly? I can't tell—he reaches into a pocket and sets two vials on the table.

"You have a source?"

Smith coughs. "Our underground membership includes doctors."

I want to weep with relief, even as I choke back a black spasm of anger at Smith for not doing this earlier. I rise shakily, approach the table, grab a vial and swallow five Duadine with a gulp of cold coffee. I close my eyes as the pills work their way down.

I sit down. "Thank you."

No response. I wave my hand around.

"What does gray light mean."

Smith looks startled—approaches me. He kneels and peers into my eyes.

"Are you in a place of gray light?"

I nod.

"Ah." Smith looks satisfied. "That. It's the place of the traveler between worlds."

Molotov woke up.

Waldo lay on his bunk, reading Borges.

"Waldo," Molotov slurred. "Are you there?"

Waldo sobbed. "Yes."

Molotov fell silent. Then:

"I had the strangest dream …. I was picked up by countless points of light, which pricked like thorns. As I ascended, sections of my body dissolved and reformed … by the time I reached the sun I was nothing but replacement parts …."

11/25/99 Molotov drifts in and out … sometimes he's hallucinatory; sometimes he seems to be revisiting moments in his past ("The mice … toxic psychosis … get the generator, Adam …."); sometimes he recalls fragments of conversation his brain registered while unconscious ("relates a *doppelgänger* myth"). Other times he seems to remember a passage he read or wrote with startling clarity ("On a warm summer afternoon … Adelchi Riccardo Mantovani … even the darkest of fallen angels can suddenly turn into a creature of light"). He has also twice uttered the words "Hi, dad."

Other times he's lucid enough, and asks questions about the shelter (located near Milwaukee, I now know) and about how we got here. I fill him in as best I can, but I know he won't remember most of it.

He wouldn't be able to talk at all, I'm sure, without the Dilaudid that Smith injects into him on a regular basis. His pain must be unspeakable.

I asked for some Dilaudid but Smith wouldn't give me any.

On another side note—Smith brought us a small turkey for Thanksgiving. I asked him to take it away.

"Why?"

"I distrust Thanksgiving turkeys."

He looked quizzical but complied.

In any case, Molotov can't eat solid food. We have to mix meat, vegetables and fruits in the blender and feed it to him through a straw.

When he was awake I asked what he meant when he said I was a "sleeper"—he rambled on about "prenatal tolerance acquisition" and "genetic affinities" and passed out again.

I've plied him with smoothies and water, sponged him down. His face is a ghastly mess, but he looks more human than he did before. He immediately asked for Dilaudid, and I seconded the request. Smith accommodated him but not me.

Molotov dozed off again. About 40 minutes later he began to rave in his sleep.

"*Clack clack clack* ... curse of the demon ... who knows what lovely, luminous garden awaits ...."

He giggled.

"Beach ... good job, Joey ... press the button ... sandy-haired ... crucifixion ... any free will ... abiding ... practiced bird ... gate of dawn ... sweetheart ... white door ... moon and its reflection ... *gotcha, sonofabitch* ... white pill ... *whoever* ... beating me forever ... *to be* ... illustrated moose ...."

Then:

"Dammit, what's with this gray light."

Waldo has a dream.

In a white hallway that glistens and breathes, a young woman with shoulder-length black hair shivers violently, gripping her upper arms.

Waldo doesn't know her.

Something terrible is happening.

"No."

He hears a *ding.* Glances to his left, sees a DEATH console.

On the monitor: 24.

Waldo grips his water pistol, but it's someone else's hand; someone else holds the gun. He tells himself to shoot.

A man sits, legs akimbo, against a floor-length window. His eyes are glazed; blood pumps through a long slash in his upper torso.

The man's eyes focus on Waldo.

His head now sits upright, without a body, on the seat of an office chair. Waldo thinks: How do I know this is an office chair?

"Amy doesn't like it," the head says evenly.

It grins. "Floor numbers go backwards in this building."

"Saw that on TV," someone interjects. It's Waldo's voice.

"Watch yourself on 24," the voice says.

Slugs rip through the door. Waldo has the impression he's in an elevator. He presses his cheek against the floor, oddly calm.

Thuck

Thuck

Then he's crying.

"Amutha … brimstone … aircraft carriers …."

Another hallway. Rows of doors on both sides.

At the end of the hallway, a white door with a sign on it: FLOOR ZERO.

Then the letters change:

REBIRTH. IT ONLY HURTS A LITTLE!

The door opens.

A figure stands on the other side, bathed in light.

Molotov voiceover: *Not a good idea to look at that too long*

Waldo tries to raise his squirtgun but finds his arm weighed down by some ponderous, viscous substance. His hand slowly rises … light flickers around the figure … the gun comes into view.

The figure steps through the door.

11/27/99 The bunk above me sagged.

"Good lord," Molotov mumbled.

He went silent. I guessed he was asleep. I worked on the journal.

"Still writing?" Molotov asked quietly.

I shut the palmtop. "How're you feeling?"

"Ah, Jesus, this pain …." He shifted on his bunk—then surprisingly, chuckled. *"Cruore ejus roseo …."*

He was quiet.

"Is there still a gray light?" I asked.

"It's here now."

"Good."

He was quiet again.

"What's that mean?" I said.

"What?"

"Cruore ejus roseo …." I tried to remember the rest.

"'By tasting His rosy blood we live to God.'"

"Yes."

"Well." He coughed. "Some see the blood as God's mercy. I don't agree."

"What does it mean to you?"

"Pain."

I didn't respond, waiting for the explanation I knew was coming.

"One of the paths to heaven available to man," Molotov went on, "is that of blood—the way of paranoia, violence, suffering. Very repetitious, a seemingly endless loop, boring … but it's one of the ways to the western lands."

"Western …?"

"The one true place."

I thought aloud. "The mice you tortured."

"You read about that? Nice work, eh?" He coughed again. "Comprehending a circle must be like heaven to a mouse."

I shivered.

"What's this light?" I wondered. "It's murky … palpable …."

"I've read about it I think. It's called the shaman's light—the light leading to a higher order."

"Is Smith creating it?"

"Smith?"

I was confused—then understood. "John Smith. The man who's helping us."

"Ah."

Molotov coughed again—an endless retch that seemed to gut him.

"I doubt it," he wheezed. "I suspect it comes from you."

I passed a hand before my face, saw trails of light follow my fingers.

"I've always believed you have powers you've never tapped." Molotov's voice was faltering. "I'm convinced that your ability to influence this particular dimension is enormous. It's just a matter of making you—comprehend a circle, as it were."

He fell silent.

"I don't understand."

He chuckled. "Well, my boy, now that we've started our little transition … it seems appropriate to tell you the true story of your birth."

I squeezed my eyes shut.

"But first," Molotov sighed, "let me rest."

"When you were born, something terrible was born with you."

Molotov lies on his bunk, speaking quietly. Waldo lies on his own bunk drinking scotch. To his surprise he isn't nervous or afraid.

"My father told me my brother was stillborn."

"A fiction. Indeed, it was almost impossible to describe the reality."

"And this—terrible thing. It has to do with Waldo?"

"Everything."

"Waldo is the thing I was born with?"

"Waldo is your way of dealing with it."

Waldo doesn't understand but moves on.

"Why didn't you tell me?"

Molotov shifts. Waldo hears him open a vial.

"You weren't ready for the truth—you'd have dismissed it as preposterous, thrown up your blocks again. It was necessary to wait for Waldo to fade."

Molotov gulps back pills. "You haven't seen him in some time, I expect."

Waldo blinks back tears.

Figure in the door

"No."

"Your Double was never your problem," he says. "Only a symptom. That Waldo of yours was guarding something too horrifying to remember."

Waldo takes a swig of scotch, then another.

"My task was to push you beyond your surrogate. Force you past this sense of threat from another self. If I could do that, I might get us closer to this—thing."

"Is that why you addicted me to Duadine?"

"And myself as well, you may have noticed," Molotov continues stiffly. "As ... 'Smith' has surely indicated by now, this is a group effort."

"What's the purpose?"

"Your brother has enormous talents. He can't be approached in the usual way. But once you headed west, I knew we might have a chance—any other effort would be doomed from the start. I believe our friends realize that now."

"And for this you made me sick?"

"Mental illness is in the eye of the beholder." His voice takes on a defensive edge. "My aim has been to create a crisis, yes."

"My brother is Richard Light?"

"Richard Light is the mask your brother wears."

"And I'm the—sleeper—who can bring you to him?"

"We're betting on that, yes."

"Why do you care?"

"There's nothing else to care about."

Waldo waits.

"I was assigned to the case," Molotov begins evenly, "in 1974 …."

11/28/99 I'm relating a series of monologues on Molotov's part, interrupted by fatigue and sleep. Smith would often sit at the table, listening.

Though what Molotov has related is fantastic, I don't doubt it. It gels with the little that I remember—my father's edgy, exaggerated reserve whenever I spoke of my mother or brother, the haunted, bewildered looks that occasionally crossed his face. He was a local sheriff, had a conservative cop's mentality, and couldn't communicate with anyone, especially me.

"If you've investigated me much," Molotov said, "you know my work has focused mainly on the production of new psychic states. Since I was a student I've been fascinated by the possibility of creating entirely new organisms. My motivation is a deep-seated disgust with the human species as it stands and a certainty that it will annihilate itself unless it quickly finds a way to achieve its next evolutionary level. I want to find a way to jump-start this process." He stops, choosing his words.

"I want to find a way to turn men into angels."

I remember something. "Fiction by fire."

"Exactly. I believe our salvation will ultimately stem from an artistic act. It will be an astonishing moment of reinvention. Our shared vision of a fire-and-brimstone apocalypse is fairly shallow, don't you think? An overeasy, sadomasochistic metaphor. No, I believe the apocalypse will be an entry, by all conscious entities in our dimension, into a new perceived reality—a group hallucination if you will."

Later:

"My work has always led me to creatures on the margins of what we call 'normalcy' … perverts … criminals … madmen …

channelers … souls pointing toward an alternate state of consciousness. I've been most gratified by my work with schizophrenics … people possessed by *others*. It's in this crowd, this noisy cluster of contending voices that I detect the most potential for developing a new life form … for here, as nowhere else, an alien reality seems to be breaking through of its own accord."

Later:

"By 1974 I'd developed enough of a reputation for both conventional reconditioning work and an interest in extreme cases that I was contacted by the U.S. government."

"There's a gap there in your bio," I thought I remembered.

"It was a classified job. You see, nineteen years earlier, an astounding and deadly creature had made its appearance a minute or so after you. It ripped your mother open. It was of a color not of this world, and it burst forth with an inconceivable violence and randomness. Every person who saw the thing died immediately—only your father and an attending nurse escaped. The nurse died a few months later in a psychiatric institution, and your father remained mentally unhinged for over a year.

"The hospital's walls restrained the monstrosity—or maybe it stayed inside of its own accord. It took a day for federal agents to send in a wheeled robot with video gear and a gripper arm. To their surprise, they found you alive, blood-drenched and bawling on the floor next to your mother. The robot dragged you out by the heel.

"Even the video images of Fish had enormous power. The first agents who looked at the screen had to be hospitalized. But still photos taken from the transmissions could be examined for a few seconds."

I thought of the picture that had knocked me to his floor. "The image in your office."

"One of the first video grabs," Molotov acknowledged. "Over a few more days it was found that Fish slipped into periods of quiescence at normal sleeping intervals—meanwhile shrinking to an identifiable size, roughly that of one of the smaller wards. So, using video to navigate, agents equipped with blinders and radio headphones entered the hospital while the thing lay quiet.

"Over several weeks they encased the room where it slept with lead and aluminum. Soon afterward, a strange *sizzling* sound came from inside—a wash of static, like a thousand voices speaking at once. The sound knocked a few men unconscious—but the box held. It was removed from the building and transported to a government laboratory."

I remembered the other photo he'd produced—the one that was overexposed, scratched, impossible to make out.

"The other image you showed me. I thought it looked like me when I was a boy."

"That was taken from a video made when Fish was five years old. It was still half interdimensional, but human features were starting to seep through. The photos grew clearer as it grew older—and less dangerous. Soon you could look at them without too much distress."

He was silent so long I thought he might have nodded off. No.

"Eventually the pictures revealed a naked youth …."

Molotov coughed—a long, brutal seizure that ended in a clutching, airless rattle.

"The thing literally ... *coagulated* ... into a mirror image of you
...."

Molotov shifted fitfully on his bunk.

The gray light persisted.

Waldo collected his thoughts on the Operation Renaissance security system.

The block. Before his death, Joey had been using the Cablemaster to transmit designs that were in fact renderings of Waldo's brother as a baby.

Joey knew what Waldo's brother looked like as a baby.

Light used an image of himself as a block for the OR file.

The check. Light used a mantra uttered by members of Rebirth.

A mantra channeled by Amutha as she died.

Light chose a phrase used by his enemies to secure his own file.

Impossible. Fucking impossible.

11/30/99 Breakfast. I fry eggs, toast bread, make coffee.

"Where was I?" Molotov says over his smoothie.

"My brother growing up."

"Ah."

He settles back, sucking at a cigar Smith brought for him.

There's something awful about watching someone smoke a cigar with very few teeth.

"By late '74 your brother was perfectly formed—not a trace of static. He looked exactly like you at the same age."

Molotov gives Waldo a prolonged look, as if picturing the young man he'd once known. An intimate expression crosses his fractured features. Waldo has no idea what Molotov is remembering, but it raises hairs on his hands and arms.

He shakes it off. "Go on."

Molotov's eyes clear. "All the boy's needs—food, hygiene—were met by robot—no one dared enter the cell. But one night I watched him on video for three hours straight and suffered no ill effects."

Molotov smiles dreamily and raises his hands—then snaps his burned fingers: *cha-cha-cha.*

"I stationed a technician at the monitor and went inside."

He shakes two Duadine from his vial and washes them down.

"Your brother struck me as the most dangerous entity I'd ever encountered. There was something intensely sinister, implacably ... *alien* about him. As I approached him I had the sensation that the walls of the cell were folding, ushering in a black, suffocating substance, cold as death, accompanied by a high-pitched twittering and gibbering, like that of bats."

I shiver and reach for my own vial.

"He crouched naked in a corner," Molotov continues, "regarding me without curiosity or fear."

"And?"

Molotov leans forward fiercely. "He said: '*Don't be afraid.*'"

I swallow three pills.

"I was astounded," he goes on. "His English was impeccable. What's more, he knew quite a bit about me and my colleagues. He even praised me for excellent handling of what he called his 'condition.'"

"You're kidding."

Molotov's eyes glaze. "'It would have taken me much more time to come through alone,' he said. I asked him who he was and where he came from—he said he didn't know. 'My earliest memory is of this place' .... I asked him how he'd learned to speak English. He said: 'I've been inside your minds for a long time.'

"Soon afterward," Molotov says, "I did something that changed my life. But that's for later, I think."

He played with his cigar, eyes glazed. "I decided he was safe to examine. It turned out there was very little unusual about him except for his telepathic abilities. Also, he had strong animal magnetism: Though he repelled some people, he fascinated others —put them under a spell of sorts.

"After a few weeks' observation—despite objections on my part— my colleagues let him move about. They established quarters for him in the lab—gave him a name—"

He chuckles ruefully.

"Rich light … get it?"

I decide to supply the rest.

"Officials visit … Light manipulates them telepathically … seduces a VIP."

Molotov throws up his hands.

"SecState, no less … I warned them, but they took me off the case."

"When did Richard join Alpha?"

Molotov's eyes soften. "I called him Rick …."

"OK, Rick. When?"

"'83."

"In what capacity?"

"VP Personnel."

I reflect. "Not bad for a 28-year-old."

Molotov shifts uncomfortably. "Afterward there were several deaths in the organization. Mostly suicides. Others quit." His eyes dart toward me. "By 1986 he was CEO."

"When did he acquire Schwarzcorp?"

"'91."

"The same year you joined Alpha."

Molotov hesitates. He isn't looking at me now. "He hired me, yes."

"Buying silence?"

"Not exactly. More a grateful gesture. He said he felt he owed me —for several reasons. So he had me spared when he bought the company I was in at the time."

"Intercorp."

"Correct." Molotov grins slyly. "What an amazing memory you have. It's almost as if you wrote my biography yourself …."

I don't let him distract me. "Did you know about the deaths at Alpha?"

"Not yet." He gives me a pained look. "But it was clear his rise was much too sudden. About the same time, some friends in government began to express concerns to me … but by then there was no way to intervene."

"Why didn't you expose him?"

Molotov waves the idea away. "Expose what? That the head of Alpha Incorporated was from—*another dimension?* No one would have believed it … and by then all official records of the project had vanished. I couldn't even get colleagues to admit they'd worked on it. I had only my lab notes, and they proved nothing … and besides …."

He looks miserable.

"Light had a file on me."

Smith returned. Paying little attention to Waldo, he deposited groceries on a counter and stepped to the bunks to check on Molotov. Given the vigorous snoring Waldo heard above him, he gathered the doctor was OK for now.

Waldo waved toward the door—meaning, beyond the shelter. "How dangerous is it out there?"

Smith studied him a moment, as if deciding whether the question merited a response. Then he shrugged and sat at the table.

"Fairly bad. You have to keep a shield up."

"Shield?"

"Make yourself think like a normal. Anxiety loops are most effective."

"I guess that makes me normal."

Smith didn't seem to appreciate the humor.

Waldo pressed on. "If we left this place—how would you protect us?"

"Think as many decoy thoughts as possible ... meanwhile, other members would focus on your image, invent alternate scenarios with you involved. The idea is to get Fish to pursue the reflections, not the reality. It's as if the universe was populated with hundreds of you." He gestured around the shelter, pointing at multiple invisible Waldos. "A hall of mirrors trick."

Waldo stood and glanced at Molotov. Asleep.

"Can you get us to Chicago?"

Smith squinted. "Why?"

"There's an Alpha subsidiary there. If I can access DEATH, I may be able to open a certain file."

"What would that accomplish?"

"I believe the file contains Light's battle plan."

12/1/99 Molotov droned from his bunk.

Shaman's light ….

None of this seemed real.

Molotov's voice:

"When I first met you I was astounded. I thought you were Light … then it came to me in a blaze of revelation: You were the *twin*, the child who'd been whisked from that hospital floor. Christ, we were such idiots we never thought to examine you. Nine months in the womb with that thing, and still alive, and it had never occurred to us that you might have powers of your own.

"If there was ever a reason to expect *folie à deux*, this was surely one ….

"It came to me instantly that you could be the answer—that the only creature who could approach that thing would be you—because only you could live with it.

"This was 1995, remember. Rebirth had contacted me some months before. They wanted to know more about Light. At the time I assumed they were government types, black operators ….

"I put you on the Alphagraph thinking I might get something useful—but nothing! Pictures of yourself in various cryptic or menacing poses, Hollywood clichés for the most part. You seemed especially fond of standing in the shadows on a street corner, looking up at your apartment. That was when I understood that you'd created a Double to guard your sanity—and resolved to bring you to your true Double, to drive you insane."

"Bastard."

"Don't think I took this lightly! I matched you dose for dose—reasoning that only if I was as mad as you could I join you in the Double's space …."

Table. Two chairs

"But if we're both mad—how do we know this is happening?"

He cackled. "How does one ever know? It's all illusion. The trick is to create an illusion that's *stronger* than the enemy's … the Yellow Emperor's magic is *stronger* than that of Fish …."

"Are you saying—I'm the Emperor?"

He coughed. "That's been considered."

"Why do you want me to take you to Fish?"

Long silence. Then Molotov said in a low voice: "To help you pull the trigger."

Waldo felt weak. "But you're wrong. I have no special powers."

"You're mistaken."

"No. Remember when you showed me that image on TV? The picture of my brother as a newborn? It knocked me out—I responded like any other human."

"I know," Molotov muttered. "I was disappointed. But then, you said you recognized it …."

"Of course I recognized it!" Waldo spat. Then he told Molotov about Joey, the OR file … then it all blurred … he told him about Dr. Dark … the attempts on his life … Marty … the setup … Amutha dying … he ground his palms into his eyes.

Molotov wept.

12/2/99 Smith is preparing for our trip.

"Cybersystems?" he asks.

"Programming outfit. They developed DEATH."

Smith glances at Molotov—asleep again. He tells me he's arranged for a dentist to visit today—another member of Rebirth.

A good thing. I hate thinking of my friend in pain.

"Smith. Are you familiar with a—*black thing*?" I sketch it with my hands. "Happens during sleep paralysis."

He nods. "Interdimensional vermin. They feed on fear."

He doesn't explain further.

"What does it mean when my … wife visits?"

He looks vaguely surprised. Then he sits down, apparently gratified that I've brought it up.

"I've sensed her. I suppose that's why I retain a bit of faith in you."

"Why do you lack faith in me?"

He eyes me vacantly. "I see my death in you."

I can't look at him.

"Does it matter if you die?"

"Doesn't it always?"

There doesn't seem much else to say.

I soldier on. "Do you really think I can help you?"

"Some believe you harbor a higher entity … a supersoul under deep cover. Personally I doubt it. I'd detect it."

"My—wife, then. Why does she give you faith in me?"

Something new crosses Smith's face—a hint of confusion, a flash of respect. But in an instant he returns to his deadpan.

"You've received a special visitation—something unusual at your level. Your wife is a fragment of grace."

Molotov had his teeth fixed—kind of. The dentist was a red-haired young man with blue eyes and chin stubble, still in dental school. For the most part he yanked out stubs of remaining teeth. But his efforts seemed to matter, and Molotov, slurring through novocaine, expressed his gratitude.

Later Molotov moaned. Waldo handed him a vial.

"You haven't told me something."

Molotov swallowed. "What."

"Your deal with BioResearch."

A sigh. "There was no deal."

"Liar."

"No. I found the same check you did. That's how I knew to go to Brownwater."

He handed back the vial; Waldo grabbed it.

"Staged attacks on you … the fabricated circumstances that killed Amutha and Marty … the fiction that turned you against me. You were played for a patsy, Waldo—from the beginning."

Waldo gulped back three Duadine. He noticed his hands were shaking.

"Either you were meant to kill Dr. Dark," Molotov said, "or he was meant to kill you."

12/4/99 We emerge into an apple orchard.

I expect a return to normal perception, but no: the same gray light, an impression of navigating through a dream. Colors are faded, unconvincing; the crunch of snow beneath our shoes is distant, out of sync. The sky looks like dawn or dusk.

It's actually around noon. It's fairly cold, but Smith has given us jackets.

We come to a rutted dirt road … a small, battered moving truck, wavering like an acid vision.

"Ah," Molotov gasps, limping. "The Bora Bora express."

I stare at him. "What?"

He grins inanely. "Popped into my mind."

Smith casts a look around, opens the back. The truck contains boxes, furniture. Smith hoists himself up, moves to the far wall, lifts a latch by the floor. A section of wall slides aside. There's about a foot of space behind it.

He looks up. "If we stop for long, assume a roadblock."

He steps back, jumps down. Hands a Glock 20 to Molotov and tucks another in his belt.

He doesn't give one to me. Probably for the best.

"Can you get us into Cybersystems?" I ask Smith.

"I'm not sure." He gazes somberly through the receding perspective of crabbed, leafless trees to where the road joins blacktop.

"My fear is they'll know we're coming."

The light source was a flashlight propped against a box. Waldo sat in an easy chair at the back of the truck. Molotov reclined on a couch, staring blearily at the ceiling.

He had just dropped five Duadine.

Waldo snapped his palmtop closed. Molotov glanced at it.

"You've written a lot by now."

Waldo nodded.

"Am I part of it?"

"Of course."

He smiled and closed his eyes.

"Perfect …."

The truck hummed along. A siren approached, making them eye the fake wall, but it passed and receded.

"How does the story end?" Molotov slurred.

Waldo stared numbly at his palmtop. "With my death."

"How do you know that?"

"I'll make sure of it."

"Can't say I blame you."

He was quiet a while.

"Death has its charms." Molotov squinted through a frame made by his fingers. "The white door."

Waldo stiffened.

"The end of the dream …" Molotov continued. "Baptize yourself in illusion; reality follows."

"You seem fond of the word 'baptism.'"

"A prerequisite for redemption, my boy … we could all use some of that …."

12/4/99 The truck stopped; we stood nervously behind the wall. The back door opened and closed; when we came out we found cheeseburgers and drinks on the floor.

I mashed up a burger with my hands and slid the warm sludge into Molotov's mouth. He washed it down with a Slurpee. He loves Cherry Coke.

Later I removed kitchen supplies from a bucket and pissed in it. When Molotov had to go he asked me to avert my eyes.

"We older men," he explained querulously. "Pathetic genitals, you understand."

"You look bad enough already, pal."

Smith let us out on the pothole-ridden parking lot of a decrepit strip motel on a sleazy route on the outskirts of what I assumed to be Chicago. We checked into a room with two beds and a cot. I took the cot.

Someone had been alerted to our arrival: clean clothes in the closet; soap, towels and other supplies in the bathroom. We took turns washing up.

After I showered and dressed I wiped off the bathroom mirror and stared at my reflection. To my surprise, I wasn't unnerved. I shaved off my beard, which had grown in.

I laid down the razor, pulled the PENIS from my pocket and pointed it at my temple.

You fuck! You fuck!

But I didn't pull the trigger. Not yet.

Smith shakes Waldo awake. 3 a.m. Sunday.

Molotov is up. Waldo drops four Duadine; Molotov takes three.

A taxi waits outside the motel.

Cybersystems is housed in a skyscraper on the north end of the Magnificent Mile. Smith pays the driver and steps onto the sidewalk. Waldo and Molotov follow.

Glass doors. Guard station inside. A man in a blue uniform leans back in a chair, reading *Guns & Ammo* magazine. He faces a bank of monitors.

To Waldo's surprise, Molotov clasps Smith's hand in his own in a tender, almost maternal manner. Smith seems discomfited and edges his hand away.

"I'm going to try something," Smith says. "But it may not work."

Waldo and Molotov nod in support, though they don't know what they're supporting.

"Remote mesmerism," Smith continues. "Like hypnosis, but telepathic. It works at close range, and only on a few people at a time. Even then the results can be uncertain."

Waldo and Molotov give him encouraging looks.

Smith nods. He breathes out and closes his eyes—then stares at the guard.

The guard rises stiffly and approaches, holding his magazine. Without looking at them, he produces a keyring and lets them in.

"Guys," he says out of nowhere, showing them the magazine. The cover has been folded back to reveal the first page of an article.

"Glock 20," he says. "Amazing firearm."

Waldo recoils, astonished. How could …?

But now was no time to be discussing the fine points of the G20 with a security guard. Smith and Molotov step forward, unaware of anything odd, and Waldo trails behind.

The guard closes the door, locks it, returns to his station. Picks up *Guns & Ammo* and leans back.

They approach some elevators. Directory on the wall. Cybersystems: 5.

They emerge from an elevator on the fifth floor. On the left a door opens into a white hallway. Rows of doors on both sides. One on the right opens into an office.

The receptionist's workstation is a DEATH console.

Waldo boots the computer, links with his setup in New York, calls up Joey's design.

"Good god," Molotov breathes. "Rick exactly …."

Waldo feeds in the image—the block dissolves.

"Your son was clearly roaming the network," Smith mutters. "Maybe he chanced on Molotov's project … image files …."

Waldo shakes his head. "I'm not sure—even if you're right, why this next piece of security?"

They wait about ten minutes—Molotov fidgeting, casting looks at the door. Meanwhile Waldo calls up a macron from the Symbols menu. When the check finally arrives he inserts the following over NAH:::AMAANAA:::NAMAANAA:

Na:::Amānā:::Namānā

Nothing. He tries:

Na Amānā Namānā

The screen clears. Waldo slumps in the chair.

"This must be a joke," Smith says.

The map of the United States reformulates. Dots appear on it. Ones over New York City … Brownwater … Milwaukee … Chicago … Aurora … Kansas City … Topeka … Colorado Springs … Kanab, Utah … Los Angeles ….

The monitor flickers—then begins squealing. Data erupt on the screen—memos—schematics—Hotmails—contracts—reports—

Waldo slams the keyboard. *"Shit!"*

Molotov groans. "What?"

"Database ventilation!"

He turns off the workstation. In the sudden silence they hear sirens. They run to a window facing the street.

A-vehicles pull up below. A-cops pound toward the front door, guns drawn.

"Damn it!" Molotov cries.

Smith draws his G20.

12/6/99 I write this in another bomb shelter

Christ, Molotov

Christ, Smith

Christ

Christ

With two pistols and a squirtgun Waldo thought they might have a chance.

An elevator in the hall was rising. They entered the stairwell; boots were charging up. They descended to the fourth floor, entered it and crouched behind a security station. Three A-cops entered the area and fanned out into surrounding hallways; behind them a larger contingent pounded up the stairs.

Waldo was in a dissociated state, seeing himself in third person. He glanced at Molotov—noted his lulled, remote expression, his languid movement.

"Smith!" Waldo barked, or thought he barked—the name came slow, low-pitched.

Smith nodded toward the stairwell.

They entered the stairs again—men shouted above. They headed down, reached the second floor. They burst into the back room of a clothing company and dashed past fashion racks to a door that led to a white hallway.

Dim wail of sirens. Floor-length window at the end of the hall, flickering with red and blue arcs from emergency lights.

Smith yanked at the nearest doors—locked. Shouts behind them; they scrambled down the hall, checking doors as they ran.

Molotov puffed miserably, beginning to hobble. He moaned and doubled over.

Waldo grabbed him around the waist, checked another door. Locked.

The door at the far end of the corridor burst open behind them. Smith went into a crouch, yanked out his G20 and shot the first A-men pouring through; the others bellowed and fell back.

Meanwhile, at the end of the hall near the window, almost carrying Molotov, Waldo found a door open.

He laughed inanely. "Look! A door!"

Smith glanced back—his eyes locked on something behind Waldo. In an airless stillness, Waldo watched a beam of light pass his left shoulder, head for Smith … who didn't move, but seemed to fold in on himself, concentrating. Then he regarded Waldo calmly—and the beam ripped off his right arm, exploded the right side of his torso and tossed him like a rag against the wall.

His G20 clattered away down the hall. Mutely, Waldo watched Smith's right lung, now visible, expand and contract as he sagged to the floor in a halo of blood.

In slo-mo, and still supporting Molotov, Waldo swung around and saw a black helicopter hovering at the window. A helmetless A-cop leaned out the cockpit. He held a very advanced weapon, even more highly classified than the PENIS: a Photon Hyperdrive and Laser Light Utilization System (PHALLUS). It was shaped much like the PENIS but without the broadened tip. It had long-term capacity and, remarkably, could shoot laser beams through most solid objects. As far as Waldo knew, it was still in development. But maybe not.

Waldo shoved Molotov through the open door into an office and dove after him; a beam sizzled by. As Molotov slumped to his knees Waldo screamed, grabbed Molotov's pistol and lurched back into the hall, confronting what looked like Waldo's startled expression as he shot a spray of bullets in rapid succession through the helicopter's cockpit window and into Waldo's head, plastering his brains against the glass.

Meanwhile Waldo heard shouts; he whirled and saw two A-cops charging down the hallway, visors down. He sprayed bullets again, missing wildly, but the men fell back. More working stiffs, he figured—none of them wants to get killed. He dragged Smith into the office, slammed the door shut and locked it.

He kneeled and cradled Smith's head. "My friend."

Smith's eyes refocused. Stunned, Waldo found him gazing at him lucidly.

Smith grimaced; blood spilled from his mouth. His lung stopped pumping—then started.

His eyes grew filmy. "This again."

The lung stopped. Smith smiled, closed his eyes and curled into Waldo's shoulder.

"If you can," he exhaled into Waldo's ear—deliberate, peaceful— "please put an end to this death business."

His legs jerked; he rattled and sagged back. Waldo and Molotov glanced at each other. Bullets blasted through the door, riddling the floor and Smith's legs; Molotov howled as blood bloomed from his midsection. Waldo dropped Smith's body, grabbed Molotov's G20 and dove behind a workstation.

The door blew open.

Three A-cops burst through. Waldo shot each of them in the neck just below their visors—*what incredible precision!* he thought— then dove for Molotov, who was going into shock. Waldo picked him up and lurched toward a window. Looked down—an alley—a dumpster, closed. Waldo grabbed a chair and threw it through the window. An A-cop approached; Waldo forced him back with a blast from the gun, then shoved Molotov through the smashed glass. Molotov bounced against the dumpster and toppled to the pavement.

Slugs spit into the windowframe. Waldo threw himself out.

The dumpster approached lazily; he watched it, alert, detached, seeing every detail on its crumpled blue surface … then he was lying on his side on asphalt, still clutching the G20.

"Molotov!"

Molotov didn't answer; his legs were twitching, teeth chattering. Above Waldo, at the window, an A-cop with an assault rifle leaned out.

Still in slo-mo, Waldo scrambled to the side, watching slugs sweep up the pavement—enter Molotov's torso. Molotov's body jerked; his eyes rolled up … Waldo rose to his knees howling and sent rapid-fire shots toward the window; this created another lull. Waldo pulled himself to his feet and stumbled past Molotov's body toward the rear of the skyscraper. Behind him were sirens, shouts.

He staggered into an alley. The alley ended at a street … he lurched toward it.

Poster on the alley wall:

REBIRTH. AIN'T IT A BITCH!

The floating man on the poster was Waldo.

Someone coughed. He looked toward the street. Saw a man with a scar on his chin.

James Gate. He grinned and raised a PHALLUS.

Waldo shrieked and sent six or seven bullets Gate's way—he seemed to phase out, then in. Meanwhile Waldo heard shouts and looked back.

A-cops pounded into the alley. Waldo fired; two fell; the others pulled away.

Sobbing, Waldo put the gun barrel in his mouth.

Don't, Amutha said calmly.

He pulled the barrel out.

Look up, Amutha said.

Waldo looked up. A woman leaned out a second-story window.

A laser beam entered the wall next to him. Waldo glanced to the left, saw Gate grinning over his PHALLUS. Waldo forced him back with a shower of ammo and looked to the right, where four A-cops were charging. He shot one of them and the others pulled back.

The world was seesawing, flickering out; Waldo looked up weeping. The woman beckoned.

"What do I do!" Waldo screamed.

She smiled. "You know what to do."

Suddenly, Waldo saw two futures before him. In one, he was shot dead. In the other, he levitated.

He tossed the G20 on the pavement but kept his water pistol.

CHUNK.

He rose.

Michael Schulze

III. JANE1

Michael Schulze

12/7/99 This bomb shelter is similar to the previous one in layout and contents, including a circular mat ringed by red glyphs.

My left arm is in a cast.

The gray light persists.

The woman's name is Smith.

Jane Smith.

Early twenties. Wide-spaced opal eyes. Shoulder-length black hair with reddish tints. Slim, sensual figure. But she summons no thoughts of sexuality, radiating only the icy, cosmic calm of her predecessor.

She carries a Glock 20 at her hip.

12/8/99 Continue.

As I levitated the alley exploded into a fiery cloud. This worked to my advantage—in the flame and confusion, maybe even some of the A-cops who saw me rise shook it off as an illusion and decided I'd been blown off my feet and was now lying dead beneath the rubble. But as I approached the window, I glanced down and saw at least two cops gazing up at it—and Jane.

Jane grabbed me, pulled me inside, led me past DEATH stations to a stairwell. I staggered down two floors to the basement, where she opened a steel door that led to a cement corridor lit by fluorescent lights in wire mesh. This led to another basement area, where a stairwell rose to the deserted lobby of an office building.

This is Wednesday, I thought. Why is this lobby deserted?

Jane propped me against a wall, ran out to the street and gestured. A gray sedan pulled up; she opened the back door, ran inside and hustled me out.

A-sirens wailed. She shoved me in the back seat; I slumped to the side. She jumped in the passenger seat and we took off.

The driver took corners at high speeds.

I passed out.

Waldo had a dream.

A beach. Sunrise or sunset.

Waves crest soundlessly against the sand. Molotov stands some distance away … pants rolled up, barefoot in the surf.

He smiles, waves.

Waldo sits at a white metal table. There's an apparatus near his right hand—an intercom?

Tinkle of laughter. Amutha sits at Waldo's side, wearing a white cover-up over a blue bikini. She shimmers … the space around her expands.

Waldo can't figure out what's different about her. Then it hits him.

She's looking at me

She laughs again, points toward the beach.

On the sand is a boy's red bicycle.

12/9/99 This Smith smokes Gauloises too.

I raise my vial and rattle it.

"Got any Duadine?"

No response. She puffs on her cigarette, filling the shelter with smoke enough to kill a dog.

I try something else. "Are you related to … 'John'?"

Her expression is flat. "He was my brother."

I'm stunned. "You know he's dead?"

I curse myself. Of course she knows.

But she shows no sign of distress. Gazing at her eyes, I think of an algorithm, an astronomical event—a cold bright curve of space. My flesh twitches convulsively.

"Christ … I'm sorry. If I could take his place I would."

"As I expect my brother told you, death is a bore."

I detect self-deception here but don't push it.

"Is Molotov really dead this time?" I wonder.

Silence. Then:

"That office we were in," she says for no apparent reason.

"You infiltrated it?"

"I'm a project manager there. Or was."

A-cops gazing up at the window

"You're compromised."

"My cover is blown." She looks vaguely irritated. "I haven't linked with the others since we got here."

"Where are we?"

"Outside Aurora, Illinois."

Aurora—dots on the map

Impossible. Too much to process.

I change the subject. "John and Molotov knew each other. Do you know how?"

She doesn't answer. I reach for the scotch again—then stop, startled by her wretched expression.

No matter how advanced, Jane is suffering. She grimaces and stubs out her cigarette.

My fault. All my fault.

"Molotov was our mother," Jane says.

Some time that night Waldo woke, feeling black tentacles of despair penetrating a shifting haze of pain … then began laughing bitterly, knowing that this woman didn't have a chance—that almost everyone he'd known during the past month had died because of him. That he was a maker of death.

12/10/99 Unlike John Smith, this one rarely leaves the shelter. I don't have to ask why.

Light is scanning for both of us.

Jane speaks little. Like the previous Smith, she often lies on the circular mat to meditate. But I never see a future in which she might levitate—or me again for that matter. Still, she invites me to try. I assume a fetal position on her mat and close my eyes.

Na Amānā Namānā, I whisper, stretching out the a's topped by macrons.

As I speak the vocables, I watch the gray light modulate to white … the room is washed with light that seems to emerge from within. The emanation is alive, aware … conveying a sense of warmth, wisdom … *beneficence* … like one of Amutha's visitations. I'm acutely, magically aware of the light, wondering how I've never seen it before; it's all so … *simple … it's been here all along* … all that's required is the *proper perspective* …. At intervals, I have the impression I'm merging with the light ….

I open my eyes. I haven't moved.

Some time later, Waldo asked Jane a question that had been on his mind.

"You're, uh … Molotov… um … how …."

She knew what he meant. "My mother's name was Artemis. She switched sexes after I was born. I was raised in a foster home, where I was loved and received a good education. But my family didn't understand me—as maybe you can imagine.

"John left his foster home and came to get me. We lived together in New Jersey. I went to high school while he did day trading. At some point I learned that Molotov was managing the Reagan Center."

"Your brother—was John his real name?"

She looked bemused. "All the males in our underground are named John. All the females are named Jane. It's a crude tactic, but it actually causes a good deal of confusion in the Interface, especially if you can internalize the names."

"Interface?"

"The place where ESP operates—telepathy, clairvoyance, precognition … think of it as a network where people like us make contact—or hide from each other."

Waldo let that sink in.

"How did you know I could levitate?"

"I didn't. But I visualized it. You did too, I'm sure."

Waldo didn't know what to say. Jane focused on smoking a Gauloise.

"Tell me about your mother."

"My biological mother. I have vague memories of her. I was two years old when she put me up for adoption." Jane looked distracted. "I kept an eye on him after I joined Rebirth."

"When was that?"

"1994—soon after my brother founded it. John and I recruited Molotov a few months afterwards. We got to know each other then."

"Why did he change his sex?"

"That puzzled me at first. He seemed fairly asexual." A pause. "I think it was an experiment."

Waldo shook his head.

Transform yourself into fiction

He could see it all play out. "One he later regretted."

"Of course." She waved the cigarette. "As he rose in the academic ranks—any serious deviance …."

She didn't finish.

Waldo looked around the shelter, depressed. The gray light persisted, but there was something sinister about it now—throbbing slightly, uncoiling … he remembered the Black Thing and felt a rush of fear … then shrank back as the Other formed across Jane's face, oily and repulsive, a thin smear of amusement hanging on its mouth.

Billions of years

Jane's face flickered back to normal. Waldo shook off a suspicion that she was the Other in disguise.

"Do we have a chance?"

"Probably not."

"So why are you helping me?"

"I'd have no chance without you. Artak convinced me of that."

"How did he convince you?"

Jane pondered her response … then shrugged.

"Artak loved you."

Waldo's throat caught.

He'd known that.

"This made no sense," she continued, "for he despised reality. He loathed the whole cruel, degrading charade of fear and desire, time and space, birth and death and rebirth … and ached with every particle of his being to reinvent it, or at least be party to its reinvention. And for some reason he loved you."

Waldo fumbled for the scotch bottle.

"As he advanced his argument that only you could possibly assassinate your brother, I dismissed it as the raving of a woman turned man who'd fallen in love with a man …." Jane's face went still and abstract. "But eventually his faith in you was too fierce to ignore … and I came, despite all the evidence, to believe him."

Waldo moaned … fingered three Duadine into his mouth with a quaking hand and sluiced them down.

Molotov, I'm so sorry

Sorry's not enough, my boy

Not even close to enough

Not even close

12/11/99 The problem with moving west is that Light/Fish's methods vary. He may choose an armed assault, as he did in Chicago. But as we get closer—especially after we cross the Rockies—he's likely to resort to more sophisticated maneuvers.

The most dangerous is the hallucination that appears normal. For example, I may believe I'm brushing my teeth when actually I'm cutting my wrist. As we near Alpha's Hollywood HQ, it will be increasingly hard to separate fact from fiction. Even a showdown with Light could be entirely hallucinated—or so Jane says.

I grimace. "These conditions are impossible."

"Not quite that bad. Remember that you can rely on me too."

"How?"

She regards me expressionlessly. "I'm adept at blackouts."

It turns out that blackouts are the psi equivalent of a computer crash. Whereas John Smith relied on noise to hide his whereabouts, Jane prefers a kind of telepathic invisibility. The trick is to cast a "net of silence," which has a limited geographic range. People within the silence will be visible but will simply not be noticed. The technique is apparently more effective than noise but has the drawback of excluding other Rebirth members.

"It's just as well," she adds. "Light might patch to us through weaker members if they know where we're going."

"Where are we going?"

"I thought you knew that."

I stiffen—don't look at her. "You've been into my palmtop."

"Yes."

I turn grudgingly, meet her eyes. "Kansas City."

We're both silent, contemplating this.

"I don't understand. The map shows not only where we've been but where we're apparently going. How is that possible?"

"Well," she speculates, "it seems clear that Joey had precognition. What's strange is that now that we know this, the map will probably direct us to our next destinations."

"But if the dots on the map are plotting our trajectory, Light already knows where we're going. He even knows we're here now."

I ponder the implications. "Do we have any free will at all?"

Jane reaches for her Gauloises. "I've discussed this with colleagues. No one is sure. The consensus seems to be that free will might operate in a limited, time-dependent manner, especially when it comes to choosing small, fairly unimportant futures. But over longer periods, especially over several lifetimes, free will no longer exists. It's a self-indulgent delusion on the part of an animal species that can't bear the thought that it has little or no control over its fate."

I'm not sure I like what I'm hearing.

She waves her cigarette, eyes like marbles. "But we have to assume from Light's lack of action that he doesn't know … isn't aware of OR. That OR is something other than we've thought."

I'm thinking ahead. "Kansas City. You've looked into it?"

"Omnicorp. A Schwarzcorp unit. Actually it's in Independence, Missouri."

"Can you get us there?"

She sucks in smoke, glances at my cast, regards my bruised face.

"Soon."

I cast a stricken look at a day-old newspaper on the table. My face squints from the front page. I look like a creature of pure evil. The public is advised to be on the alert for a terrorist who killed five security officers in Chicago.

No mention of the bodies of Molotov and John Smith.

I shudder. "Can't wait that long."

Jane gives me a look. Annoyance? Weariness?

More like disgust.

She stubs out her cigarette, reaches into a drawer and pulls out two Duadine vials. I gasp with relief.

She tosses the vials to me—I make a grab for them with my right hand but bat them away. They roll beneath the bunk bed.

I get to my knees, scrabbling on the tile, unashamed, not thinking to be ashamed.

Waldo woke from a troubled dream in which Joey's final designs melded oddly with images of A-Police charging down endless white corridors and a vast interstellar creature expiring in shuddering agony, sometimes in the guise of Marty, sometimes as Molotov, sometimes as himself, a cosmic crucifixion, all reality dying in this creature's weary, compassionate heart … Molotov's voice: *even the darkest of fallen angels* … Joey separating into slime, Brownwater exploding into flame, John Smith dying in his arms, lung pumping feebly … Amutha in his arms, bleeding and blind and dying; he sobbed as she whispered words he couldn't make out … *I'm sorry*, he screamed, and the words reverberated through rainbows of lifetimes to a luminous place where a white door opened … a white door approaching to the *clack clack clack* of a turning wheel and painted in red on the door are the words HI, DAD.

He heard the bunk above him squeak.

Waldo's throat caught. "Jane," he whispered, feeling tears roll down his cheeks.

He couldn't speak for a moment. "I keep crying …."

"I know."

"I want to end it."

"You'll do that."

He wiped the tears off.

"Jane," he tried again.

"Yes?"

"When I looked up at the window and you were there … Amutha told me to look up."

She didn't respond.

"Did you know I killed her?"

He could sense her choosing her words. "I read about that part, yes."

"Where is she now? Can you tell me that?"

Silence.

"That's the thing, Waldo," she said finally. "When Amutha spoke to you, I felt my mouth moving."

12/12/99 I keep waking, falling back to sleep … in a dream … or was it … my naked limbs fusing with Amutha's in soft white light, mouths searching and melding, hands gripping my ass as she opens herself to me. An electric *sizzle* races through but there's no paralysis now; in a timeless, electric stillness I enter Amutha and feel her legs wrapped around my hips, dazzled by her blind face staring at me like a mosaic of a dreaming saint.

The electricity follows the pulse of our lovemaking; as I move deeper into her we fold into each other; we're a single organism in a cocoon of white light. There's no building toward orgasm here, only the ebb and flow of our bodies, restful as the rhythm of the ocean or of blood … sweet, calm, astonishingly generous.

And then … I hear Amutha's voice as if whispered in my ear.

You'll make life, Rick

I sit up on my bunk bed.

I'm sure that's what she said.

Rick

Jane appeared in the evening. There was nothing especially different about her, but Waldo detected a new element nonetheless —something soft, vaguely affectionate, at rest. As she unbagged some canned goods, her back to him, he found himself regarding the lines of her hands, the curve of her neck or a hip, finding in these details something more than feminine loveliness … there was an actual *transparency* to Jane today, as if, with a touch of a finger, he could scrape the surface and reveal the shimmering spirit body her mortal body contained—a hushed, gracious entity.

He didn't want her sexually. She was out of his league. But Waldo wondered: Had Jane somehow merged with Amutha last night?

She cooked dinner in the microwave. As they finished eating she gave him a brief, nakedly human look.

But maybe Waldo imagined that.

She produced a keyring. The keys moved toward him. His hand closed around them.

"You drive," she said.

12/12/99 Wooded area. Bitterly cold, low clouds that might hold snow. I know it's dark, but the gray light imparts details I might not otherwise see.

To the right a field, a split-rail fence. The fence is flat, unreal—a cheap cardboard prop halfheartedly erected to lend a dab of realism to a poorly articulated, chimerical tableau.

To the left a dirt road. Gray car.

It's an automatic; I can drive pretty well with one hand. Meanwhile Jane concentrates on making us invisible. Queer feeling … like cotton stuffed in the brain. Sounds are muted, as if heard underwater … when we speak, the words come unnaturally slow, low-pitched.

We've decided to use expressways. The advantage is speed, the disadvantage possible roadblocks.

Even worse—let's say the database ventilation at Cybersystems triggered a dump into a file. Say my OR session was saved.

Approaching Des Moines. In a wet, bitter snowfall Jane emerges from a rest stop bathroom, clad in jeans, a black coat. She stretches on a bench beneath a pine, blank face pointed at the gray sky.

Please, Light, you remote, uncaring sonofabitch. Don't take this vicious charade any further. Stop this.

Stop.

Jane gets nervous. At the wheel now, she leaves the expressway, passes through mid-size towns. Waldo's brain is still clogged, the world around him a gray blur … department store … car lots … forms, clusters, ciphers, meaningless. He washes down five Duadine with a pint of scotch … heading west south of I-80.

Stop for gas. Waldo buries his head in a map as Jane operates the pump. She pays the clerk in his store, returns to the car … tosses Waldo a newspaper.

His face on the front page still. Waldo is now known to be responsible for the destruction of much of Brownwater. Alpha Inc. offers a handsome reward for his arrest. ASS chief James Gate vows to avenge the deaths of his men.

There's no apparent reason for Stanton's murder spree. However, he has a history of mental instability and violent acts. One psychologist who has reviewed his clinical record considers him "a classic paranoid schizophrenic"—"At critical moments he may literally be possessed by a secondary personality. I suspect that at his most homicidal, he's not Waldo Stanton at all but his alter ego."

Waldo sees bubbletop lights on an overpass. Jane concentrates furiously.

They get back on the expressway.

Headlights illuminate a billboard … cigarette ad. On a beach, youths clutch each other with delight, laughing into the camera. None of them are smoking.

Pasted across a girl's eyes:

REBIRTH. IT'S TIME TO END IT!

12/13/99 Pull into a roadside park. I type in the car; Jane sits on a bench by a brook, huddled in a coat. The snow has let up.

Moonlight leaks through a gap in the brightening clouds—a gold, runny light mingled with gray, spilling pale ovals and points on Jane's black hair and jacket and the sluggish water.

For a while she was smoking a cigarette. Now she holds her head in her hands.

I go to her, shivering, shuffling through an inch or two of snow … sounds are a second or so off. The gurgle of the brook is off-kilter, uncoordinated with the water's movement.

As I approach, it becomes clear that her fingers touch her face at certain points. I sit beside her, wrap a blanket about her shoulders.

"What's wrong."

"Pressure," she mutters. She points to her temples. "Here." To the space between her eyes. "Here."

She grits her teeth. "This *sizzling* sound …."

Waldo feared that Light's men would intercept them. But without any other good alternative, and with Omnicorp nearby, they decided to proceed.

Driving in early morning about twenty miles from Independence. Snow fell again.

"Jane."

"Yes."

She stared at the broken center line pouring past, wavering behind the smeared glass.

"Why haven't we been stopped? Killed?"

"I'm not sure. Possibly we're supposed to make something happen."

Waldo brought up the obvious. "Tell that to the A-Police. They weren't shooting to miss at Cybersystems."

She gave him a glance he found hard to decipher. Amusement?

"Maybe."

"What do you mean?"

No response.

Waldo shook his head.

"Christ …."

They drove a while in silence.

"Another possibility," Waldo said. "OR is a trap."

"I doubt it. Why would Light announce he knows who you are—who we are?"

"To make us curious," Waldo tried. "Lead us on. Draw us toward him."

"Maybe," she said again. She fingered the gun at her hip. "What seems certain is that the situation has been orchestrated." She gave him a significant look. *"Who's* doing the orchestrating—that's another question."

It depends on your definition of whoever

Waldo broke into a sweat—tried to get a grip. As this happened he realized, as sometimes occurs in dreams, that he was dreaming … Jane, the car, the monotonous motion of the windshield wipers, the broken center line passing beneath them … languid … stately … unreal ….

North of town. Crumbling pavement, decrepit hotels, industrial buildings, parking lots. The snow had turned to rain.

Remembering a book he read once—*The Lucid Dreamer.*

No distinction between the moon and its reflection

12/13/99 It turned out that Omnicorp was to the south. We decided to approach by back roads, using a wide circling route.

We drove about fifteen minutes. I felt a stab of apprehension and glanced at Jane.

She was frowning. "Stop."

We were on a road in a state forest. I pulled to the side, glanced at the dashboard clock. Close to 8 a.m.

"Roadblock," I muttered.

She nodded. I dropped two Duadine.

We sat without speaking. I stiffened as lights approached behind us … a white truck roared past; on its side, smeared with snow, I saw the letters GOD.

My vision wavered, and for a moment I saw the big picture … my cop father crouched in a chair, all stoicism gone, face wracked with confusion and pain … Amutha naked in my arms that first, dazzling night, blind eyes wide … and everything that followed, precise and pellucid, the entire sweep of my life in one high-speed download … and I understood not with my brain or my heart but with my flesh and my bones that it was all prearranged, all of it, not just Light's vicious, mocking, incomprehensible plot but every second of every minute of every day from my unlucky conception to my imminent death.

Immediately it was over, and I stared at the vanishing taillights of the GOD truck, anxiety gone and now feeling awash with a dull, sad compassion, a bittersweet ache.

I glanced at Jane; her eyes were lidded, peaceful. I wondered how much of this she'd sensed.

"What's the plan."

She blinked … emerged from her remote place. "Let's keep going. I can handle this."

I contemplated her a moment—made to get back on the road. She stopped me with a hand.

"It would be easier if you were out of sight."

I write this on my palmtop in the trunk, with a flashlight.

The car slows—Waldo goes dark.

They stop. Muffled male voice—then Jane's, low and cool. In his mind's eye Waldo pictures the result of her remote mesmerism: maybe a businessman—rumpled suit, loose tie—coming home from a sales call.

Crunch of feet on gravel toward the trunk.

"You said you live nearby?" a male voice asks.

Waldo's heart sinks.

Jane forgot to shroud the license plate.

He raises his water pistol to his face. Jane makes an explanation he can't hear.

"Cover him," the voice barks. "Get his keys."

Seconds later the trunk door lifts; rain spatters his face; lights glare in. Black silhouettes. Waldo kicks the door open and points his PENIS at them.

"Don't move or you'll experience a nightmare you'll never forget."

The silhouettes back off. Incredulous, Waldo edges out of the trunk. Two A-cops without helmets, clearly afraid. Waldo begins to gloat—then something slaps him on the neck.

As he falls he drops his water pistol. Meanwhile he watches as Jane emerges from the car and begins firing at something to the left. Someone grabs Waldo's jacket and drags him behind an A-car.

A-cop. Terrified. One of his partners lies sprawled on the pavement, writhing. A third has taken refuge beside another A-car. The A-cop jams a G20 in Waldo's mouth.

"Gotcha, sonofabitch."

A red flower blooms on the cop's forehead. His body jerks to the side, landing on Waldo's left knee; there's a *pop*; Waldo hears himself howling. Meanwhile, divorced somehow from this remote, annoying noise, he dully watches Jane standing by the second A-car, shooting the third cop in the back of the head.

The kid on Waldo's knee rattles—kicks a few times and goes still.

Jane kneels by Waldo's side. He gazes at her through a red haze. "Help."

She lifts him up; he hops to the passenger door, opens it. Before he sits down he bangs his knee into place … then the world goes silver. Beside him, Jane arches back and cries out.

Waldo tumbles in slo-mo into a place without time or space.

He comes to on the pavement. Beside him, Jane stares vacantly at nothing. Waldo sees an entry wound on her upper chest. Blood pools on the snow beneath her back.

Waldo feels for a pulse in her neck. Nothing.

Waldo shrieks.

In a daze, he looks around. An A-cop, blood spurting from his gut, staggers toward him, G20 pointed vaguely in Waldo's direction. The cop moans and slumps to his knees … topples forward on his face.

Waldo gathers Jane's body to him and weeps.

When he pulls away he sees that her face is smeared with blood. He feels his neck; his hand comes away red. He lays her down, takes off his coat, rips out part of the lining and wraps it around his wound.

The cold brings him to some sort of focus … he looks down the road in both directions.

No lights.

He locates his squirtgun, jams it in his belt, gets to his feet and hobbles toward the cop who had died on top of him. He goes through the young man's pockets, finds a keyring. Then he struggles with the corpse, yanking off its black jacket and boots and pants. He stumbles to an A-car and finds a helmet with a visor.

Clutching the disguise, Waldo sits in the A-car's driver's seat. The keys don't work. They work in the second car. He retrieves his palmtop from Jane's car, reaches down to grab her gun—then stops.

No. Even now.

He leaves the G20 where it is, tosses his palmtop into the A-car and takes off.

In the rearview mirror, he watches Jane's dead body receding.

The rain is intensifying. Still no traffic. Sobbing, Waldo drives about five miles, comes to an intersection—takes a right, then another, and spots the entrance to a campground. A carved wooden sign says "Welcome to Oh! Boy!" Waldo pulls in, snapping a chain stretched between two posts.

Gravel parking lot. Deserted mess hall. Wood cabins. Black lake.

Waldo drives the A-car to the back of the campground and parks it behind a cabin.

Then, for the next twelve hours or so, Waldo remains still in the driver's seat, only leaving to urinate or vomit.

He mourns the death of Amutha. Dead at his hand. He mourns the deaths of Marty and Molotov. His friends John and Jane, serving him loyally despite dismal odds. All of them dead because of him. And the cops. Just doing their jobs. Dead. Dead.

Please put an end to this death business

Occasionally the radio crackles with nearly unintelligible reports. At one point it erupts into frenzied shouts as the bodies near the A-car are discovered. The reports are so confused that Waldo can't determine the number of dead.

For some reason no one interrupts him. The A-police seem muddled, searching everyplace except here. No one notices the snapped chain near the road. It's as if he's been deliberately left alone.

Waldo wants to end it. If he could kill himself with a water pistol, he would. Instead he quakes before a vision of a rock circling without purpose in interstellar space, infested with human vermin. Mindlessly orbiting a flickering, dying light. Dying. Soon to be dead. A rock where you can kill and others can kill you, and it doesn't matter because nothing exists in the first place.

Waldo sleeps.

Just before dawn, he updates his journal. Then he drops six Duadine, starts the car and goes hunting.

12/14/99 I left the campground and drove around at random. No sirens. I turned on the radio, but there was no mention of the disaster I'd left behind. I drifted past strip malls … fast food joints … pawn shops … payday loan offices ….

Then, surprisingly, I came across several acres surrounded by a tall fence with barbed wire pointed outward. A sign on the fence with a road behind it. In faded black letters, the sign said "Omnicorp. A division of Schwarzcorp." In the distance, I saw an office building three stories high. The bottom story was lit.

I rammed the A-car through the fence and headed for the building.

I parked in a Visitor's spot. Stuffed the water gun in my belt, tucked the palmtop in my shirt pocket, made sure I still had my Duadine, and pulled on the A-cop uniform, positioning my wounded left arm within the black jacket. Wrapped some fresh coat lining around my neck and donned the helmet. Left the A-car and strode toward a lit window.

I pressed against the wall, edged toward the window and looked in. A laboratory. Three men in white lab coats, backs to me. They grouped around a DEATH console.

Images flickered on the monitor …. Wasn't this weird, I thought? Why would they do this, at the crack of dawn, on the first floor? Why would they do it in front of a window?

The monitor showed a boy on a chair. Maybe ten or twelve years old. Dressed in a white hospital gown. His arms and legs were bound to the chair with leather straps. He seemed to be asleep.

A tech spoke something into the boy's ear and stepped away.

Nothing happened for a while. Then the boy's eyes rolled up; his head rocked back and forth, and he began to convulse. The techs pressed closer. The boy's body arched back; his tongue protruded … he jerked violently three times.

The video image filled with static, dissolved in a blur … the techs blocked my view. Then one turned and seemed to look directly at me.

I shrank to the side and pressed against the wall again. Forced myself to calm down, then looked back in the window.

The video picture had stabilized. On it, I saw four techs. The chair lay on its side in a pool of blood, straps broken. One tech righted the chair; two others dragged what looked like a large side of beef toward a door, leaving a long smear of blood on the floor.

The fourth onscreen tech approached the camera. I tried the window—open! What were the chances of that? I inched the bottom of the window forward and saw the tech's drawn face fill the screen.

"Product failure again, Tom. Those Yellowstone assholes." He wiped his face. "Send a report to Whitmore."

The Omnicorp techs switched off the DEATH console and left the room.

Waldo pushed the window all the way open. Struggling to protect his left arm, he pulled himself up, toppled forward and fell with a grunt on the office floor.

He stumbled forward and booted up DEATH. Logged into OR. Got to the map of the United States.

What?

The file had been modified. Date/time stamp: 12:14:99 00:00—last midnight. A time-triggered switch?

Now different dots appeared on the map, and more text appeared below it:

FICTIONALIZER

Research and Development

Red

1

Acusystems:::Kanab, UT:::Whitmore, Arnold:::A

BioResearch:::Brownwater, MI:::Gomez, Marvin:::S

Biotechnics:::Colorado Springs, CO:::Nelson, Bernard:::A

Consolidated Chemical:::Colter Bay, WY:::Morgan, Ernst:::S

Cybersystems:::Chicago, IL:::Elmore, Martin:::A

Omnicorp:::Independence, MO:::Allen, Peter:::S

[------]

Waldo stared at the screen. Dots also appeared over New York City and L.A.

Six satellite offices—three Alpha ("A"), three Schwarzcorp ("S") —each, it seemed, collaborating on a deep classified ("Red") operation reporting to Light ("1").

He scanned the company names. Technology. Biology. Chemicals.

Boy arching back

If he assumed correctly, the "Yellowstone assholes" were employees of Consolidated Chemical in Wyoming. These people were supplying "product"—the Fictionalizer?—to a company whose testing unit had just reported via video.

Assume Biotechnics. Had the boy just died in Colorado?

If so, a report had quickly gone from Nelson at Biotechnics (Alpha) to Allen at Omnicorp (Schwarzcorp), then to Whitmore at Acusystems (Alpha).

Complex.

Which was of course what his brother wanted. Waldo thought of the dummy companies, camouflaged units, subsidiaries masquerading as competitors that made up Light's empire—the intricacies, overlaps, circuitous pathways, underground connections. He regarded the names on the screens—how many relays through other offices, and at other levels, were taking place? And hadn't he seen another testing lab at BioResearch? Of course most or all of these centers had such labs … he imagined them shuttling information back and forth, some pertinent, some not, some relevant only to other compartmentalized programs ….

Waldo guessed that no one involved knew the full extent of the OR project, except Light.

Waldo gazed at the bottom left of the screen:

[------]

Simple password, probably. Six characters.

He glanced at a clock. 8:43 a.m.

He entered the DEATH security module. Shouts, military barking —probably someone had discovered the stolen A-car.

Waldo logged off OR.

"Dammit!" a voice shouted. "Clear the building! *Clear it!*"

Boots pounded up the hallway outside. A hand rattled the door; the boots thumped past.

Waldo drew his PENIS and strode to the door. No sounds. He opened the door and peered out. Empty white hallway. He lowered the visor on his helmet, stepped out, closed the door and hurried toward the right end of the hall.

He came to a door, opened it and peered through. Saw more or less what he expected, but in his brittle, quasi-hallucinatory state the scene incited a fit of weariness and revulsion ... it was so pathetically ... *unimaginative* ... couldn't someone think of *something else* ... three A-cops approached, checking doors on both sides.

Waldo had a brutal flash of understanding: *This will never end*

There would *always* be A-cops approaching … but never quite connecting, their only purpose being to subjugate, to instill fear. How long, he considered sadly but with a sort of lucid wonder, had he existed in this rat's maze of hallways with black shapes closing in, their menace merely a function of his own self-loathing … how long would he inflict this nightmare on himself … what unspeakable pain had visited him, or had he caused, that it should repeat itself like this ….

Fatigued and resigned, Waldo lowered his A-visor and stepped through the door. He headed toward the cops, leading with his right side to hopefully hide his empty left arm.

The cop on the right squinted at him. "Hey," he said, reaching for his G20.

"It's Miller," Waldo said.

The cop on the left frowned and pulled his gun. "Don't know no Miller."

Slo-mo again. Waldo brandishes his water pistol, then hears a footstep behind him and spins around. Too late … a fourth A-cop, materializing from nowhere, has wrapped his arm around Waldo's throat and is poking something hard into his waist. Waldo grapples with the cop, terrified yet oddly detached, as if watching TV. A knee presses into his left thigh; the floor approaches … *pop* … Waldo screams, watching a character in a TV show scream. His helmet hits the floor and flies off; he skids forward … a hand grips his right wrist; his right arm jerks behind him and he screams again. Pain sears through his broken left arm; he gazes through a pulsing pink cloud at an A-cop. The cop raises a club … the TV picture flickers out.

Water splashes his face … his head cracks cement … he looks up past two A-cops at a gray sky. The cops are dragging him across a parking lot in a sleety rain. He sees an A-car approaching.

It stops. Waldo stares up at the front passenger door. The window rolls down; one of the A-cops peers inside.

Woman's voice: "Thank you, soldier. Mr. Gate will handle this."

The cop straightens. "Ma'am!"

Waldo is picked up roughly; the back door opens; his face smashes onto a seat.

From his twisted position he sees two figures up front. He senses someone beside him.

He passes out again. When he comes to the car is moving.

"He's awake," the woman says.

The figure beside him turns to him. The face is in shadow.

"How do you feel," the figure croaks.

Waldo sobs.

Molotov.

12/15/99 Another safe house.

I had a dream. The familiar electricity was pulsing through, and I had the impression of a sinister black shape on my chest … but at the same time I saw it as a cluster of black shapes, breathing globules at the edges of a white door. Techs in white coats dragged a side of beef toward the door, halting momentarily to lug it over the splayed feet of a dead A-cop. The techs seemed to be speaking, but their lips weren't moving … a mix of fragments: "… *garbled data ... beasts at the gate ... convoluted process ... Big Man ...* see *... sucks him down ... reasonable approximation of a human being ...*" and other snatches I couldn't make out. Though the fragments overlapped, it seemed like the same person was speaking each one—or typing, for I also heard a *clacking* noise.

Then it struck me: It was *my* voice, *my* writing … and just as that happened I saw the password prompt in the OR file—[------]—and knew exactly what those six characters had to be.

Molotov lies on the top bunk, oscillating between unconsciousness and delirium.

Jane lies in a corner on a cot. She's slept for over a day.

Waldo sees he's been given a fresh change of clothes. And a sponge bath, he thinks.

Yesterday Jane peeled back her bandages to show him her entry and exit wounds. The entry wound appeared just below the left collarbone. The bullet had exited to the right, missing her spine. In return, and by way of self-justification, Waldo showed her the flesh wound on his neck.

The pain would have been unbearable for both Molotov and Jane if not for the ambulance driver, who brings Dilaudid every day. In addition, a high school girl arrives twice a day to lay hands on them.

As for Waldo, he's asked for Dilaudid without success. He gets Motrin.

Jane remains alert despite her terrible injury. "You bastard," she says evenly. "How could you leave me?"

"I thought you were dead!"

She sucks at a cigarette. She's traded her Gauloises for marijuana.

"Why are you doing this? Why are you still helping me?" Waldo asks.

She waves the question away. "Orders. From the Executive Council."

"Council?"

"No one knows who leads us. Which makes sense. What if one of us is captured? Interrogated?"

"I don't want your help. Please don't get hurt for me again."

She regards him stonily—then emits a low laugh.

And there it is: A *frisson* sweeps over him, and he sees Amutha's and Jane's faces overlain. He can't reconcile the images—one face arctic, interstellar … melded with a vision of radiance, the kind, resolute face of the creature who had embraced him in dream.

"Who am I helping?" Jane asks. "Who the hell are you, Waldo Stanton?"

He can't answer that.

Once she finishes her joint she fills him in.

When she was shot she slid instantly into trance. A Rebirth member in an ice-cream truck, Looney Tunes music blaring despite the early hour, screeched to a halt by her side soon afterward.

A week earlier, Molotov, nearly gone, had been slid into an ambulance driven by another Rebirth member. But incredibly, none of the wounds was lethal. One near the left kidney, one on the left side of his chest, two near but not over his heart, one just missing his liver.

According to Jane, there were five Rebirth members stationed around the skyscraper that held Cybersystems—the ambulance driver, a delivery man, a streetwalker, a cook in an all-nite restaurant, and a woman in a sedan painted and kitted out to look like an A-car—all instructed to try to get them out of trouble if needed.

The ambulance holding Molotov had sped about a mile to a closed movie theater, where a girl had jumped in the back. She was the high school student Waldo had met—a serious, no-nonsense teenager skilled in psychic healing. Laying hands on Molotov, she kept him alive until they reached a safe house.

A few days later, she did the same for Jane — who, once she was able, bundled Molotov into the dummy A-car and headed for Omnicorp.

Molotov mutters in his bunk. "Bottom of my heart ... cross between your eyes ... Time for me to *swallow* it, brother ...."

Waldo reaches for his vial.

12/17/99 A moan.

"Enough, thanks ... I've tested this pain theory quite enough."

Molotov lies on his bunk bed, looking like hell—raw multicolored patches across his upper chest, bullet wounds on his gut like angry red gopher holes. The ambulance driver is changing his bandages. Molotov ignores him for the most part, rocking slightly, eyes slits.

Sometimes his body drips with sweat. At other times he shivers with cold.

Duadine pills dance in his jumping hand ... he downs them, tilts back a bottle of scotch. The alcohol spills down his chin.

Suddenly his eyes widen. He sits up and looks around, making the ambulance driver step back.

"Where's ... Smith?"

I don't know how to respond.

"I'm sorry ...."

Molotov considers the ceiling a while ... then rolls away, weeping. His sobs modulate into a drawn-out moan, combined with snivels, grunts, gurgles, and groans, slowly subsiding into helpless, pitiful whimpering.

Finally he regains control. He even manages a broken, cynical chuckle, as if recalling the Rebirth dogma about death. He rolls back toward us, snot dribbling over his upper lip. He attempts a smile but produces only a grotesque, suffering leer.

I hand him a wad of tissues. Affection creeps into his burnt-out eyes. "You're too kind," he murmurs, wiping the snot away and tucking the wad inside his blanket, for future use it seems.

The ambulance driver resumes his task. I wish he would hurry up and put Molotov's shirt back on. Meanwhile I try to imagine a woman but see only a sexless, disfigured crone. Every vein stands out on his wrinkled gray hands, while the bare feet poking from his chinos appear papery and insect-like.

Molotov raises a quivering hand. "Stop staring, my boy. You make me feel self-conscious ... almost as if there's something wrong with my appearance."

He laughs at his bad joke, then groans as something inside him hurts.

"You worry about me too much. After all, I'm sure it's ...." He doubles over, embarking on one of his wretched coughs.

"... I'm sure it's because of you ... I'm alive at all ...."

The attack ends in an interminable gagging wheeze.

Waldo had a vision. He wasn't sure whether he was sleeping.

The vision resembled a TV promotional spot.

In it, exquisitely formed couples in bathing suits walked or floated hand in hand in a dazzling white haze to the music of steel drums.

Waldo understood that he was in a world where death no longer existed, where illness, pain and anxiety had all been eliminated. It struck him that no one here ate, urinated, or defecated. They wore bodies because it gave them pleasure to do so, and could remove them if they chose, as easily as they could their bathing suits.

Waldo knew the name of this place.

12/19/99 Over dinner I've recounted my experiences at Omnicorp to Molotov and Jane, with particular attention to the atrocity I glimpsed on the DEATH monitor. I've told them I believe Light's plan involves the development of a drug or technology that can produce physical metamorphosis in human beings.

Molotov sits in the gray light. He gazes at me vacantly, appearing to ponder something else—then grins hideously and snaps *cha-cha-cha*. Jane hands him a Slurpee, which he sucks down with relish.

He lights a cigar and begins to pontificate in rapid fire.

"Tame—tabloid stuff. But not inconsistent with Fish's broader agenda." He grows contemplative. "One thinks of the cybernetic principle *Information overload equals pattern recognition*. That moment of hushed awe and overwhelming compassion when the light comes through the door—"

I stop eating.

Opens its mouth

Molotov punches the cigar in the air, eyes glazed. "—and one is absorbed by the final act, the fierce visitation that obliterates all, atonement before the fist of fire, surrender to a brand new order ...."

He hunches forward, drumming fingers on the table.

"So yes, one can see how violent change in the human organism could prefigure a broader metamorphosis ... a universal New Year if you will." He blinks, then grins. "But it's all still fairly banal, don't you think? Genetic experiments, mutants ... haven't we seen this before? In grade B movies? You'd think Fish would have more imagination."

Molotov glances at Jane. "Certainly, he's playing up the melodrama and dreary, pathetic paranoia in our own clearly predetermined narrative." His expression grows crafty. "As if we were *lab mice*."

Unperturbed, Jane lights a joint.

"Don't forget," she murmurs. "Physical alteration may be a side effect. If the actual metamorphosis is perceptual—"

"Aha!" Molotov cries.

I reach for my Duadine.

"Lucid dreaming …" Molotov continues.

I curl around the vial.

Days passed. Molotov and Jane recovered quickly—largely, Waldo thought, due to the ministrations of the high school girl, who had truly impressive hands.

For Waldo, something had changed in the gray light. It persisted, but white patches appeared more often, and overall he had a sense of less oppression, more expansiveness—optimism.

They considered their options. This safe house was in Topeka. Clearly they needed to get to Biotechnics in Colorado Springs. This seemed suicidal, as every facility associated with OR was bound to be under heavy guard. But Jane thought she might be able to manipulate the perceptions of anyone they might encounter long enough to get them in and out.

The more serious problem was that while she did this, her shield would be down—and Light would surely be scanning every OR site. She'd been trying to teach blackout to Waldo, but he couldn't do it.

Molotov, true to form, refused to take this as a negative—though occasionally he'd shown signs of impatience.

"This is really a nuisance my boy ... this primary identity of yours is a goddam *jamming* device. I must say I expected more progress by now." He coughed, observing Waldo cagily through bloodshot eyes. "The solution of course is trauma. Trauma so intense, so devastating ...."

Molotov reflected. When he spoke again it was as if to himself.

"Perhaps only something close to death could accomplish it ...."

Waldo wasn't reassured by what he heard. He wondered whether this was the real reason he was being taken west—to lead him to some unspeakably painful episode that would cause him to shed himself like a snakeskin, uncovering a new Waldo.

They decided their objective was twofold:

1) Learn more about Light's human transfiguration operation.
2) Reenter the OR file.

Waldo told Jane and Molotov that he thought he could access the next level.

Jane's look—lidded. Had she been reading Waldo's journal?

Had she guessed what he knew?

12/25/99 Today is Christmas, the purported day when our Savior was born to atone for our sins, wriggling on the cross like a worm on a hook.

The problem is I don't feel very saved right now.

Amutha came to me again in a dream.

Gauzy light … so beautiful. Her eyes weren't blind. As in the dream of the beach, she gazed at me tranquilly. I woke, sad at her leaving yet suffused with a remnant of her quietude.

From my bunk I regarded Jane meditating on her mat. She lay facing the wall, back to me, legs pulled to her stomach. I felt glad I wasn't facing her, glad that my sorry human affection for her could be experienced in solitude, uncompromised by her steady impersonality.

I've read of Aleister Crowley and others, of their magical acts called "workings" in which a fellow human—often a sexual partner—is found to be, or is conjured to be, an avatar of an otherworldly being. I'd always assumed these reports were delusional and self-serving, but now I suspect that isn't true. Amutha seems to be operating through Jane, and regarding her, I feel deeply for Jane and understand that this is what Amutha wants.

I watch the slow rise and fall of Jane's shoulder. I imagine the exit wound on her upper back.

Above me, Molotov mumbles something in his sleep.

I reach for my vial.

In the early afternoon of Sunday, December 26, Waldo removed his left-arm cast and they prepared to move out.

To his surprise, the ambulance driver, streetwalker, high school girl, delivery man, cook, ice-cream truck driver, and the woman he'd met in the bogus A-car turned out to give them a going-away party. Apart from Jane, they all got drunk on scotch. Waldo was touched.

Their guests left. About a half-hour later, Jane, Waldo, and Molotov emerged into a copse of trees. Beyond it was a postcard farmhouse surrounded by snow. The place had the look of something staged, a hastily assembled set for a rural drama— *Oklahoma, Of Mice and Men.* Waldo suppressed a desire to approach a tree and press it, wondering if it might topple back or maybe waver and disappear.

Molotov cackled weakly. "Look at that *silly* house."

Waldo wondered if the next step would be something even simpler —a ragged box drawn with crayon in a child's hand, with a crooked chimney, curlicues of smoke, and the three of them appearing as stick figures nearby.

Waldo glanced at Molotov. "You see it?"

He giggled. "You're the one writing this, Waldo … you really should work on your technique."

Waldo turned to Jane. "What about you?"

"I don't know what you're talking about."

They walked down the road and came to a black hearse. Inside was a coffin. Mahogany, purple velour, evidently built for a hefty corpse.

If they heard three raps from Jane they were to climb in and shut the lid.

12/26/99 Before Jane put us in the back of the hearse, she tossed us the flashlight and two more vials. For a while Molotov and I bent over our stashes, counting the pills. Once I found him glancing at me, feverish, covetous—a loathsome, predatory gargoyle.

I gave him a long look; his eyes cleared, then grew startled and anxious; he turned away.

Jane is taking side roads. We should reach Biotechnics around two a.m.

Gas station. Jane eyes the red tip of a joint as she leans against the wall near a women's restroom.

The black shapes have been revisiting me over the past few days, morphing menacingly at the edges of my vision. I ask Jane about them.

"They visit people at their physical and spiritual nadirs. But they're also seen as bringers of rejuvenation, of rebirth—I've heard them called 'beasts at the gate,' 'dogs at the door' ...."

I rub my eyes.

U.S. map. Colorado Springs.

Somewhere along the way the hearse pulled to the side and stopped.

Three raps.

"Christ," Molotov whispered, eyes wide—then doubled over, trying to suppress a coughing jag. Waldo checked his PENIS, clapped a hand over Molotov's mouth and jerked him toward the coffin.

Waldo's palm grew damp as Molotov hacked into it. He shoved Molotov inside, dropped on top of him and tugged the lid shut.

They squirmed around in darkness, settled side by side. The stench was awful. Molotov wasn't healing completely; some of his wounds were suppurating.

"God," he hissed. "Can she do this?"

Waldo felt less worried about Jane handling a roadblock than about the probability that their psychic defenses were down. As if on cue, he felt a brutal stab between his eyes and clapped a hand to his face, moaning, certain that Light had homed in.

Molotov breathed raggedly next to him.

After a moment the pain receded … seconds later it seemed unreal. Then the hearse began moving—apparently Jane had passed through.

Was this futile? Waldo thought. Would Light contact his men; would they come after the vehicle they'd just cleared? He had a vision of Jane slumped over the wheel … of fire consuming the hearse, of everyone writhing together in flames.

He made to open the lid but stopped, reflecting that there was no proof Jane was free … maybe A-cops had seen through her, were escorting her somewhere.

Christ—they'd made no arrangement for getting out of the coffin once they'd got in.

Molotov embarked on a retch that ended in a long, wheezing rattle. Despite the circumstances, Waldo couldn't imagine staying with him; the smell was intensifying and he was appalled to find himself feeling a furtive, dirty intimacy with this wounded animal, this woman/man reduced to a hodgepodge of bruises and oozing orifices, who'd died and risen and died and risen again and was now little more than a gruesome zombie animated only by the ferocity of its will.

"I'm sorry," Molotov whispered, and let out a long fart.

Waldo kicked open the lid.

12/27/99 We stopped at a rest area and relieved ourselves at different spots in the woods. We reconnoitered at a picnic table beneath a pine tree and hunched forward in the cold, covered with blankets, squinting up at the counterfeit sky.

I dropped four Duadine. Molotov did the same.

Jane filled us in. She'd indeed been stopped by A-police; she'd handed them imagined papers indicating that she was a black male employee of a funeral parlor. They'd glanced in the back and waved her on.

I grew despondent, increasingly certain our cover had been blown. And sure enough, just then a squad of A-cars appeared on the highway heading west, lights out and sirens silent.

It seemed the opposition was preparing for our arrival.

Back in the hearse. Molotov sat on the coffin, doing something utterly nauseating. A wound in his left upper torso was especially bad—he'd removed the bandage and was using it to poke at the bruised, loathsome flesh, inserting it into the lips of the wound … raising the bandage to his face, as if to decipher the hidden meaning of the designs of blood and pus that had been made there.

Finally Waldo begged him to stop. Molotov gave him a startled, haunted look, as if he'd forgotten Waldo's presence—then, embarrassed, replaced the bandage. Waldo felt revolted again as Molotov wiped ooze from the bandage and flicked it away.

"Why were you doing that," Waldo muttered.

"Doing what?" Molotov sits cross-legged on the hearse's floor, averting his gaze.

"Why were you—playing—with your wound?"

No answer. Then Molotov turns, eyes clear, direct, maniacal … bending toward Waldo in the hunched, enervated posture Waldo remembers from his days in therapy.

"It's odd—I've wanted to speak to you about this but haven't found a way." He pauses, looking anxious. "You know of my fascination with reinvention." His eyes dart toward the front of the hearse. "And by now, I expect, you've learned I've engaged in some … reinvention of my own."

Waldo hesitates, unsure how to reply.

"Yes."

Molotov blinks—settles against the wall, closes his eyes. Then he shrugs and chuckles. "It's funny how the enlightened are the worst gossips."

"It wasn't—"

Molotov waves him off. "I know …." His relief radiates out; it's clear he's ready to reveal his sex-change secret.

"You know I had children?"

"I've wondered why you never mentioned them."

"I didn't because I was such a bad parent."

Molotov reflects, his eyes fixed on a troubling memory. Waldo lets time pass.

"Who was the father?"

Molotov gives him a significant look. "I think you know."

Waldo thinks about it—it hits him.

"Christ—"

Molotov nods, satisfied. "I was in my early thirties when your brother developed into a copy of you. He was young, super-intelligent, intensely charismatic. When I proposed to marry him I thought the idea would be rejected on the spot. But DARPA officials were surprisingly receptive."

"You married my brother?"

"I didn't see why not. They didn't either. At this point he'd shed all semblance of his former self. He had no health issues. He was normal in every way except for his telepathic abilities—which, let's face it, many people have. The government had spent millions keeping him in quarantine. Why not let him out into the world while being observed by someone they trusted? I could file reports."

"So you had—kids?"

"Two."

"John? Jane?"

"Those are the names you know."

Waldo tears up. "God, Molotov. I'm so sorry about John. I had no idea."

Molotov rubs a finger against his bare, blasted gums. His expression grows haunted, shifty—but not disconsolate, not like Waldo expects.

Waldo sees the whole picture. "So you're my sister-in-law? Or were? John was my nephew? Jane is my niece?"

Molotov nods, looking pathetic.

"Jeez, that's almost too perfect to be true."

Molotov shrugs European style—lips puckered, palms up, eyes wide, almost comical—meaning: *What can I say?*

"What happened to the kids?"

Molotov averts his face. "Rick and I gave them up for adoption."

"Why?"

"After a few years we realized that neither of us was any good at raising children. I was too busy with academic work. Rick had

259

started his climb up the corporate ladder. We agreed that it'd be better for the kids if we found good homes for them—wealthy people in safe neighborhoods, excellent schools—all that. So we did. I still think it was a good decision."

He gives Waldo a pained, searching look.

"Still, I kept track. I was pleased for them—and especially proud of my son's success at day trading. That gave him the bankroll to launch Rebirth, which he eventually sold to a company connected in some way to Alpha."

"Why did you divorce?"

Molotov swipes his hair back—the portion that hadn't been burned off. "Because I hated myself. So I gradually began to hate Rick. It's a difficult situation when you inhabit a body you detest —and, as I learned, your partner suffers too. Also, Rick abused me. Not physically but verbally. He often grew impatient with normal humans, and I was usually the one on the receiving end. After a while we realized we didn't like the marriage anymore— so we ended it."

I think about it—and laugh. "So that's why you sometimes give me lingering looks."

Molotov blushes—pink splotches amid his green and brown bruises. To spare him, I change the subject. "Did DARPA get involved again?"

"I think so—I suspect Rick was under surveillance for many years. But at this point it was clear he'd become a familiar type— a smooth, ambitious businessman who'd stop at nothing to get rich and gain power. So the military people eventually lost interest, I think."

Silence. Molotov rubs his gums again.

"Since Rick is a highly advanced being, I'm not surprised that I gave birth to two advanced souls. And somehow, you fathered an advanced being too." He croaks out a sardonic laugh. "A strange coincidence, don't you think?"

Waldo doesn't follow.

Molotov's grin freezes—disappears. "You have to understand that, as I've had to painfully acknowledge, nothing I've done in my entire life—nothing I could imagine inflicting on myself—not the agonies of birth—not holding a flame beneath my chin—not cutting myself—not overdosing on hallucinogens—not even my —" Waldo is surprised by the delicacy of what comes next. "—my little procedure … not any experiment, not any excess, not any atrocity I self-administered could stop me from being … *me*. This pitiful semblance of a human being, this hideous bag of festering guts, this decaying testament to wasted potential."

Molotov's eyes are closed now … he's lost in thought, rocking on his knees.

"The sad, excruciating fact was that I seemed to spring back automatically from whatever trauma I induced, slightly weaker but game as ever, ready for the next hand of abuse I could deal to myself … it became miserably repetitious, depressingly futile. But *this*—"

He pats his body, running his hands over damaged areas, wincing with pain as he digs his fingers in.

"*This* is different, *this* is something that finally registers. Back in the last safe house, you may have noticed, I spent long periods in the bathroom behind the curtain."

Waldo nods. He'd wondered about that—assumed it was constipation.

Molotov gives him a long, penetrating look, somehow more repellent than the scene with the bandage.

"I was studying myself in the mirror. The *wounds*, the wounds on my body look increasingly like a language … I know I'm changing, and I suspect the wounds are an outward manifestation of that metamorphosis. Behind the plastic curtain, I would gaze at them, transfixed by their shapes and patterns, just as I've been transfixed by kitchen or bathroom tiles while on LSD. And the more I stared at them, the more they began to … *mean* something. I feel I'm on the verge of understanding, incredibly close …." He scowls. "But it's not there yet, so maddening …."

Molotov presses his hands to his face.

"Maybe, with one or two more wounds in the proper places, I'll reach critical mass and it will all come together, and I'll finally comprehend who or what I've become … the *wounds* will teach me … am I making sense?"

Waldo feels tears coming.

"Yes, Molotov," he whispers. "You're making sense."

12/28/99 The hearse stopped. There were no raps but I was seized by jitters.

The handle clicked. The door swung open; a cold wind whistled in.

It was a clear day with a light fall of snow. Snowflakes glittered on Jane's hair and shoulders. I regarded her ringed with a crystalline aura, an angel bathed in white.

"Look at this," she said, gesturing.

We got out. A lookout, four inches or so of snow. A few ridges away in the dawn light, a mountain reared up, its glaciered top fuzzing into pearl-gray clouds to create a fairytale tableau.

A sign said: Pikes Peak.

Molotov stood unsteadily, gazing at the scene. Watching him, I felt my irritation with him dissipate … slowly replaced by a numb wave of sadness and guilt. Worse, as he'd come so close to death —twice—and seemed unlikely to live much longer, I understood that, as part of the privileges granted to the dying, he was regarding this picture through a special lens, seeing it from a perspective I hadn't yet achieved. I felt a stab of jealousy.

"I rounded Colorado Springs so we could scout Biotechnics from a height," Jane said. "It's good I did. Look."

She pointed to the left. A valley there held a sprawl of low industrial buildings with an occasional stubby smokestack. Trucks sat around them, some backed up to loading bays.

"Farther," she said.

I saw a smear of light and movement in an adjacent valley. Jane handed me binoculars; I peered through them. Cars parked haphazardly by a river … tents, bonfires, people milling about in snow.

Near a fire, what looked like words. I adjusted the binoculars.

Sign stuck in the ground: **DEATH TO ALPHA!**

They spent a few hours on the lookout, napping in shifts. It was clear that their timing was phenomenal. The coming demonstration would provide a distraction from their own activities.

The timing was impossibly good.

It had stopped snowing. Molotov sat at a picnic table, wrapped in coverings, shivering.

Meanwhile Jane lay in a fetal position on her mat in the back of the hearse. *"Amānā ... "* she whispered. *"Namānā ...."*

Waldo wondered: Could Jane see into the future while meditating? Could she teleport to the other side of the mountains, where the unreal would increasingly replace the real?

No. Just meditating.

Inky shapes coiled in. Then something hard poked Waldo's right temple.

"Mr. Stanton." A woman's voice. He glanced at Molotov, saw a figure bending over him. The figure held a Glock 20.

"You should all come with us," the woman said. "You can bring your mat," she said to Jane.

After some fruitless argument, they were ushered to the back of a red van, where they sat amid a batch of protest signs.

12/28/99 Molotov is delirious again.

"Take me there … strap me down … never die till I die in you …
ah, god, my sweet, that setting sun … heaven to a mouse … how
much I love you … sweet boy … your face … the world was
made for you, you make the world … any place you say … the
beach … you need lessons …."

Sometimes I wonder if Molotov isn't actually raving. Maybe he's
visualizing a future that could occur if we all play our cards right.

The van moves along. Molotov seems to recover.

"You know what?" he mutters. "I've always wanted to become
transhuman. But lately I've been thinking … to achieve that, I
need to become—a *teacher*." He shakes his head. "Not a teacher
of adults—I've done that." He casts a look at Waldo and Jane,
wanting desperately to be understood.

"I want to be a teacher of a child. I want to teach that child some
simple thing … the ABCs, maybe, or … whittling." A tear rolls
down his smashed left cheek. "Something simple."

Then, grinning through tears: "But I guess it's too late for that."

In a slo-mo, priestly gesture, he raises his arms and snaps his
fingers: *cha-cha-cha.*

The van stops. The back door opens. Jane2—as Waldo now thinks of her—beckons Jane1 (as he now thinks of her) and Waldo out and hustles them toward a large gray tent. Meanwhile, a man Waldo now thinks of as John2 carries Molotov, unconscious, behind them.

Waldo takes a moment to step aside, pretend to cough, and drop three Duadine.

The tent houses a command center. To the left, next to some kerosene heaters, stands a row of TVs, each displaying a different scene—a young man speaking rapidly into the camera, A-cars halted at angles at an intersection, a shot of a TV anchorman, with an inset showing an office building with a sign saying "Biotechnics. Biology for Your Future." Other monitors show protesters crouching by tents erected in the snow, warming themselves with coffee or tea, leaning against cars, checking watches, smoking cigarettes or joints.

To the right is a long plastic folding table surrounded by folding chairs on which sit a number of people, including an elderly man with small, round, rimless glasses who looks familiar to Waldo for some reason. Jane2 and John2 bend over him, conferring in low tones. Molotov has been deposited on a cot near the TVs.

The old man glances at Waldo and starts. His eyes grow wide. Then he collects himself, though he still regards Waldo curiously.

The old man nods, and Jane2 waves them over. She's attractive, self-assured, about Jane1's age. John2—in his mid-thirties, maybe —seems shy, almost meek.

Jane2 pulls back her coat, grips her hips. A Glock 20 pokes from her belt.

"We're pleased you're here," she says. "We hope you can help us."

Jane1 shakes her head. "Don't count on it. We might make your situation much more dangerous."

Jane2 gives the old man an uneasy look. He continues to stare at Waldo.

John2 clears his throat. "This is the first time we've openly challenged one of the biotech units. We're pretty certain Biotechnics is at the center of it."

"The media are losing interest in us," Jane2 says. "We need something dramatic to win them back. Just a few seconds of you on TV would do that."

Jane1 shakes her head pessimistically—then shifts gears. "How did you find us."

Jane2 seems distracted. The old man gives her a furtive look. "Some of us have received the same training you have," he says.

Jane1's mouth tightens. "If you can find us, Light can."

Waldo is suddenly aware that everyone in the tent is listening in. They peer at the old man, who nods sagely. "That's a risk we'll take."

Waldo looks into the man's wizened scholar's face and wants to weep. The man's bravado is compelling—but Waldo can't ignore how doomed this operation is, how pathetically useless.

"Who are you," he says thickly.

Then it hits him.

A-POLICE PASS FIRST TEST

New York Times—when? A million years ago.

The elderly man with round spectacles being dragged away. Next to the photo of James Gate.

Waldo makes a guess. "Do you run all the protests?"

"Most of them," the old man responds. "In truth, my agenda is a bit different from that of"—he gestures toward the TVs—"others out there. I'm part of a small group that is occasionally given guidance."

"From an Executive Council?" Waldo tries.

The old man blinks. No answer.

"What's your name?" Waldo asks.

The old man takes off his glasses and peers through them, as if searching for streaks. "You can address me as John, of course."

Waldo decides to think of him as John Prime.

12/28/99 Jane2 sits with me in the back of the red van. Slender, friendly, with ash blond hair falling just below her shoulders. She wears a fragrance I can't identify, something tropical … frangipani, pineapple, orange blossoms. I'm aroused.

Glancing at her, I start as I glimpse Amutha's eyes … and wonder if Jane2, too, will emerge as a version of my dead wife, a new expression of her seraphic body.

In demonic counterpoint, black shadows swell in the van's corners, just beyond my range of vision. By now I suspect they'll never leave—though, with devious masochistic logic, I also understand that the moment I accept this, some inner protection will fail me and that's when they'll attack. Indeed, as I write this, they swarm closer, pulsing with expectancy. Only by resuming my grim, wearisome stance of watchfulness can I induce them to retreat to their peripheral haunts.

Jane2 opens two beers, gives me one. "You're a legend, Mr. Stanton."

"Waldo."

"Waldo." She gives me a frank, inviting look. I'm captivated; I want to kiss her … it dawns on me that I'm gazing at her mouth. She knows it; I feel myself flush. She offers a swift benevolent smile.

"The entire resistance movement has been inspired by you. It's widely believed that only someone with superhero powers could've eluded so many well-armed A-cops. You've become something of a Robin Hood figure—actually a cross between Robin Hood, Jesus Christ and the Fantastic Four."

I gulp from my can. "Suitably schizophrenic."

Her face darkens. "That backfired on Alpha, you know. It turns out that many people seem to like the thought that you could be" —she gazes at me quizzically, as if trying to decide for herself— "mentally ill. I guess they figure that only a madman could defeat the real lunatics who oppress us with their murderous 'public safety' scams."

I blink, still attentive to the breathing shadows. "I was a contributor to those scams. I sold brainwashing equipment."

She regards me sympathetically. "John contributed too." (John2, I understand.) "He manufactured a serum used in military interrogations."

I open my vial, remove three Duadine. I offer her one.

"Sorry—I'm told that's for you."

"What about Molotov?" I ask, swallowing the pills.

"A special case. Everyone considers him a conduit to you. He does what he wants—or did." She hesitates. "Is he dying?"

Tears well up in me from nowhere. I make a light comment to fend them off.

"Aren't we supposed to stick to John and Jane?"

She laughs. "Yes, but you and Molotov aren't initiated into Rebirth. When we think it's necessary, we use code names. We have several for you."

"Like what?"

"Don't ask me why, but we often call you Mr. Sunset."

As Waldo sat in the van updating his journal, he sensed the inquisitive tendrils of Jane2's attention probing his brain … though she appeared absorbed in a book: *The Millennial Prophesies*. The cover showed the sun on a horizon, much like the Alpha logo.

This mental incursion alarmed him, as it betrayed a hole in Jane1's blackout—but Waldo was losing faith in the blackout in any case. And there was an intimacy to this insertion that rivaled sex; he enjoyed Jane2's curiosity and would have given her free rein of his head if he didn't have to keep watch on the throbbing black ectomorphs, which were growing more insistent.

"Why are you writing?"

It dawned on him that she'd spoken. He looked up—she regarded him, artless and affectionate. The book was in her lap.

"I don't know. It's a disease. Getting worse."

She appeared to understand, but he doubted it.

"What are you writing about?" she continued.

"Events as they occur." Waldo's speech sounded odd to him—remote, tinny, unreal. "They seem to involve … a trajectory." He pushed a finger through the air.

"Where does the trajectory end?"

Waldo stared at her blankly.

The white room

The words emerged in slo-mo:

"A table … two chairs …."

12/29/99 The van's door slid open around 2 a.m. Jane2 and I followed John2 into the tent. Jane1 and John Prime sat inside, sharing a joint.

"Waldo, welcome," John Prime said, smiling a little creepily. "I was hoping to get a briefing from you—learn your take on things."

I was starting to reply when a voice broke in. "I had the strangest dream …."

Molotov sat up on his cot, fingering bandages on his torso, swinging his legs back and forth over the edge.

"I was in a garden," he continued slowly, lisping as always, "gnawing at an apple that was also a pill …. I had the impression it was Duadine, but perhaps it was something else … the consciousness of *every sentient entity ever conceived* was within that pill, starting with our first blind stirrings in primeval ooze … I was *breathless,* I tell you …."

I grinned, weak with relief. "You're back."

He glowered. "Not necessarily so good to *be* back. You can have no idea what I experienced … I was like a *god*, I tell you … a god spread out on a cross of time and space …."

I felt queasy.

Big Man

John Prime cleared his throat. "Very interesting. Welcome to our war room, Doctor."

Molotov leered and rubbed his palms together. "'War room.' I like the sound of that. Depths of mirrors … clatter of weapons …."

"We'd appreciate your advice." John Prime hunched forward. "Jane has been explaining your mission to L.A. Our own people have had no success trying this—no one can get close. One member entered Nevada a few years ago but was killed by lightning."

"In a desert?" I asked.

He gazed at me woodenly.

Jane1 spoke up. "I've explained that we can't be filmed. Our cover is too weak."

I felt a pulse between my eyes. She rubbed her forehead absently.

John Prime shrugged. "We accept that of course. And we'll help you any way we can. Like you—but through somewhat different means—we've concluded that Light is involved in bioengineering schemes that are killing off human test subjects. We'll announce that to the press this morning, charge that the testing is taking place at Biotechnics—though actually we're not certain of that—and stage a fracas. Hopefully this will create enough of a diversion for you to slip inside."

John2 waved a joint that Jane1 had given him. "What we're most worried about is you. We can't see how you expect to get to Light."

Molotov cackled weakly. "Don't worry about us. Our friend here has tricks up his sleeve even he doesn't know about."

I let that pass. "My understanding is we're doomed anyhow if we don't."

John Prime nodded approval. "If you get in and out of the building, some of us will join you—help you move west."

I took in what he was saying. Despair rushed in.

These people were about to die.

John Prime tugged a trunk from beneath a table and opened it. "I have a feeling, despite your combined talents …." He pulled out some A-helmets and A-uniforms. "You're going to need camouflage."

The A-uniforms weren't very convincing. Waldo filled out his well enough, but Jane1 was too petite for an A-cop, and no amount of black leather could make Molotov look young.

They huddled in the back of the van in early morning. Jane2 and John2 kept watch on the front seat. Snow fell heavily. Outside a chant was building:

DEATH TO ALPHA! DEATH TO ALPHA!

"Entrances here, here, here," John Prime said, pointing to photos of Biotechnics HQ. "Heavily guarded of course, but you may be able to get through."

Waldo glanced at Jane1. Her expression was lidded and remote.

"During your mission," John Prime continued, "we'll make sure everyone's focus is here." He pointed to a left-side door. "We can keep things stirred up for about a half hour—you'll have to move fast. We suggest you do what no one expects." He pointed to the front door.

Waldo and Jane1 nodded robotically at this suicidal proposal.

John Prime checked his watch. "In about ten minutes things will intensify. When you hear gunfire and screams, move out."

"You know what you're doing?" Waldo said.

John Prime grinned demurely. "Loudspeakers … fake blood."

"What if things escalate," Jane1 asked.

"We'll take that as it comes."

"You're risking a lot for us," Molotov wheezed—then doubled over retching.

John Prime's eyes darted toward Waldo, grim and fatigued. He rose heavily and leaned over the front seat, gazing pensively at the protesters gathering in the snow.

"Nothing we do is ultimately for you."

John2 had pulled the van closer to Biotechnics. The chant had become a roar:

DEATH TO ALPHA! DEATH TO ALPHA! DEATH TO ALPHA!

Waldo donned his A-suit and waited for his cue.

12/29/99 By the time the shots start my head feels like it's stuffed with a towel, and I know Jane1 has mustered every force she has. I peer outside, regarding the melee—a shrieking crowd rushing the building, signs bobbing … A-cops fending off projectiles with shields, beating the nearest protesters with clubs. To the rear of the crowd, a young man lies sprawled on the snow in a circle of blood.

A-cops kneel at the corners of the building, readying assault rifles.

We have only Jane's G20. Molotov and I haven't been given real guns—it seems we're both considered too unstable now. But I still pack my trusty PENIS.

About a dozen A-Police stand at the front door, eyeing the disturbance. As I watch, one of them brandishes a rifle and sprints toward his fellows to the left. Others follow.

I look back. "Ready?"

Jane1 nods while casting a guarded look at her mother.

"You OK, Molotov?" He absolutely insists on going with us. None of us is enthusiastic about this—his presence isn't needed, and he'll slow us down. I've been thinking of ways to keep him in the van, such as knocking him out. But most of the time I've just hoped he'd pass out again.

About thirty minutes ago, John Prime gave him a hefty dose of Dilaudid, part of the team's impressive medical kit. It seems to be working.

I asked for Dilaudid, but John Prime said no.

"Let's go," Molotov gasps, holding a fist to his mouth.

Then he has a thought, flashes me a look of manic glee—crawls forward and reaches behind my ear. He produces a vial, shakes four Duadine into his palm, downs them. Then he gives me some.

He croaks out a laugh. "We have things we're intended to discover … no?"

I swallow five Duadine.

We pull down our visors, leave the van. Jane1's blackout effort is now so intense that the scene before me—the building, the protesters, the cops—is dislocated and jerky, like old film running on a bad sprocket. It's clear that people in the area don't take us in visually. The biggest danger we seem to face is bumping into protesters by accident. As we advance, their cries seem unreal—a hollow, contrived roar from a far-off sports stadium in a dream. My legs are weak; I feel drunk … slo-mo has clicked in again.

We climb steps to the Biotechnics entrance. We suddenly register with some guards, who nod at us and step aside. We breeze through automatic doors without incident.

A deserted reception area. To the right and left stretch white corridors with closed windowless doors.

I point to a door at the far end of the reception area that says STAIRS. We open the door and consider our two options. I choose up.

A door on the first landing says MARKET RESEARCH.

Molotov breathes harshly but is keeping pace. I open the door gingerly.

Office. Deserted. Cubicles with DEATH workstations.

Molotov giggles. "Now we're talking."

I sit at a workstation, boot it up, log on.

Below us, dim gunshots, muffled screams.

"Hurry," Jane1 says.

"I can't."

Finally I enter OR … pass the block … key the mantra ….

FICTIONALIZER

Research and Development

Red

1

The map showing the Fictionalizer R&D centers remains. I stare at the second check.

[------]

Six characters.

Sadness washes in. I start crying.

I move the cursor to the blanks, and from a vast, melancholy distance watch my hands type:

HI DAD

The screen clears.

"Christ," Molotov mutters.

Below us, a shot.

Words materialize on the screen: HI DAD! How you doing?

Below them, characters scroll rapidly past.

"Chemical formula," Molotov says.

Jane1 jerks her head up.

Boots clomp up the stairs. She reaches for her G20.

"Get ready."

Waldo had spotted a door at the far end of the Market Research unit. Jane1 had seen it too. They could only hope that it didn't lead into a manager's office or some other cul-de-sac.

Waldo didn't have time to back out of the file. They ran toward the door, half dragging Molotov.

Meanwhile the door behind them banged open; they heard shouts; Waldo looked back and saw four A-cops pouring through, brandishing assault rifles. He blinked ... in the gray light, the cops were faceless, amorphous, fluid black shapes ... they seemed connected somehow, at the shoulders or hips, a single, pulsating, protoplasmic blob of menace .... Jeez, Waldo mused, these thugs were looking more like Vermin every second.

His thought was interrupted when a bullet splintered the door by his head and his face erupted in pain. Waldo waved his water pistol blindly while Jane1 fired at the invaders, hitting at least two. Through a fog of impending blackout Waldo watched a spray of red across the office's white walls, the gray fabric of the cubicles and the screen of the DEATH console where the words HI DAD! still mocked him and the chemical formula still scrolled by.

Waldo doubled up, pressing a hand to his right cheek, as Jane1 opened the door. Stairs led up, but that course seemed unwise. A door to the left said LEVEL SUB-ONE / AUTHORIZED PERSONNEL ONLY. The door was locked, but Jane1 fired into the handle twice and kicked the door open. They staggered into a stairway that led steeply down, hearing shouts and boots approaching.

Blood ran down the upper arm of Waldo's A-uniform and dripped off his elbow.

This stairwell was crude, with bare cement walls and lights protected by wire mesh. The inside of the door was padded. Out of the padding sprang three iron grips, which were bookended by holes on the walls on either side. An alcove to the right held an iron bar. Jane1 grabbed the bar and fitted it into the grips and holes. They turned and peered down the stairs.

What about this stairwell required a barricade? Why the sound insulation?

Waldo had a glimmer of understanding but not enough. Meanwhile the door shook; someone bellowed and pounded. Before they could react a laser beam slashed through the padding, sizzling between Molotov and Jane1; they bolted down the stairs as another beam flashed over their heads.

Jane1 helped Molotov descend the stairs. Waldo was having trouble with his own footing. Above them something slammed rhythmically at the door.

They came to a cramped cement corridor lit by buzzing fluorescent lights. Windowless doors lined each side of the corridor. On the far end was a door painted white.

They made their way through the corridor, checking the doors. All locked. The far door held a sign that said LEVEL SUB-TWO / AUTHORIZED PERSONNEL ONLY. Jane1 tried it—unlocked.

"What a stroke of good fortune," Molotov laughed bleakly, then retched.

Stairs going down. This time they came to a cement corridor that stretched in both directions. They headed right, checking a new set of doors; Waldo had almost given up trying when a doorknob turned.

The door opened into darkness. Above them, muffled shouts. Waldo glanced at the door at the end of the corridor.

"Which way."

"Inside," Jane1 decided.

A door above slammed open … boots approached.

Waldo led them inside, closed the door, turned the lock. This was a futile gesture, as his blood on the floor would certainly lead their attackers to the door and they'd blast it open.

They stood motionless, eyes adjusting. The room wasn't completely dark. They saw a bluish glow before them, broken by vertical black stripes. As Waldo regarded the glow it shifted—a white spark popped up and blinked out.

In that instant, Waldo felt the darkness become palpable … he crouched and pressed a hand to his forehead. A thick, malignant substance was wrapping itself about him, suffocating, murderous … it felt like all the badness in him combined, along with every moment of terror he'd ever experienced, raw black evil pressing in, squeezing out all oxygen, all light.

Molotov: "Good god … what's this *feeling* …."

Jane1: "Pay no attention! Don't make them stronger!"

Click … she's found the light switch. Waldo stares in shock at the sight before him, feeling the Vermin pause.

In a filthy cage against a cement wall, surrounded by lab tables, video gear, and a collection of surgical instruments on a steel tray, lies what appears to be a quarter of a middle-aged man, with other elements overlain or interspersed. There's a naked right thigh, a hairy forearm, two burly shoulders topped by an unshaven face with unseeing, dark black eyes. From the man's shaggy, dirt-caked hair spring what could be twine, vegetable tendrils or electrical wiring. The torso has been replaced by what appears to be part of a large black mammal, a sea cow maybe, though there are moving, liquescent components that don't call to mind any animal, and the place where the stomach should be is filled with a strange racing electricity that Waldo believes produced the white spark they just saw. The hips and legs are even harder to categorize: a mélange of flesh and hair and blood and bone flickering in and out, mingling somehow with an impression of pale faces on rain-swept streets; dead insects, musical passages and algebraic equations; broken-down buildings and seedy alleys and sick coughs of drunks; and what should have been feet appearing as a dance of sour memories and rainbow arcs of twisted space disappearing into a far distance impossible to reconcile with the cramped dimensions of the shit-stained cage.

Shouts outside.

The atrocity's eyes focus on them—grow wild. It moves … Waldo watches stunned as it noses the cage door open, slithers out, falls with a wet *plop* to the floor, and uses its shoulders to wriggle toward them.

It opens a toothless mouth and groans.

Someone tries the lab door, pounds it. Someone barks orders … a silence. Waldo glances at Jane1 as the Vermin coil back in.

"Down!" he shouts.

They fall to the floor … a PHALLUS beam sizzles through, passing to the left of a lab table. A second burst enters the floor near Molotov. The third is a horizontal sweep that approaches the atrocity, which grins obscenely and leans into the light.

The atrocity explodes … sparks fly through the room, mixed with smoking fragments of flesh. The lab distends, and a long drawn-out sound yawns out from the thing's dissolving body … a piercing shriek of mad laughter that quickly fades away, leaving an icy blue contrail and the electric smell of burnt ozone.

Encouraged bellows in the hall. Someone fires into the door.

There's no way out of the lab. The only opening is a round grate in the floor near the cage—an outlet for the atrocity's wastes, Waldo assumes. He shimmies forward and peers through the grate at black liquid about five feet down.

Someone fires a second time. Waldo tries the grate—it moves. He pulls it aside as someone fires again.

He tosses his helmet away. Jane1 and Molotov follow suit.

Waldo drops into the sewage, retching … he finds his footing; the stream comes to just above his waist. The Vermin are crippling now; in a moment they'll shove him down and he'll sink below the surface.

Another shot. Molotov plops into the sewage beside him.

A light downstream … black stripes.

Jane1 lowers herself, replacing the grate before she drops.

Another shot—thud of a door kicked open. Cheers.

Waldo peers at the light. The sewage is emptying through bars.

"This way."

There are shouts at the grate. Waldo is maybe fifteen feet away when he hears it being moved behind them. He laughs helplessly —a weak, spasmodic, yelping sound.

Even if they reach the outlet, what good will that do?

Waldo crams his palmtop in his mouth, makes sure his water pistol is secure, checks his Duadine vial, squeezes his eyes shut and dives into the sewage.

The Vermin take over. In his blindness, in this suffocating slime, they wrap about him like a rubber suit, sending black probing feelers into his body, particularly the space between his eyes. As the shapes cluster and worsen, seeming to gibber with insectile glee, it occurs to him that, in an act of impossibly cruel cosmic malevolence and sick humor, he's been fated to die like this, in a sewer with shit wrapped around his face and tormented by avenging demons; he's going to die like an animal in a sewer and that's precisely what God has intended for this particular sick, unworthy, murdering sonofabitch.

In the gray light, items in the sewer are faintly visible. Waldo is amazed by the variety of artifacts. Shit-clotted toilet paper, of course, along with shitty tissues, condoms, menstrual pads, diapers. Medical waste: syringes, plastic gloves, antiseptic pads long past being antiseptic … human and monkey parts, eyes, tongues, hearts, kidneys, intestines … shitty wallets, purses, toothbrushes, toothpaste tubes, floss sticks … Post-its, memo pads, calendar pages, street maps, crossword puzzles, scraps of Yellow Pages, all clumped into shit balls, shit clusters … fake eyelashes, fake fingernails, fake teeth … credit cards, Medicare cards, transit cards … bubblegum wrappers crusted with shit … plastic items: shit-covered plastic bottles, bottle caps, drinking straws, cups, pill bottles, combs … cigarette stubs, cigarette packs … bumper stickers (I CLIMBED MOUNT WASHINGTON!) … Christmas ornaments, party hats, noise makers … a dead cat, a dead dog, a dead rat, a hairy, shit-clotted lump of something dead … a filthy banana peel (The joke's on you, Waldo!) … and above all the cloying, awful smell of shit, shit, and more shit, enough shit to drown the human race for eternity in shit.

Waldo desperately needs air … the palmtop slides back into his throat and he begins to choke. This fills him with another spasm of helpless silent laughter … *swallow your words, boy … suck 'em down* ….

Waldo surfaces, wipes his eyes clean and glances behind him to see a small round object descending on a cord through the opened grate. Molotov, struggling a few yards behind Waldo and Jane1, has spotted the object and gives Waldo a terrified look.

Then, impossibly, he cackles. "Go on … keep moving … we have work to do …."

Pop … the round object explodes, releasing a cloud of yellow gas. It washes over Molotov, and blood begins drooling from his eyes, nose, and mouth.

"Leave her," Jane1 mutters.

Molotov's teeth chatter. *"Cruore ejus …."* He shakes his head wearily, as if the joke has worn thin. His eyes roll up; he gurgles … then sinks beneath the sewage. A black bubble burbles up.

The gas moves toward them. Waldo's eyes and nostrils burn. He glances at Jane1 and sees tears streaking her face.

She tests the bars at the outlet. Firm.

Waldo's knees buckle … he sags toward the sewage, glad at the thought of joining Molotov.

Two hands hold his cheeks. A voice in his ear.

Don't give up, sweetheart ... our boy wants you to go on

Waldo convulses, wracked with sobs, retching, imagining a white form before him, an unspeakably beautiful white form, the form of a woman cradling his head in her hands and speaking to him with unlimited compassion and forgiveness.

Go on

Waldo sobs, cringing blindly before the profundity of his ugliness, the twisting, fragmented horror inside ....

Then he sees two futures before him. To the left, the outlet has no bars. To the right, bars.

He chooses.

CHUNK.

Waldo and Jane1 pass through.

12/30/99 I write this in the back of a GOD truck.

The GOD package delivery franchise is owned by Rebirth. A fund-raising arm.

We're headed west.

My poor friend.

My poor, demented friend.

Christ, I'm so sick of this.

I'll give this palmtop to Jane2. I never want to see it again.

IV. LIGHT

Michael Schulze

After the passage through the outlet Waldo's memory grew hazy. He knew he floated, sometimes in sewage, sometimes in dirty water—the Vermin gradually receding, then vanishing, leaving a pleasant narcotic wash of release.

He bumped into a barrier … found his footing, raised his head, spotted a cement arch lit by floodlights. Jane1 rose beside him, gasping. They saw a short cement wall topped by a walkway that led to stairs and a white door marked EXIT.

Jane1 pulled her G20 from the ooze and waved it toward the door. They slogged over … the walkway was about a foot overhead. Waldo threw up his palmtop, water pistol and vial and pulled himself up, groaning as pain slammed into his left arm. Jane tossed up her gun and followed him.

A laugh rose from Waldo's stomach, high and creepy. He watched himself laugh; he was off to the side, seeing himself crouched, slathered with shit, eyes and teeth shining white, succumbing to hypothermia.

Giggling, he rose to his feet and headed for the door.

He opened it. Snow bit at his face.

A white Hummer stretch limo stood at the curb of a small, empty parking lot ringed by snow-covered pines.

It was a limo for the richest of the rich, driven by a chauffeur with Jane2 by his side. And it had a hot tub in back.

"Yes!" Waldo cried.

Soap, washcloths, towels, shampoo. Jane1 stepped into the tub, unrolled a screen from the ceiling and undressed. She handed her A-uniform and other clothes past the screen to Waldo, who lowered a side window and threw them out. As she washed and shampooed he found some blankets in a cupboard near the floor. He handed one to Jane1, and she stepped out wrapped in it while gripping her G20.

His turn. He emerged covered in a blanket and clutching his few possessions. He and Jane1 opened the rest of the windows and did their best to clean the interior. Up front, Jane2 and the chauffeur hung their heads out their windows until they'd stopped retching.

"Christ," Jane2 breathed. "Do you really have to submerge yourself in shit to get where you want to go?"

Waldo spit out a bitter laugh. "How did you know to bring the stretch?"

Jane2 looked puzzled. "It was the only vehicle left in the local Rebirth motor pool. The rest had been taken by protesters. We use this limo to impersonate bigwigs."

Pregnant pause.

"Molotov?" Jane2 asked gingerly.

Waldo saw an image of his friend slipping beneath shit, gassed, bleeding. He shook his head to chase the thought away.

"I think he might actually be dead."

They fell silent. Jane1 toweled and combed her hair repeatedly, even after it was clean and dry. Her girlish vanity was surprising and endearingly human; it made Waldo feel a wave of affection for her.

Meanwhile he found scotch in a compartment, ice in a bucket, and poured drinks. Everyone imbibed, including the chauffeur—a garrulous semi-retired fellow with a former career in the Green Berets.

They drove west through the Rockies. Eventually they pulled into a highway rest stop, where they came upon a GOD truck. The chauffeur parked behind it.

Snow fell; mountains reared in the waning light. The truck's driver's door opened and John Prime stepped out, looking pleased. He gestured for them to approach. Waldo and the two Janes exited the limo—regretfully—while John Prime opened the back of the truck. As he did, two metal steps slid out below the door.

John Prime gave a thumbs-up to the limo driver, who returned the gesture. His vehicle faded away in the snow-glazed distance, heading east.

The back of the truck held a pile of white linens. To the left of them, a pile of mats and blankets.

"Good lord," John Prime beamed at Jane1 and Waldo, who huddled in their blankets. "Don't you two have anything better to wear?"

They didn't like the joke.

Waldo thought about asking how they'd been located, but he knew the answer.

John Prime's eyes darted toward Jane1. "I understand that Molotov has passed." He grew reflective. "Poor fellow—if one could call him that." Too late, he recognized his misstep. "No offense, Jane."

Jane1 and Waldo gave him hard looks.

John Prime grinned uneasily, then gestured toward the cargo area. "C'mon. It's cold out here."

Waldo stumbled back to the limo to grab the scotch, then followed the two Janes in. John Prime came up behind them and guided them to the white linen.

"Look," he said too cheerily. "All for you." It was a pile of white GOD uniforms. Jane2 held them up. White pants. White shirt with the word GOD on the left pocket. A parka with raised collar, with the word GOD over the left breast. White baseball caps with the word GOD above the brim. White shoes. There was even GOD underwear—panties and boxer briefs with the word GOD on the elastic bands.

There were five uniforms. They fumbled around, trying not to look as each got dressed. A uniform for Molotov lay unclaimed on the floor.

John Prime suited up last, zipping up his parka with a flourish.

"There. We shall all be as GODs."

Groans.

John Prime proceeded to the other pile. "And we also have mats … you might like this one, Jane—"

To everyone's surprise, Jane1 let out a restrained coo. It was her mandala mat.

Waldo wanted answers. "John—if you're all open to connections from others, why hasn't Light tuned in too? Every floor of Biotechnics should have been packed with cops before we got there."

"Clearly Light is being blocked," John Prime said guardedly.

Waldo rubbed his forehead. "I don't feel a blackout."

"Indeed." John Prime kept his eyes on him. "Odd, isn't it."

Jane2 watched them both. Meanwhile Jane1 looked away from her mat. "Where's John," she said—meaning John2.

Jane2 pretended to be absorbed in tying her shoes. John Prime reached behind the blanket pile and removed four flashlights. He turned them on and began placing them in different locations.

His eyes were shielded by a glare on his glasses. "John led a charge at a side door … it wasn't part of the plan. He and some others fell. But several got through." John Prime paused.

"It's strange. The vainglory I mean …."

He removed his glasses and rubbed them with a corner of his GOD parka, peering at Waldo.

"So very unlike John … almost as if he was under some sort of spell."

Waldo shifted uncomfortably.

"So what happened at Biotechnics?" John Prime asked.

"We entered some sublevels," Waldo told him. "Came across an experiment—much worse than I imagined. Almost as if my brother was trying to recapture his youth. Parts of the creature were definitely interdimensional."

John Prime leaned forward. "So Light is trying to … clone his early self?"

Waldo didn't look at him. He really hadn't thought it through.

Of course … his brother was working to manufacture a *host* of Fish. Waldo envisioned an army in black A-garb goose-stepping past, thousands of black helmets shading implacable faces, each of them Waldo's.

John Prime drove. Jane1 slept next to him. In the back, Waldo and Jane2 sat on mats, wrapped in blankets and trading swallows of scotch.

After a while the GOD truck stopped and John Prime opened the back door. Behind him loomed two mountain peaks framing a dark snow-driven sky.

John Prime had parked on a gravel pull-off recently cleared of snow. They stepped out to a world muffled of sound. To his surprise, Waldo experienced no sense of Vermin or spectral Waldos. He inhaled clear cold air and for the first time in a long while felt alert and unafraid.

He dropped two Duadine.

They all sat wrapped in blankets at a picnic table. The moon glimmered over a ridge. They finished off the scotch. Then John Prime stood and drew a line in the snow with his GOD shoe. He turned toward them smiling.

"Welcome to the Continental Divide."

"I understand this isn't a good thing," Waldo said.

John Prime sat down. "True. But I suspect we can beat Light's hallucinations this time." He peered at Waldo. "We just need a little professional assistance."

Waldo glared at him. "I'm just a tech guy from Manhattan."

"Don't underestimate yourself," Jane2 murmured. "You've come far. You can do this."

Waldo laughed bitterly. Then the laugh seemed to expand. It pealed out amid the frozen mountains with stars reeling behind them, galaxies merging and imploding light-years in the past, through nebulas, luminous gas, interstellar dust, alternative futures, all of it clumsy, farcical, useless … no rhyme or reason to any of it, from the deaths of blind, mindless protozoans to the final gruesome, ignominious collapse of the uncaring cosmos.

"Sure," he said. "No problem."

Jane1 rode up front as before. Everyone agreed that given the seriousness of her wounds, she should share the cabin with the driver.

Waldo considered pointing to the wound on his neck but decided that was a bad idea.

In the cargo area, Jane2 signed off on her cell phone. This was how she communicated with John Prime while he drove. Waldo had told her it was dangerous, but she thought it didn't matter.

"Light knows where we are," she said evenly. "He just doesn't care."

No roadblocks. Waldo expected to hear sirens or helicopters, but nothing.

At this point he wanted to find another DEATH station and access OR—less to capture the formula than to revisit the "Hi, Dad!" greeting. Just to look at it.

Our boy wants you to go on

But this would be pointless. By this time, at any Alpha or Schwarzcorp facility he might invade, the OR file would be erased —or rather, a dummy file would be inserted to lead him astray.

No—the only way to end this now would be to confront Richard Light.

Waldo looked up. Jane2 gazed at him knowingly.

He asked Jane2 to call John Prime again and give him her phone.

John Prime answered. "Jane?"

"Waldo."

"What do you need?"

"Where are we headed?"

"Kanab. The next step on the map, correct?"

"That would distract us."

John Prime didn't respond right away.

"If you say so."

"I think you know where to go."

Waldo had a dream. He was making love to a blend of Amutha and Jane1, but this time there was an element of Jane2 … along with Molotov in her younger, female aspect. All of them merging, less sex than an electric intertwining on a white sheet in an empty room. *Make life … Rick … he's getting it …* the voices like light-shot smoke moving about them, rising slowly out through the twist and arch of their phantom bodies and that familiar *sizzle* into a cool, calm, shining mosaic, wrap of limbs and rhythm of days unfolding like a white rose.

He woke and found himself curled with Jane2 on a mat beneath two blankets on the truck's floor.

They were naked. Her left leg curled over his stomach. Her vulva touched his genitals.

He didn't remember what had happened.

Rhythmic sound of the truck.

Jane2's face lay inches from his. Lips parted in sleep. Her head rested on his left arm.

There was no hint of hostility to the close, leaping shadows that pressed around them. Instead, the shadows contributed to a soothing intimacy, blending easily, in slow gradations, with a cocoon of white light.

His left hand was asleep. He removed his arm carefully, lowering Jane2's head with his right hand while clenching, unclenching his left fingers.

What a sweet, caring girl. He was glad his body was clean.

He glanced at her. She was awake. She regarded him smiling … then curled into him, nuzzling his neck.

Waldo pressed into her.

Midmorning. Rest stop north of Cedar City. Jane1 bought food.

Cold, with a brisk wind and a bit of snowfall.

Jane2 sat, hip touching his, at a picnic table beneath a scrawny pine, eating a cheeseburger. To Waldo's gratification, she held his hand. Their eyes didn't meet, but her calm, unaffected fondness overwhelmed him.

John Prime and Jane1 sat across from them, eyeing them discreetly.

Jane2 finished eating, detached her hand, pulled a joint from her GOD parka. Waldo grinned at her, beatific.

Another rest stop. Blankets. Picnic table. Food, drinks. They feel giddy; they speak fuzzily about lack of sleep. No mention of the danger before them.

Jane1, it seems clear, has no intention of reintroducing the blackout. Everyone seems willing to place their fate in Waldo's hands. Waldo himself is starting to suspect that he might have some astounding psychic ability that can hold his brother at bay.

How else explain the lack of Vermin? He hasn't sensed them for a while, not even at the farthest corners of his eyes. Meanwhile the GOD group remains bathed in a milky haze that Waldo knows is good.

Sharing a blanket, John Prime and Jane2 hunch over *The Millennial Prophesies*. They exclaim as they come to a passage. It turns out the book mentions Fish.

"Listen," Jane2 says. "Illusion will increasingly resemble substance, substance illusion—until illusion overtakes us."

John Prime looks up at Waldo. "The Fictionalizer." He shakes his head. "Of course, that explains it—what I've been feeling since I met you. This sensation of ... *unreality* ...."

He waves at some trucks near the picnic table.

"Look over there—try as I might, I can't detect any *detail*. No scruff marks, bumper stickers—nothing!" He passes a hand over his eyes. "I can't focus on small things, can't isolate them. It's just a row of generic vehicles, might as well be painted on canvas. And I suspect that, if we sat here all day, no driver would appear and get in ... nothing would happen that doesn't support the overall ... *storyline*. Christ almighty—" He looks around laughing. "Everything is so damned *contrived!*"

"Funny you should say that." Jane2 holds up her book. "It's getting harder to read this thing—some of the pages are blurring."

Jane1 nods. "I feel it too. It seems Waldo has this influence."

"It could be Light's," Waldo cautions.

"Color," John Prime presses on. "Do you see how it's draining out?" He gestures about. "White, black … snatch of red, bit of blue … the colors of dreams you might say. It's like the world is bleaching."

"We don't like that," a voice says evenly.

Waldo freezes. Jane1 goes for her belt.

"Don't try it."

Jane1 grips her pistol but doesn't pull it out.

Waldo looks around. Somehow, in the past few moments, soundlessly, they've been surrounded by several dozen A-police with assault rifles and Glock 20s.

"Place the gun on the table, Jane," the voice says. "If you or anyone else tries to fuck with our brains, we'll kill you."

Jane1 places her gun on the table.

"All of you—put your hands up."

Their blankets fall away as they raise their hands.

The crowd of A-cops parts. ASS chief James Gate steps through. He wears a black leather trench coat with an "A" on the lapel and holds a G20. He presses the gun to John Prime's temple and smiles calmly at the group.

"Wow, nice uniforms. All white—I like the logos. Not too big, not too small—very fashion-forward."

No one speaks. Gate turns his attention to Waldo.

"What's up, shithead?"

Waldo stares ahead, unblinking.

"As you know," Gate continues, "we've had a bitch of a time getting to this point." He eyes the cops. "You've killed a number of my men."

The cops mutter and shift about edgily.

John Prime coughs. Then, to everyone's surprise, he tips the barrel of Gate's G20 to the side with a finger and leans toward Waldo, eyeing him fiercely. "Waldo," he murmurs, low and quick, "there's something you need to know. When we met, I realized I'd seen you before—or someone like you. I've attended one Executive Council meeting in my life. There was only one other person in that room. That person looked and spoke exactly like you."

"Oh, fuck this shit," Gate says, and shoots John Prime in the head.

John Prime's brains splash across Jane2. She shrieks and jerks to the side, pawing at her face.

Waldo cries out. Jane1 moans.

The A-cops cheer as John Prime's corpse topples to the ground.

Jane2 pries a bone fragment from her cheek, hysterical. Gate gazes about absently, waving his gun.

"Who's next?"

Waldo found himself in another limo. This time his hands were shackled.

Jane1 sat beside him, also shackled, gazing blankly out the window. Jane2, drenched with blood, sat across from them, shackled, her eyes empty.

Waldo found a way to open his Duadine vial and swallow three pills. As always, it seemed, he was crying—a purgation without release.

Gate sat up front next to the driver, an A-cop. They'd turned on the radio. Evangelical rant.

You are approaching a higher order

Can you see it, brother? Can you see how close you are?

Acusystems: a five-story gray-brick building in an industrial park west of Kanab. When they arrived it was surrounded by A-police.

An opening appeared in the cordon. The limo passed through it to an underground parking area, from which they proceeded deeper to a smaller garage that held a dozen or so A-cops. They trained G20s and assault rifles on the two Janes and Waldo while Gate led them from the car.

Jane1 was impassive. Jane2 had revived somewhat but still hadn't spoken. Waldo was a miserable mess.

They entered a reception area, where Gate spoke briefly to a man in a white lab coat. Then cops began hustling the two Janes away …. Jane2 glanced back at Waldo, startled and afraid. Terror and horror crashed in as Waldo watched the Janes go.

They were ushered through a door. Waldo shrieked and swung on Gate. "Bastard!"

Three or four A-cops seized him; one held a pistol to his throat.

"Don't hurt them!" Waldo screamed.

Gate regarded him without expression, then turned to another technician.

Small white room. No windows. Fluorescent lights. Metal cot. Toilet. Waldo's hands and feet were shackled.

One of the places they confined test subjects, he thought.

They'd let him keep his PENIS. What's the harm in a squirtgun? But they'd taken his Duadine.

Waldo knew he couldn't stay there long. He'd go into withdrawal and die.

He decided that would be fine.

The cell door opens; two cops enter, one with a G20 and one with an assault rifle. They remove Waldo's shackles, pull him out roughly and lead him stumbling down a white corridor to an elevator.

They rise to the fifth floor and enter an office. A door at the back says GATE. The cops knock, receive an OK through shoulder mikes and open the door.

They enter an expansive, semicircular enclave with floor-length windows, a bank of monitors, and a large glass-topped desk holding a DEATH console, a phone, an intercom, and other executive-type peripherals. James Gate sits on a black leather chair behind the desk, fingering his PHALLUS and gazing out at an impressive desert view.

Gate gestures languidly toward a chair with leather straps on the arms and legs. The cops sit Waldo down and buckle him in. Gate nods; they bow slightly and leave.

Gate continues to look out the windows. "Color country, they call it." He glances at Waldo, curious. "Can you see colors these days, Waldo?"

Waldo doesn't respond. He's watching a white mist still lingering around him. Irrationally, he tells himself that as long as the whiteness remains, the two Janes can't be dead.

Gate holds up Waldo's palmtop. "I've been reading your journal —what I can make of it. You're a very bad writer. Some of the action sequences are OK … though they grow a little monotonous. Almost like a recurring bad dream." He sighs and swings around, places his laser gun on the desk, reaches into a drawer and removes Waldo's Duadine vial.

Waldo shudders. Gate smiles, studying the label.

"May induce paranoid psychosis when ingested in large amounts."
He gives Waldo a significant look. "The patient may experience
difficulty distinguishing between reality and fantasy."

Waldo says nothing. Gate pops open the cap, pours pills onto his
palm.

Waldo's face twitches.

"I imagine you'd like some."

Waldo nods.

"How many? Ten? Fifteen?"

"Three would be fine."

Gate places three pills on the desk, pours back the rest, caps the
vial and returns it to the drawer.

Waldo tries to suppress a look of naked hunger—unsuccessfully,
given Gate's bemused expression. Waldo feels shame mingling
with a visceral rush of greed and relief.

Gate steps around his desk and pours the pills into Waldo's mouth.

"There. That should make everything OK … right, you vile,
stinking, cop-killing junky?"

Waldo feels the pills slide down his throat, a long, slow,
vertiginous tingle.

Gate returns to his chair. He picks up his laser gun and peers at
Waldo through the sight.

"I received a message," he says finally. "My employer tells me that, despite your remarkable resemblance to him, there's no family connection. Waldo Stanton is what everyone always thought he was, including yourself—a nobody, a loser, despite your success with brainwashing, an opportunity already tossed to the winds thanks to your stupidity and incompetence."

Waldo does nothing, says nothing. He's waiting for the Duadine to kick in.

"In this case," Gate continues in a low voice, "you're a particularly deluded loser, a pawn in a chess game between my employer and a group of business rivals who've concocted an inane story about a battle of supernatural entities named 'Fish' and 'Yellow Emperor' and gotten you so messed up with pharmaceutical hypnotics you believe it."

Waldo feels a stab of sick uncertainty.

This was possible.

He speaks feebly. "Why would they take the trouble … the setups with Amutha … Marty … so complex. And the OR file—"

Gate's face darkens. "Moron. The file is a plant. Someone from the other camp infiltrated our system—we didn't even know it was there. We've looked over that 'chemical formula'—a bunch of nonsense characters."

He settles back. Waldo sees a glimmer of pity in his eyes.

"They did it to string you along …. If you weren't so befuddled with drugs you'd see it all clearly."

"Why me," Waldo whimpers.

"Because of the physical resemblance, obviously. The opposition needs an avatar, and the existence of a presumed twin encourages acceptance of their mythology. And it's working. Since your homicidal rampage, the underground Rebirth has garnered hundreds of recruits. We've had a tough time rooting them out— we can't have spies in our business, you understand."

Waldo stares at him. "What's your business, exactly."

Gate shrugs, waving the PHALLUS lazily. "Bioengineering, as you've seen. There is indeed a Fictionalizer; that much the opposition knows—they just don't know what it is yet. And that bothers them. So they invent this OR file to get you and others pursuing it … I mean, really." He leans forward, incredulous, taking pleasure in his clincher.

"Why would we protect a file with details relating to your family life? A mantra used by the opposition? Why would we do something so absurd?"

Waldo closes his eyes.

Gate keeps it up. "And this stupid cross-country action/adventure scenario. All this crap about real versus unreal." Gate leans forward sneering. "It's *all real,* Waldo … *all of it is real,* except for the horseshit sloshing around between your ears."

Waldo tries something. "The different futures …."

Gate shakes his head sadly. "It's hard to tell what you mean, since your journal is so incoherent in those parts. But let's take the section where you encounter bars in a sewer outlet. I sent people to check." He stabs a finger against his desk. *"There are no bars in that outlet.* The fact is you chose the only future you could—the one that was real in the first place." He grins tautly. "So CHUNK that in your pipe and smoke it … the future is set, and you can't control it any more than I can shoot shit out my nose."

Waldo sags against his chair. His last try.

"Amutha … her voice …."

Gate snorts. "Doesn't take a Sigmund Freud to figure *that* one out, junky."

Time passes. Waldo loses track of how long. Meanwhile Gate ignores him—signs documents, works in DEATH, plays with a paperclip. People come and go—assistants, technicians in lab coats, cops. Gate gives orders. Some cops have shoulder mikes and speak into them. Waldo barely pays attention.

At a time when the office is clear, he rouses himself. "What's going to happen."

Gate blinks, then squares his shoulders. He gathers some papers and neatens them.

"You, of course," he says without looking at Waldo, "may die."

Waldo nods dully.

Gate looks up. "Or change."

"How's that?"

Gate steps from behind his desk and approaches the chair. He leans over Waldo, crafty, casual—almost chummy.

"Change. Metamorphose. You know"—he mimics swallowing something. "Turn into something you aren't. Which I'd think you'd welcome."

Waldo moans.

Gate guffaws eerily. Waldo hears his voice, jovial, insinuating, like a game-show host's. "C'mon, Waldo, be a sport—we're always on the lookout for new subjects …."

"Please don't do this."

"I'd think you'd be honored. It's not every day a guy like you gets to make history."

Gate chuckles. "'Make history' … I'll have to remember that …."

Waldo twists on the chair, suffocating, seeing the Other's toothless mouth, leaning toward it.

"The Fictionalizer, you understand, is a very sophisticated drug. You see, Waldo—look at me—"

Gate grabs Waldo's cheeks and peers into his face. No trace of amusement now. His eyes are small points; the scar on his chin throbs.

"The Fictionalizer is a hypnotic. A very powerful one. So powerful that it affects the collective unconscious. Do you understand the meaning of this?"

Waldo nods, tears streaming down his cheeks.

Gate examines him a moment—then releases his face and strides toward some monitors.

"Maybe it will help if I give you an example."

He picks up a remote, clicks it. One of the monitors brightens.

Jane2 sits strapped to a chair in a bare white room. She wears a white hospital gown. Her face has been wiped off, but her hair is still bloody. She glares fiercely at a technician, who takes notes on a clipboard a few feet away.

Waldo squeezes his eyes shut, trying desperately to imagine two futures. One: they're in Acusystems. Two: they're not.

Nothing. There's only one future available, and it's an abomination.

"The meaning, if I must tell you," Gate's voice drills in, "is that the moment your friend here is made to believe something, every other conscious entity in the universe will believe it too."

He returns to his desk, sits in his chair and leans back, holding the remote.

Waldo opens his eyes just as a technician forces something down Jane2's throat.

"Imagine." Gate points the remote at the monitor. "Here we have a synthetic substance that can alter reality on command. Anything we tell your friend to think will literally—*happen.* And will continue to happen unless we change the suggestion. If we tell her there's a coffee machine in the room—a coffee machine will appear, and it will make coffee.

"Think about corporate applications. Let's say you have a couple of tons of useless vaccine—it does nothing. It's basically a placebo. You could create an illusion of a pandemic that only this vaccine can resist, and you'd become a multibillionaire, dialing global terror up or down as required.

"Think of geopolitics. If you controlled the Fictionalizer, you could make enemies go away. Entire countries could appear or disappear on the map. Can you imagine what a government would pay for that capability? Face it, Waldo—this technology will make your Cablemaster look like a pop-up toaster."

Gate checks his watch.

"And if we tell Jane here, say, that she's a moose ...."

"Please," Waldo pleads. "She's just a girl."

Gate laughs softly. "'Girl.' Have you ever thought about that? It's a product of consensus—unconscious, but a group decision nonetheless. We're merely going to change what Jane means to the universe, so to speak."

Waldo struggles. "You can't! You know it won't work!"

Gate nods reflectively. "I must admit that's been the case so far. We've made some messes, as you've seen." He brightens. "But hey—there's always a first time, right?"

He bends over an intercom and punches a button.

"Deliver the suggestion."

On the monitor, Jane2 appears unconscious. The technician whispers in her ear.

Gate watches the scene absently. "But I'm convinced we're on the right track. At this point, synthesis is the only problem—and we're almost there ...."

The technician leaves the picture. Jane2 remains unconscious.

Suddenly her eyes shoot open—then roll out of their sockets. Her head snaps back and forth. She arches back convulsing, straining against the straps, tongue sticking out … then jerks once, twice.

Waldo cries out as Jane2's arms disintegrate into a tornado of static.

"This is normal," Gate says calmly. "The structure takes some time to rearrange."

Jane2's mouth gapes in a silent scream as her lower body dissolves. Meanwhile Waldo hears a high-pitched twittering, like that of bats, combined with a violent whistling wind and a familiar electric *sizzle* … the static has moved up her torso. Then, still shrieking silently, Jane2 is swallowed up entirely, and the room fills with swirling intimations of form, a hissing, angry cloud resembling the image in Molotov's office that had knocked Waldo to the floor. Words roar through him like objects in interstellar space: *fugitive … fingernails … photograph … beach … child's history … 24 … bloom … fallen angels … bright curve … gate of dawn …* mingling with a tumultuous stadium sound that is the same as the point of light approaching his forehead. Madness sweeps over him, keening and gibbering; he knows that in a moment it will be irreversible … but then the static coagulates; the light fades and the sound diminishes and sanity seeps back.

Waldo sees on the monitor a huge, flopping sac covered with coarse black hairs.

Then, unbelievably, the sac morphs into a moose.

"Christ!" Gate shouts into the intercom. "Is it alive?"

"I believe so, sir!"

The animal takes wobbly steps.

Every detail is exact. Stumpy tail. Knobby legs. Small horns—an adolescent male moose. At the same time, as it passes the overturned chair with broken straps, heading blindly toward the far wall, it looks crafted, fake, like an illustrated animal in a sporting magazine.

As the moose reaches the wall, tremors seize it.

"No," Gate mutters.

The moose goes still. Then its hindquarters dissolve into an interdimensional miasma. It can't be described. The problem is that the brain translates each element into its nearest previously experienced equivalent: spiraling picnic tables intersecting with green wrestling matches in frangipani sirens, merging time frames frowning at a fly swatter, smelly lizard-eyed aliens made of oak tree's amazement, logarithmic equations with a stretch limo in a state of castor oil, makeshift pizza toppings amid a delirious smell of quaking ozone, motorcycle parts, rose petals, wiring diagrams melding with astrological tables, yellow sandpaper scratching against wasted dreams and scattered industrial toothpaste. Then the cloud of nothing and everything disappears soundlessly.

The moose collapses, its destroyed rear end spewing blood, intestines, sparks, and interdimensional sprays, contrails, tendrils, and vortexes.

"Damn it!" Gate cries, slumping back in his chair. On the monitor, technicians rush in and begin dragging the carcass from the room.

"That was close," Gate whispers to no one in particular as an onscreen tech wheels in a mop and bucket.

Waldo retches dryly.

"But in a moment of remarkable timing," Gate goes on, "we received two other releases of the prototype in today's delivery."

Waldo retches some more.

"We hadn't planned any tests for this evening. Best to lie low after the mess at Biotechnics. But then, when I heard you were nearby" —Gate smiles—"I asked some of our people to stay late."

"Someone will talk," Waldo gasps.

"Who—our employees? Really, Waldo, I'm surprised. Only three people in our organization know we're working with humans. As far as these techs are concerned, this is just another project using test animals."

Now Waldo throws up for real, on his knees and on the floor. He jerks himself back and forth without speaking, vomit dribbling down his chin.

The Cablemaster ... they were using it on their employees.

"And fortunately," Gate continues smoothly, "as we happen to have been provided with more test subjects ...."

"If you hurt Jane I'll kill you!" Waldo screams.

"Oh no. It's not her I'm referring to." Gate pauses. "I meant another friend of yours."

Waldo stops struggling, confused.

Then it hits him. A sob rises in his throat.

"This can't be happening ... Christ ...."

He hangs his head crying. Gate leans over the intercom. "Bring him—or her—in."

Waldo looks up at the monitor. A technician leads in a crabbed, hobbling figure in a white hospital gown.

The figure's blasted, blind eyes stare at nothing. It appears half dead. The tech helps it face the camera. It grins hideously and waves.

"Waldo, are you there?" it croaks. "Janes?"

It's Molotov.

Three a.m. Sign on the border:

WELCOME TO CALIFORNIA!
THE GOLDEN STATE

Pasted on the sign, a poster.

REBIRTH. YOU'RE GETTING THERE!

Screaming, screaming in the brain ... Waldo was terrified for Molotov of course—and afraid also for Jane1. It was clear that Molotov thought she was with Waldo, which meant she hadn't been with Molotov.

He sobbed ... remembering Gate's comment about Duadine, suspecting this was all hallucination—in any case, wishing fiercely it were so.

"Don't kill him."

It was as if Molotov could see him. "Don't cry, Waldo. All that weeping ... so unnecessary. It's probably a result of the medication."

Waldo looked up ... saw Molotov's bruised, smashed-in face, eyes grisly and radiant.

Waldo cried harder as a technician entered the picture. Meanwhile Molotov passed a hand over his blasted body.

"There's nothing here to save. And besides—" He sensed the presence of the technician and flashed his old mad grin. "My friend here has been kind enough to explain the procedure. I'm excited about it."

Molotov coughed, bending double. Blood spattered the floor beneath his head. After a while he straightened and wiped his mouth.

Gate spoke into the intercom. "You sure he's up for this?"

The technician glanced at the camera. "The physical condition shouldn't matter, sir."

"Yes, yes, I know, but still ... Christ ...."

"Whoever you are—James Gate, is it?" Molotov spoke into space. "I suspect it's you, though no one will confirm this." He looked anxious. "I really do want to go through with this. Every man has his fate, and Waldo, if he's alive, can tell you that in many ways my entire life has led to this moment …." He gestured again at his body. "For I really want so badly to … *change*, you see … you mustn't take this opportunity away, not when I've come so far." He stumbled forward and came to the overturned chair. He felt its contours, then shoved it toward the technician.

"Could you get another chair, please? Something with … *decent* straps?"

Awkward silence. Gate cleared his throat.

"Of course, doctor. We planned to get one."

Stunned, the tech left the picture. He returned with a new chair, which he placed near Molotov.

Molotov felt around on it. "Ah."

The tech removed the other chair. Meanwhile Molotov turned back to what he thought was the camera. His gaze was about 45 degrees off.

"The only thing I ask is—please don't hurt Waldo or the two Janes. They've conducted themselves in innocence and good faith. Any damage they've done to your operation was purely the result" —he chose his words—"of excessive idealism. You're aware, I'm sure, that they're victims of an enormous conspiracy."

He embarked on another coughing jag. When he was done he faced what he thought was the camera again.

"They're there, aren't they?" His voice was querulous. He coughed into his fist; blood dripped off it.

"Waldo and both Janes are there, right? They're alive, aren't they, Mr. Gate?"

Tears rolled down Waldo's cheeks. Gate reflected, then bent to the intercom.

"Yes," gruffly. "They're all here."

Molotov tried to smile, but the result was a hellish rictus.

"Mr. Gate," he said quietly. "I understand that if this procedure works, you can turn me into anything you want. Which means I could *become* anything I want, if you agree to try it. Is that true?"

Gate didn't answer right away. Then—was he privately cursing the tech? Given the man's resolute concentration on his clipboard, Waldo suspected so—bent.

"Yes, doctor. Theoretically, you could become anything you want."

Molotov's expression was both beatific and grotesque. "Well … *that*, as you may know, is a subject that has occupied me for many years." He grew pensive. "Have you ever wondered, Mr. Gate, what it would be like to not be damned?"

The technician stopped writing. Gate's expression grew lidded and irritable.

Molotov tried to smile charitably. "That's the only question that should really concern us, isn't it? How to become an angel? Yet we constantly distract ourselves with the degrading minutiae of avoiding death in this filthy hovel of time-space, watching our wastes piling up around us. I tell you, Mr. Gate, I've spent decades wondering what it would be like to be an angel. My thinking on this matter has gone through a number of changes …."

Christ, Waldo thought. Even in this state, Molotov was holding forth. He hobbled about the room, waving an arm professorially. Waldo laughed brokenly.

"At first I had grand cosmic visions," Molotov expounded.

Gate listened, jaw slack.

"I saw myself as a being of light, a still thing within a point of perfect stillness, with entire universes flaring and dying within my limbs."

Molotov pondered a moment—then laughed softly.

"At other times, I figured it might suffice to simply be beautiful or handsome. Or to be a teacher of a child."

Waldo hung his head.

"But you know what I've been thinking?" Molotov had somehow found the camera and seemed to gaze into it, serene.

Gate stared impatiently at the ceiling. "What."

"I want to go right to the top. Next to the seat of God, along with Jesus Christ."

Then, grinning through tears, in a slo-mo, priestly gesture, he raised his arms. But instead of snapping his fingers, he reached behind his right ear, produced something invisible, and held it up to an imagined sky.

"Take me to heaven, Mr. Gate."

Gate's voice comes through. "Harry."

"Yes."

"Strap him in."

Molotov sighs as he's secured to the chair's arms and legs.

"Please," Waldo whispers. "Stop."

Molotov seems uncertain. "Will you turn me into an angel, Mr. Gate?"

Gate regards Molotov warily. He murmurs into his intercom. Harry's eyes grow wide with surprise, concern, and doubt. Gate and Harry have a tense whispered conversation.

Finally Harry steps aside and buries his head in his clipboard again. Gate clears his throat and bends.

"Sure. Not a problem."

Madness creeps into Molotov's face. "Principle behind confession. Fiction by fire. Whatever it is, I expect you morons will make a muck of it."

Waldo struggles again, shrieking at Gate—part of him watching himself, hearing his mouth produce garbled, incomprehensible sounds.

"Waldo," Molotov says. "Janes. Don't worry about me. I have a feeling this Fictionalizer will ultimately be used in ways our hosts can't predict."

He glances at where he thinks Harry is. "Do it."

Molotov squeezes his blind eyes shut, opens his mouth and sticks out his tongue.

"No!" Waldo bellows.

Harry places his clipboard on a table and removes something from his pocket.

Waldo slumps back, wishing he could interpose his other Waldo somehow, a Waldo who might somehow reverse this horror.

Harry, clearly troubled, places a tablet on Molotov's tongue. Molotov swallows. Harry backs away.

Molotov looks up serenely. "Stop crying, Waldo," he says. "It's time to *stop crying*."

Waldo tries to stop.

"OK," Molotov slurs. His head droops—his eyes flutter, then close. "Tell me what I'm finally to be …."

After a minute or so, Molotov passes out.

Harry bends and whispers something in his ear.

Waldo watches. Gate leans forward, raps the desk with his knuckles.

"Let this one work," he murmurs.

Harry leaves the screen. Molotov sits slumped in the chair.

Then, with a sigh, he arches back, raises his face toward the ceiling … passes through his straps … and slowly levitates, without a struggle, toward an expanding circle of light.

Waldo laughs.

"Christ," Gate breathes.

The room's walls bend, twist, dissolve … the screen blossoms into whiteness, blissful and compassionate … as if for a moment Waldo is allowed, like a child at a spectacle, to watch the slow upward struggle of brutish, undeserved consciousness toward an immense, loving radiance.

Waldo laughs deliriously, feeling the light reach through the monitor and embrace him. He watches Molotov, blind face pointed to the heavens, arms outstretched, feet dangling, slowly rising toward a glistening, rotating white rose.

Then, in the middle of the rose, the Devil appears.

Once again, Waldo's memory supplies the nearest alternative to a phenomenon his brain can't fathom. A few years ago, he had watched, while Amutha listened to, a black and white film called *Curse of the Demon* (1958). The Devil looks like that creature.

Gate chortles. "What the fuck is an angel, Waldo? White robe? Wings? Harp? Give me a fucking break. Angels don't exist, you know that." He waves the thought away.

"I can't do heaven … but maybe I can do hell …."

Molotov senses the monstrosity above him and starts to struggle. The Devil engulfs the white rose and morphs into something at the edge of imagination. Massive, twisted, brown horns; gloating scarlet eyes; black roiling body; arms ending in clutched claws the size of aircraft carriers. Bared, sharpened teeth surround a gaping mouth that grows wider as it approaches Molotov.

Molotov shrieks.

Gate cackles and strokes his PHALLUS. Harry looks on appalled.

The widening maw holds all Hell inside … flames shooting up
from seas of fire … cinders raining down … numberless writhing
naked human forms crying out to be delivered to death as they
boil in rivers of white-hot coals, burning iron, brimstone …
people buried in muck upside down, buried to their necks in
volcanic fire … tortured on racks, in iron maidens, on crosses,
genitals and knees and feet and hands ripped from bodies, howling
souls split into quarters by charging horses … raped, sodomized,
disemboweled, watching their intestines circle on sizzling spits …
meanwhile, smells somehow begin oozing through the monitor,
sulfur, exploding ozone, urine, shit, burning tires, burnt tar, burnt
hair, burnt flesh … white hot hate merging with ancient,
intractable evil and relentless pain.

As Molotov screams, the Devil's arms transform into swarming
tentacles with pulsating suckers. The tentacles surround Molotov
and yank him toward the Devil's mouth.

The Devil swallows Molotov and sucks him down into Hell.

The room was now empty except for Harry.

Gate slumped back in his chair, rubbed his face. "Amazing."

After a moment he shook his head and bent to the intercom. "Did you see it?"

No answer right away.

"Yes," Harry's voice came finally—feeble, shocked, afraid.

Gate looked dreamy. "Did we succeed?"

"Hard to tell. Dr. Molotov has disappeared."

"Let's do some more tests. Meanwhile, write this up. If we can really get the Devil to eat people on command, there might be commercial opportunities here."

Harry bent over and threw up on the floor.

Meanwhile Waldo felt calm, perfectly calm … quiet, focused, alert … **CHUNK** … he raised his arms, unsurprised to find them free of straps, just as Molotov's had been. His hands were quasi-transparent.

He rose from his chair, noting that his legs, too, were free. In a slo-mo dream state, he watched himself crouch—then launched himself across the desk, scattering a pen set, Rolodex, stapler, calendar pad … thinking to himself, what *cheesy props* … absently regarding his hands, now reformulated and heading toward Gate.

Gate was raising his laser pistol as Waldo sprawled into him … *pop*, Waldo's left knee, *shit shit* … Waldo rolled, holding his knee, groaning, while Gate's body landed on his, and through a sliver of vision Waldo saw that Gate still held the laser … he gripped Gate's hair, lifted his head, tried to poke out his eyes; Gate got a hand in the way, then used it to grab Waldo's face. They rolled about on the floor.

They slammed into the desk, fighting for the PHALLUS. Waldo grabbed Gate's right hand; Gate punched Waldo's face with his left. Waldo tried to slam a knee between Gate's legs but Gate got there first. A red missile of pain rammed into Waldo's brain, then brutally exploded; he gasped, released Gate's hand and doubled up.

When Waldo came to his left cheek lay in a puddle on the floor.

Waldo stared at Gate sideways. Gate leaned panting against the window, training the PHALLUS on him.

Waldo's knee had popped back into place, but the pain remained intense. A smell registered. Vomit.

Suddenly, without warning, the Vermin ooze back in, pulsing against Waldo's chest and face.

"I told you that if you fucked with me I'd kill you," Gate says. He rises, steps forward and presses the laser pistol between Waldo's eyes.

Waldo regards him. He's surprised to feel no fear.

There's a long, slow, glowing moment in which Waldo is no longer in Gate's office. He's in a room where Gate merges with the Other. Waldo sits at a table across from Gate/Other in white light.

The Vermin flee, flapping black wings.

What do I do, Amutha

Her reply is hard to decipher.

Find Floor Zero

Waldo is in Gate's office again, on the floor, staring past the weapon in his face.

The words rise from Waldo's gut: "I forgive you."

Gate looks startled. "What?"

Waldo peers into Gate's eyes. In fact, he feels something stronger than forgiveness. Friendship, compassion—he thinks he may even be smiling fuzzily, eager to share his incomprehensibly brotherly feeling toward Gate, and taken aback and a little disappointed to see Gate's expression grow afraid.

"I forgive you," Waldo repeats.

It's like he can read Gate's mind. *What the—no one—Light, you—this wasn't—*

Gate's eyes glaze ... sweat breaks out on his face; the laser gun quivers. It snaps away from Waldo and Gate staggers back, shaking. He gazes at Waldo desperately.

"No."

Waldo feels deliberate, kind, oddly officious. "Careful," he says as Gate sags back against the window. "Don't hurt yourself."

Gate's expression grows crafty.

"C'mon, Waldo. I'm just a spook. I'll do anything for anybody if they pay me enough. I could work for you."

Waldo has picked himself up. He absently wipes his cheek.

"Well …." He raises a palm, honestly apologetic. "I'm not sure I'm the one in charge here."

Gate's eyes dart. "You want Light? I can do that. I can get you to that sonofabitch."

"That may be." Waldo feels earnest, like a junior negotiator eager to reach a conclusion that will leave them both satisfied. "But I have a feeling my brother and I will meet in any case."

"You cocksucker," Gate snarls. Then he raises the laser gun to his neck and cuts his head off.

Gate's upper torso dissolves in a red cloud, and his head lofts slowly into the air, staring at the ceiling. Waldo follows the arc of the head with numb interest, watching it ricochet off the window, leaving a bloody patch on the glass, and sail back toward the lower body, which has collapsed into a bloody mess with the PHALLUS on top. Glancing against the desk, the head caroms off the floor and soars into the air again, and in still sad amazement Waldo realizes that the eyes, like those of a just-severed fish head, are still registering the final inputs of life, that the brain is still trying to puzzle out this strange turn of events. And in something like poetic justice, the head hurtles into the chair Waldo has just vacated, bounces about between the arms a bit, and comes to rest, tilted to the left but mainly upright, its eyes still open and glassy, gazing blindly at Waldo.

The head's mouth opens, as if about to speak—then closes. Blood from the severed neck pools in the seat.

In a daze, Waldo plods to Gate's chair, sits, checks the DEATH security module.

On the monitor, A-police keep watch in various corridors and surround the building.

Gate's office isn't under surveillance. No one has seen them.

"Mr. Gate."

On the monitor, Harry stands in the empty room. "Do we proceed with a third test?"

Waldo freezes. *Jane1.*

Brain reeling, Waldo curses himself … meanwhile he recalls Gate's voice. A bit lower than his own, but not too different … remarkably like Waldo's, in fact.

He leans into the intercom. "The girl?"

Harry frowns suspiciously—Waldo thinks he's been made. But it's not that.

"Uh, no, sir … I thought you'd been told."

Dread swarms in. "Told?"

Harry looks perplexed. "She attempted psychic manipulation and was liquidated."

Ah god, ah god … Waldo curls up in Gate's chair, burying his face in his hands, choking back a scream.

"Sir?" Harry says.

Waldo can't answer … he reaches for the drawer, opens it. Removes the Duadine vial … the pills scatter across the desk.

"Mr. Gate," Harry says, nervous. "I was referring to Stanton. Should we proceed?"

Waldo knows he's blowing it but can't speak. His hands peck at the pills. One, two … he crams six more into his palm and jams them in his mouth.

"Sir?" Harry fidgets with his clipboard.

Waldo forces the pills down, gagging. Harry begins to edge out of the picture.

"No," Waldo gets out. Harry stops, relieved.

Waldo wipes his mouth. "We have more to learn from Stanton."

He falls silent. Harry waits expectantly.

"Let's call it a night."

Harry looks pleased. "Whatever you say, sir. Good night."

The monitor goes dark.

Waldo thinks a moment—then logs onto OR.

This is the best place to do it. Gate's ID won't ring any bells. But would the file still be there?

No dice—it's gone. Instead, words appear on the screen, which Waldo at first takes to be an error message.

Then he reads: **TOO LATE, BROTHER. THE WYOMING GROUP JUST SENT ME A PERFECTED PROTOTYPE.**

Waldo doubles up, pressing fingers to his face. Meanwhile the screen flickers, then clears.

THANKS FOR TAKING CARE OF GATE.

Sunrise. Cajon Junction.

For the past few hours they'd been battling fatigue hallucinations
—phantom creatures scuttling across the road. Twice they'd
almost lost control.

They were taking a circling route through mountains to avoid A-
cops.

Heading toward Wrightwood.

Klaxons sound. Waldo checks security. A-cars screech around the Acusystems building; A-cops check hallways door to door. Other cops pound up steps.

A door crashes outside Gate's office. Bellows.

Waldo doesn't have time to think. He scrapes the Duadine pills into the vial and jams it in his pocket. He checks his PENIS—present. He limps to Gate's remains and picks up the laser pistol.

The door bursts open and cops pour in, brandishing rifles and G20s. Bullets riddle the monitor, splinter the desk, smash through the window. Waldo gazes at them with detached interest.

Five menacing figures.

Sizzle

He lurches through the carnage toward the open door as two more cops appear.

Sizzle

Waldo looks around. Same old white hallway. Same old white doors.

At the far end of the hall a door hangs open. Waldo strides toward it. In the doorway, another cop appears, a cipher.

Sizzle

Waldo enters a stairwell. Boots pound up the stairs. He aims the laser at the lower landing. Two cops round the corner.

Sizzle

A few seconds later a laser beam angles up through the floor at his feet. Waldo sends a shot through the floor and glances up. The stairs end at a small landing and a metal door.

A beam cuts across the floor in front of him, then angles back. He jumps out of its path and sends another shot through the floor. A scream.

He hobbles to the landing, undoes a bolt on the door, opens it. Staggers out into a frigid evening.

Tar-and-pebble roof. Klaxons, sirens. Searchlights cut across the sky.

No other roofs nearby. Waldo has no idea what to do.

Searchlights rake the roof, blinding him, and through the cacophony he hears a *chop-chop-chop*—then his hair blows back; pebbles bite his face. Bathed in stunning light, he shades his eyes and makes out black shapes hovering above.

Two helicopters. Waldo sweeps his laser at the nearest one—the beam enters the metal; nothing happens. A beam passes his face; he glances back at the door.

Two A-cops crouch in the doorway. One holds an assault rifle, the other a PHALLUS. Waldo limps behind a brick chimney—though this, of course, provides no protection from the laser. Brick spits from the chimney; a beam passes over his head; the roof explodes at his feet—then something slaps his right side, knocking him to his knees.

About three feet away, tar and pebbles spit in a line moving toward him … the slugs pass inches away. Waldo looks up at the nearest chopper. In the cockpit, he makes out an A-cop with an assault rifle.

Sizzle

The chopper veers away unsteadily. A beam slashes into the roof near Waldo's right elbow. He rolls, heading for a ventilation unit. He stops behind it. The cops have advanced a few yards and are pointing their weapons at him.

Sizzle

Waldo rolls again and sends a wave of light toward the second chopper, with no result. He hears a screeching metallic sound. Looking behind him, he sees the first chopper rounding back. It has tilted to the side so that its rotor scrapes the roof about twenty yards away. The chopper hurtles toward Waldo, searchlight pointed at the sky. A rotor blade crumples, dragging a sheet of flame behind it.

Waldo claps his hands over his face.

The rotor passes a few yards to his left. He feels a searing wind as the chopper's body passes overhead … for a moment he's engulfed in smoke and heat. Then he hears a *crack* from the chimney as it's ripped from the roof, and the chopper lands with a force that rocks the building. Gagging on smoke, Waldo watches as the machine advances like a crippled animal toward the door, screeching, grinding, groaning … it plows into the wall to the right of the door and stops. One of the cops in the cockpit flops unconscious or dead onto the roof.

Waldo rolls to his back and eyes the second chopper. The pilot and shooter stare at the crash, mouths open. Their faces turn to Waldo, and his eyes lock on theirs. They grimace.

Sizzle

The chopper hovers a moment, then banks to the left. Waldo watches as it disappears beneath the roof.

He's dizzy. He forces himself to sit, vacantly examining blood spilling from the right side of his waist.

Screams from below … a bone-rattling *boom* as the second chopper crashes.

"Waldo," someone says.

Waldo glances to his right and curses. An A-cop holding a G20 stands near the wrecked chopper, wreathed in smoke. Waldo flops onto his stomach, preparing to fire.

"Waldo," she says again.

The chopper emits a burst of flame … the cop lifts the helmet's visor, and in the glare he sees her face.

Jane1.

"Jane!" Waldo cries.

There she is, wearing an A-cop uniform down to the boots. Beautiful, icy, inscrutable Jane1 … he steps forward, wanting to take her in his arms. He wants to tell her how much he loves and respects and admires her and how glad he is to see her. How grateful he is for everything she's done for him and is doing now.

But she'd never put up with that.

She nods toward his right side, where his GOD uniform is bright red. She also takes in his PHALLUS. "Seems you've been busy."

He glances down guiltily. "Didn't want to. But they killed Jane."

Feeling creeps into her eyes. Heartsickness—desolation? But her face soon resumes its stony façade.

She shakes her head, hefts the G20 and approaches him. She clasps his hand.

He feels no fear. Everything will be fine now.

Jane1 returns to the door, slams it shut, grabs a piece of broken prop and tilts it beneath the doorknob. "Quick," she says, pointing to the chopper.

They run to it and glance inside the cockpit. The pilot slumps insensible against the controls. They turn their attention to the cop on the roof. They remove his helmet and jacket, rip off his boots and pull off his pants. They hear rotors … look up and see two more black helicopters in the distance.

Waldo suits up. Pounds on the door, shouts. No time for the boots. Jane tosses away the prop piece and yanks open the door, revealing three confused A-cops. Waldo waves them through.

"Men down!" he shouts. "Men down!"

The cops lurch onto the roof. Waldo's white GOD shoes poke through the bottom of his A-uniform, but they don't notice.

Below them, two more A-cops charge up to the fifth floor and into the office. Shouts of horror, vomiting. One of the cops screams into what is probably a shoulder mike.

They step down to the fifth floor. One of the A-cops dashes from the office and begins frantically punching an elevator's DOWN button. Jane1 and Waldo continue down the stairs.

Jane1 hands Waldo a shoulder mike. As more cops rush up, he begins shouting nonsense into it.

"Clear sector four! Man the barricades! Fuel the pump station!"

Fourth floor. Two A-cops run past them up the stairs, brandishing rifles.

Third floor. Waldo still shouts into the mike. Second floor. Waldo feels dizzy and grips his side.

The first floor is a madhouse. A-cops, men in suits who seem to supervise them, radio equipment, a DEATH console set up in a corner with security videos playing. Kanab cops in blue uniforms argue with suits over jurisdiction. Small elderly women in green uniforms and white aprons thread through the crowd, distributing coffee and donuts. The men take a few bites or slurps and continue to shout at each other. No one notices Waldo's shoes.

Jane1 pulls Waldo into the men's room, which is empty. Strangely so, given all the people in the lobby. But Waldo's pain chases that thought away.

Jane1 grabs paper towels from a dispenser and raises his A-jacket and GOD parka. The wound isn't deep but still squirts blood. Jane1 crams the towels into it, making Waldo cry out.

"Keep the towels there," Jane1 commands, grabbing Waldo's right hand and pressing it to his side. She guides him out of the men's room into the first-floor chaos. They wend their way through the milling, futile throng and step through a glass door into the dim evening light.

Cement steps descend to a street clogged with A-police, Kanab police, state police, fire trucks, news trucks and emergency medical vehicles. Rotating lights cast a mad dance of red and blue. Jane1 guides Waldo around the corner of the building, where they find a bench and sit.

"Put your head in your hands," Jane1 instructs. He does; she does too. Now they're two A-cops recovering from traumatic stress. Waldo tucks his feet beneath the bench.

"How did you escape?" he hisses.

"Tell you later."

Jane1 scans the cars before them. Police have arrived so frantically that some of the cars are still running. She locks her attention on a brown Ford sedan—probably owned by an off-duty local cop.

Jane1 jumps into the driver's seat while Waldo lands in the back. They take off.

Wrightwood, Sunset Motel, about 3 a.m. Twin beds.

Jane1 pulled the Ford behind the motel. They shoved the A-uniforms and weapons in the trunk. Jane1, in her GOD uniform, got a room while Waldo kept out of sight.

Once she'd guided Waldo to a bed, Jane1 found an all-nite pharmacy and returned with cigarettes, rubbing alcohol, bandages, tape, needles, thread, safety pins, over-the-counter painkillers. She did her best with Waldo's wound while he clamped his teeth on a Gideon Bible.

She also brought food—chips, cookies, hot dogs from a rotary stove, garnishes in packets. They sat on the beds and dove in—neither had eaten in some time.

Afterward Waldo dropped two Duadine while Jane1 lit an American cigarette. No Gauloises or marijuana here in the middle of the night.

"How did Jane die," Jane1 asked quietly.

Waldo explained about the Fictionalizer but didn't say much about Jane2—just that she hadn't survived the experiment.

"Something else," he said. She studied him.

"They had Molotov. Fished him out of the sewer. He was blind but alive."

Jane1 seemed gratified—then grew grave as she saw Waldo's expression.

"And?"

"They experimented with him too … it turned out badly."

Jane1 squinted.

"Is he dead?" Waldo anticipated her. "I have no idea."

They fell silent. Then, out of nowhere, Jane1 said: "Do you know what today is?"

He shook his head.

"New Year's Day."

Waldo laughed brokenly—then grimaced with pain and gripped his side.

They settled into the beds and got some sleep.

7 a.m. Rested. Showered. Waldo dropped four Duadine.

Five pills left. Oddly, he didn't feel concerned.

This motel had a coin-operated washer and dryer. Jane1 brought back two clean GOD uniforms. She'd closed the hole in Waldo's uniform with safety pins.

"Jane," Waldo said. "Fill me in."

She looked almost shy. "An A-cop took me to a small white room. It was half finished—there were studs, pipes, dangling wires. He had a G20. He took off my handcuffs but shackled me to a pipe on the wall, then sat on a folding chair.

"I could have tried hypnotizing him, but we started to talk. He took off his helmet and shoulder mike. He was an overweight, homely guy—buck teeth, pimples. He told me he was nineteen years old. His name was Bob.

"Bob wasn't making much money. He complained that his job wasn't worth it. He didn't have a happy marriage—very little sex. He swore that he'd never killed anyone and never would. I commiserated with him.

"Then I offered to suck his dick and fuck him."

"Jane!" Waldo gasped.

She gave him a look of feigned surprise.

"Anyhow," she continued, "Bob was game. He unshackled me and let me get out of my clothes. Then he laid his gun on the floor, took off his boots and uniform and came for me.

"I punched him in the nose twice, hard, and he slumped to his knees. I grabbed his gun and trained it on him. Then I told him to press his face to the ground. He swore at me but obeyed. I used some wires to tie him up.

"At this point Bob was naked except for his socks. He glared at me—without too much hostility, I thought; he almost seemed relieved. Meanwhile I put the GOD uniform back on, pulled his A-uniform over it and yanked on his boots. I picked up his shoulder mike and spoke into it.

"Someone responded. Keeping my voice low, I reported that the subject had tried to use mind control and had been eliminated. This seemed to work."

Then Jane1 had rifled through Bob's A-pants. His wallet held over $500 in cash, which seemed at odds with his complaints about money. Then it came to her.

"Holiday pay?"

Bob nodded.

"Sorry," she said while removing the bills along with coins from one of his pockets.

Bob shrugged philosophically. "Easy come easy go."

Jane1 continued: "I holstered his gun, put on his helmet and found my way to the main floor. No one noticed. I took the stairwell to the fifth floor. The office there was splashed with blood and full of cops; I knew that if you were in there you were dead. So I went to the roof."

Waldo chortled. "You're amazing. Wonderful."

Suddenly fear for Jane1's life overwhelmed him. He sat next to her on her bed and touched her shoulder.

"You've gotten us this far. Let me do this part."

She shook her head, detached his hand and reached for her cigarette pack. "No. We'll finish it."

For some reason he believed her.

At this point he didn't believe a word Gate had said.

They take stock. Jane1 has Bob's G20. Waldo has Gate's PHALLUS and his water pistol.

They leave the motel and drive toward L.A.

Around 9 a.m. Jane1 pulls off the road and enters a town. She checks the Yellow Pages and then drives to an Army Navy store, where she buys a pair of black boots for Waldo. The boots aren't A–issue, but they're better than Waldo's GOD shoes, which he crams in the pockets of his A-jacket in the trunk.

As they descend toward Glendale, traffic picks up—especially oncoming. It's strange: Some cars blare their horns, while others dodge crazily between lanes, as if trying to drive east fast.

As they near Hollywood, they come to a rise and see why.

Below them, Hollywood is an armed camp. Along every visible stretch of road stand black A-cars, troop trucks, vans, jeeps, fire trucks, ambulances. Cops mill about everywhere. In the sky black helicopters and news helicopters chop back and forth. The activity is most intense around a black skyscraper near the Hollywood Bowl.

The skyscraper, Waldo knows from TV news and annual reports, is Alpha HQ. Sixty-six stories tall, tapering to a point at the top, like an obelisk.

Jane1 pulls around to the back of a gas station. "Maybe we should forget this," Waldo mutters.

She shakes her head. "We can handle it."

They grab their A-uniforms and pull them over their GOD ones. They get back in and Jane1 eases the car down the road.

They come to a roadblock manned by a dozen or so A-cops armed with assault rifles. The cops don't know what to make of the Ford, but when they see Waldo's laser gun they step back and wave them on.

Ah—their ticket. Only the most senior A-cops would rate a PHALLUS.

Jane1 drives on. They come to a place of heavy traffic. They inch forward until they reach Santa Monica Boulevard.

So it goes. After they pass two more roadblocks Waldo begins to laugh quietly.

"Shut up," Jane1 says.

She takes a right. They approach HQ. It's a block wide at the base.

Jane1 turns left. On the side of the building they see a Parking sign. Jane1 pulls in.

A ramp slopes beneath the building. It's guarded, but the A-cops wave them past. They descend and enter a garage full of more cops.

Jane1 pulls into a slot between two black vans. Waldo downs three Duadine.

Two left.

They leave the car and spot an EXIT sign. They head toward it casually, passing a cluster of A-cops who pay them no heed.

They open a door to a cement stairwell.

The lobby is modern corporate—white tile, mirrors, stainless steel. Twenty or thirty A-cops mill about. Video cameras on the walls. Elevators to the rear, behind a security guard sitting at a desk.

As Waldo and Jane1 approach the guard, other cops notice the PHALLUS and part before them.

Waldo leans close to the guard. "Mr. Light's office."

The guard stares at the laser. He waves toward the elevators. "Top floor."

"We need to join our men. Where are they?"

"Men on the 48th, 24th, third floor. Elevator stops there. Then take the stairs."

"How do you mean?"

"Floor numbers go backwards in this building."

Waldo blinks.

Floor numbers

He pushes through a turnstyle and strides to the elevator banks. One bank has elevators for each floor in the lower building—66-48. Other elevators go straight to the 48th floor but no farther.

He gets it. His brother would want to occupy the first floor, at the top.

He returns to the guard. "Tell me more."

The guard wipes his forehead with a coffee napkin and looks around for backup. It's clear that none of the A-cops wants to come close.

"Men on the third and second floors. The only office on the first floor is Mr. Light's. He gets in from the roof—a helipad. No one ever sees him."

"Good man."

The guard looks gratified.

"Who'd know if Mr. Light is in," Waldo continues.

"His assistant."

"Can you call this person? It's important."

The guard picks up a phone, punches some numbers. Someone answers; Waldo grabs the receiver.

"Who is this?"

"Gary."

"OK, Gary, this is Allen Whitmore at Acusystems. May I speak to Mr. Light?"

"I'm sorry, Mr. Whitmore, he's in a meeting."

"Did he get my package?"

"Yessir—he received it yesterday."

"Please tell him I'll call back."

Waldo replaces the receiver. "Who controls the chopper?" he asks the guard.

"Mr. Light."

"How."

"Gary calls when Mr. Light needs it."

"It doesn't stay on the roof."

"No, it returns to the hangar at his estate."

"Is the stairwell to the first floor locked?"

"Yes."

"Who has the keys?"

"Jerry on the third floor."

"Jerry's working now?"

"Yes."

"Can you describe him?"

The guard glowers suspiciously. He gestures toward his head.

"Old guy—bald."

"Good. You've been very helpful."

The guard glances at the PHALLUS and nods, relieved.

Waldo and Jane1 proceed to the elevator bank. Waldo presses a button that will take them without stopping to the 48th floor.

"Alert 66!" a man's voice barks from a speaker on the wall. "Alert!"

A-cops glance around feverishly—some raise assault rifles or G20s, while a few crouch in shooting positions.

"Intruders near the elevators!" the voice shouts. "One is Stanton! Shoot on sight!"

Ding ... a light blinks on; an elevator door opens.

Suddenly every A-cop in the lobby is pointing his weapon in one direction.

Waldo brandishes his PHALLUS. "Hold your fire! You may kill us, but five or six of you will be cut in half first!"

The A-cops eye each other uneasily. Some lower their guns. Jane1 and Waldo step into the elevator, and the door closes.

They drop to the floor, expecting a barrage of bullets. Nothing.

"Amateurs," Jane1 breathes. Waldo clutches her hand.

The elevator rises. As it does, they hear guns blasting below.

Jane1 detaches her hand, rolls to her back and yanks back the slide on her Glock. "The next floor will be tougher. Some of them may have lasers." Waldo slides to his back next to her.

"Great."

"Alert 48!" comes a dim voice.

Ding.

Rifle fire smashes through the door. Still on his back, Waldo passes the laser through, zigzagging the beam about.

Screams. Silence.

The door opens. They crawl into a white hallway splashed with blood and body parts. Rags of flesh and black leather studded with splinters of bone. The hand of a detached arm clutches a G20. An A-cop lies in a corner, staring at the ceiling and emitting a death rattle. Another cop, minus a leg, drags himself toward a bloody assault rifle.

Jane1 steps over and shoots him in the head. Waldo gazes at her dazedly as the body jerks to the floor.

Jane1 turns to an elevator bank about twenty feet away. 48-24.

Waldo glances at a video camera on the wall. "They saw that on TV," Jane1 says. "Watch yourself on 24."

He shakes his head wearily.

Watch yourself

Jane1 strides to the elevator bank and punches UP.

Ding. One of the doors opens. They get in. There are buttons for every floor.

"Which one," Jane1 says.

"24."

She nods and pushes the button. As the elevator rises they press against the side walls. Waldo holds down the CLOSE button, hoping this will keep them from getting stopped along the way.

Waldo looks at Jane1 and moans. Her eyes are squeezed shut—face bloodless. She shivers, gripping her upper arms.

Waldo understands. "Jane. Don't let Light do this."

"What's that sound," she mumbles.

Waldo glances at the floor indicator: 42.

"Fight it," he hisses.

But already she's on her knees … the G20 clatters to the floor. She presses her fingers to her temples and third eye.

Waldo grabs her by the shoulders. "You can beat him!"

"Amy …." Her voice is strangled. "Amy doesn't like it …."

35.

"Dammit!" Waldo pleads.

Jane1 bares her teeth, rocking back and forth. Then something flashes in her eyes … a mix of terror, hope, affection, and grim irony.

"Amy's mad," she mutters.

Waldo knows who Amy is. Jane1's real name.

Ding. 24.

Slugs and laser beams slash through the door—*sizzle*. Waldo shrieks and fires back—*sizzle*. Silence falls.

Despite the damage to it, the door opens. Two A-cops stand amid four dead ones. One holds an assault rifle, another a PHALLUS. Waldo slashes first, and both cops collapse in a bloody heap.

Meanwhile Amy lurches past him. She heads for the stairwell, holding the G20 in her cupped hands like some precious alien artifact.

"Mama …" she whimpers.

Two more A-cops appear. Both hold lasers.

"Amy!" Waldo screams. "Jane!"

She smiles fuzzily. She tries to point her gun at the cops, but it skews to the side.

"I've been so lonely," she murmurs.

Sizzle. Her torso spews blood—she spins.

Waldo screams and kills both cops. He rushes over and kneels by Amy's side in a puddle of blood.

She gazes at him, radiant, sad, subdued. She regards Waldo imploringly, but he knows she's seeing someone else.

"Please … make me warm …."

Sizzle. A laser beam sweeps past Waldo's shoulder. Waldo howls and kills an approaching A-cop as another beam leaves the man's gun.

Waldo glances back at Amy, seeing everything in slo-mo and with perfect clarity.

The beam approaches her with stop-action precision … Amy meets his eyes, and he comprehends that she sees him now and is calm.

Sweetheart

Body parts and fragments of A-uniform and GOD uniform thud to the floor.

Waldo sloshes to the next elevator bank, his face a psychotic mask.

24-3. He presses UP.

Ding.

In the elevator, he presses the 4 button, then vomits.

18.

He looks up. A drop ceiling. He shoves a middle panel up and to the side.

Trap door. He reaches up, pops the door open. Checks the floor indicator.

10.

Waldo grabs at the opening, yanks himself up. He rises into a brick shaft illuminated at intervals by bulbs in metal mesh. He passes a black metal door with the number 7 painted on it in white. He pulls up his legs as the elevator reaches floor 4.

The elevator stops. *Ding.*

Gunshots below … he looks down dispassionately, watching slugs burst through and lasers play about. He shuts the trap door, looks to his right—a metal ladder runs up the side of the shaft. He scuttles over and grabs the ladder's rims.

A crash. Bellows, shouts.

The ladder stops at floor 3. Above it, the elevator cable leads to a black maw of machinery.

Waldo climbs. A laser beam slashes past him on the right. He pauses and pours his PHALLUS through the elevator's roof, moving it about in a slow circle.

Screams.

Waldo comes to the bottom of door 3. Beneath him, the elevator's trap door crashes open and an A-cop appears in the opening, pulling his right arm through. Meanwhile slugs rip through door 3, creating a lazy dance of light in the shaft.

The cop in the opening sends off a beam, which sizzles through brick at Waldo's left; Waldo rakes his laser across him; his head dissolves and he topples back through. Meanwhile so much artillery has hit door 3 that it hangs half open … Waldo hears boots, yells; two cops poke their heads into the shaft.

Sizzle

More beams pour up from below … Waldo glances at the elevator cable and leaps for it.

He's calm, serene … he transfers the laser gun to his left hand … his right hand reaches out; he grabs the cable and spins clockwise.

He registers the gaping, ruined door and sees three A-cops in the opening, gripping assault rifles. Waldo releases the cable and feels himself float toward them—meanwhile opening up with the PHALLUS. One cop shrieks and dies as Waldo's right foot finds the door's bottom lip ... he watches another cop split in two as he topples forward onto the third floor. He jerks to the side, seeing slugs riddle the floor next to him, and rolls to his stomach.

Sizzle

Sobbing, Waldo looks about. No other cops—just a man in a guard's uniform, quivering behind a desk, hands clamped over his bald head.

Waldo hears boots in the stairwell—frenzied shouts.

"Jerry." He's amazed by the evenness of his voice. "Give me your keys."

Shuddering, Jerry pulls a keyring from his waist and tosses it toward him. It skitters across the floor.

Cops burst through the stairwell door. Jerry screams.

Sizzle

One of the cops, holding a G20, keeps coming. By now Waldo has lost respect for this weapon ... so it's with astonishment that he feels something slam into his left hand. He moans and holds the hand up ... sees a neat hole in the middle, drooling blood.

Sizzle

Bloody flesh rains down, mingled with shreds of black leather. Jerry retches onto his desk.

Waldo looks around. About ten feet away is a door marked STAIRS.

Waldo tucks the PHALLUS beneath an armpit, grabs the keys, staggers toward the stairwell.

Sweat pours down his face. His teeth are chattering.

The fourth key works. The stairwell is empty. Waldo stumbles up, fighting off nausea, gripping his laser in good and bad hands.

On floor 2 he pauses. He throws off his A-helmet, shrugs off his A-jacket, removes his A-pants. Takes off the black Army Navy boots and replaces them with his GOD shoes.

Now he stands in a GOD uniform marred only by some safety pins and smears of blood.

He opens the door marked 2, steps through it and is clubbed across the face.

Crying out, Waldo reeled to the side, clutching his face …
meanwhile he watched the laser gun twirl in his right forefinger,
then leave his hand.

He dropped to the floor. In a white cloud thick as cotton, Waldo
lay on a smooth, cool surface. He felt serene, even goofy.

He gave a strangled laugh at the picture above him: three A-cops,
visors down, images of black menace … clubs raised, tips fused in
a phosphorescent haze. They appeared solemn, priestly … Waldo
giggled and then choked as a club smashed his mouth.

Then the other clubs fell.

In some far-off part of his brain, Waldo saw the clubs descending.
He heard a *thuck … thuck … thuck* and felt a vague sensation of
pressure here and there. But he also had the impression that the
clubs were only approaching, not landing, in a slow methodical
rain that mesmerized him with their mathematical precision and
stately grace.

Meanwhile the cops themselves seemed to be shrinking,
modulating into something more remote and abstract. In fact they
didn't look like cops at all but rather beastly dwarves, hunched
and hairy, with insane yet mournful red eyes and snapping fangs.
Deep within Waldo's head, but at the same time all around him, he
heard a keening, grunting, and gnashing, mingled with deep
groans and long, high wails of terror that rose into shrieks of
startled, impossible pain. Meanwhile he remained peaceful,
contented beneath the rain of blows, grateful that he was finally
about to take his place among the damned.

He looked up at the creatures beating him and laughed, realizing
that he was finally seeing the Vermin in their true shape and
understanding that they held no grudge against him. Rather, they

were fulfilling their monotonous role again and again, sad-sack actors going through motions, working stiffs, disinterested ghosts.

They've been beating me forever

He lay there, a patient on an operating table, arms and legs spread as if nailed there … accepting the blows like gifts, each blow serving to strengthen him somehow. In a cool white cocoon he heard the gnashing and grunting, the moans and groans and screams blend into a single high, penetrating, insect buzz, a cold, electric white noise passing like a wind through the point between his eyes, and he felt his mouth spread in a smile.

Thuck

Thuck

Thuck

Waldo grinned through his teeth, seeing the clubs raised perfectly still above him, gazing without fear into the unfocused, distracted, strangely gentle and knowing faces of the bored beasts.

His body was expanding, opening like a flower toward the stunted, pathetic creatures and the clubs that he now desired with all his soul. Beyond the ring of clubs, within the phosphorescent glow where their tips fused, he saw Amutha's face floating, Amutha smiling, gazing into his eyes, shattering, graceful, his wife welcoming him home.

I love you, Waldo whispered.

To Amutha, to the beasts, to all the damned, all the angels, all the blind, uncomprehending souls twisting in purgatory. To Marty. To Molotov. To the Janes and the Johns. To his dead son. To all the dead.

I love you

The beasts vanished.

Waldo wakes on the second floor landing.

No cops. No beasts.

He sits. He sees no evidence of beating. His left hand has a hole in it but has stopped bleeding. His clothes look good. No safety pins. No blood. Just Waldo dressed in the crisp white uniform of a GOD delivery driver.

He doesn't know where his laser went. All he has is his squirtgun.

Waldo stands up. He is in a luminousness that blurs borders. His field of vision embraces vague shapes, glowing as if illuminated from within.

He ascends steps deliberately. He comes to a door marked 1.

His hand appears on the doorknob.

He enters a waiting area. A young man crouches behind a desk— staring, shivering. He holds a G20 but can't seem to raise it.

"Gary," Waldo says.

Gary's mouth opens and closes. No sound comes. Finally he nods —then, apparently relieved to find something working, nods again.

Behind Gary is an office door. A sign on it says LIGHT. Waldo gestures toward it with his PENIS.

"Is he in there?"

Gary gives the door a stricken look, nods.

"Alone?"

Nod.

Something shifts in Waldo's brain. His limbs relax. "Go."

Gary lurches toward the stairwell. His mouth opens again—nothing. He backs into the stairwell and vanishes.

Waldo turns toward the door. It opens into an office similar to Gate's, looking out on the Hollywood Hills.

A desk. A DEATH console. On the screen, a chemical formula scrolls past.

The office is deserted.

Waldo looks about, sees another door, unmarked. It opens into a stairwell. Here he encounters a security measure he's never seen before. What were once fifteen or twenty stairs have folded in on themselves, creating a flat, steeply inclined surface.

Waldo checks his water pistol. Half full. He steps to a water cooler and tops it off. Returns to the flattened stairs.

Waldo contemplates how to reach the next landing. He decides to let his futures choose.

Amutha's voice: *See, sweetheart*

CHUNK.

He rises and approaches a white door.

Levitating near the landing, Waldo tries the doorknob. Unlocked. He nudges the door forward. Light pours through the crack.

Waldo pushes the door open and floats past it. His feet settle on the floor like those of a practiced bird.

He stands before a blaze of light. His eyes adjust.

Sharply sloping walls end in a pyramid-shaped ceiling. The tip of the skyscraper.

The room contains three shimmering objects: a table and two chairs.

A man sits on one of the chairs. He's dressed in a white GOD suit. But in his case, the GOD logo is on the right breast, not the left, and it's not exactly aligned with Waldo's own.

He's Waldo.

Call them Waldo1 and Waldo2. Waldo2 is the person Waldo1 has been calling Richard Light, or Fish, or the Other.

Waldo1 has the feeling he's gazing into a mirror—reinforced by Waldo2's gestures, which imitate Waldo1's in subtle ways. As Waldo1 raises his right hand to wipe his forehead, Waldo2's left hand rises and rubs his chin. As an experiment, Waldo1 raises his left hand to his eyebrow. Waldo2 raises his right hand to his nose.

Waldo1 approaches the table slowly ... Waldo2 hunches forward, his face inscrutable. As Waldo1 draws near they both point toward the empty chair—Waldo1 with his right hand, Waldo2 with his left. Waldo1 sits in the chair and faces his Twin.

No, Waldo1 is wrong. Waldo2 isn't inscrutable. There's something in his eyes ... bitterness, melancholy ... an element of hot resentment. This is a profoundly human face, pinched with anxiety and—now that Waldo1 examines it closely—fear.

In fact, Waldo1 realizes he's the inscrutable one—he senses he's delivering the same dead reptilian gaze that he knew from John1 and Jane1. And indeed, he feels distant, arctic, inhuman—a sensation mingled with a flood of relief at finally having run this brutal gauntlet, along with a pleasurable stab of disdain at his brother for having failed to liquidate him.

Waldo1 points to Waldo2's hands. Waldo2 makes no gesture in return.

"You're not armed," Waldo1 says.

Waldo2 clears his throat. "It's not necessary."

Their voices sound alike, but not exactly.

They regard each other. Waldo1 grows uncomfortable. He gestures about the room. Waldo2's left arm does something similar but not the same.

"Nice place," Waldo1 says. "Odd decor."

"Yes. I come here to think." Waldo2 grins wryly. "Floor Zero, so to speak."

Waldo1 processes this.

Waldo2 looks bemused. "You did a nice job with the collapsed stairs."

Waldo1 tries to summon back his anger. But it feels out of place, grotesque even, given Waldo2's absence of resistance. Waldo1 has rehearsed this moment so often—this faceoff, this payback, good guy vs. bad guy. But now the lines he calls to memory have a stilted and self-conscious quality—the lines of a bad actor reciting a bad script.

Waldo1 glances at Waldo2's GOD logo and frowns. Waldo2 glances at Waldo1's GOD logo and chuckles.

"Guaranteed on time …. Happy New Year, Waldo."

Waldo1 ignores him. "What's going on."

Waldo2 looks perplexed. Then he cracks a strange, sad smile. "All right. Actually it makes sense. One thinks of so many B movies, with the villain revealing all at the end … though it does give one pause, seeing that you're the one calling the shots."

Waldo1 doesn't know what he means.

Waldo2 leans back in his chair. "Well. Where to begin."

Waldo1's vision wavers. "Amutha."

The light is intensifying, making Waldo2 grow fainter. But his face, somehow, is more visible than the rest of him.

Waldo1 produces a vial and swallows his last two Duadine. Waldo2 produces a vial and swallows two hits of Dr. Omega.

"I never should have succumbed to it," Waldo2 says.

"What do you mean."

"My desire to stop you. Especially"—his face grows anguished— "my willingness to engage in murder to do it."

Waldo2 grimaces. Waldo1 grins tautly for no reason.

Waldo1 could swear he hears sounds of battle—grunts, shouts, clangs of steel against steel … shrieks of agony.

"Looking back," Waldo2 says bitterly, "it's clear it was a setup. But it had got to the point"—he laughs, causing Waldo1 to cough —"where I couldn't take the suspense."

They study each other.

"I've watched you for years now," Waldo2 says, "waiting for a move. The whole thing was driving me insane. And then this *idea* came up, and it seemed the perfect thing." He shakes his head ruefully. "That was a setup too, of course."

Waldo1 comprehends. "Your idea," he says evenly. "It killed my wife."

Waldo2's face tightens with dread. "But you have to understand how desperate I was."

"No. I don't have to understand that." Waldo1 pulls out his water pistol and starts playing with it.

Waldo2's eyes cloud over.

"I guess you don't."

Silence. Waldo2 drums his fingers on the table, making Waldo1 do the same, but in a different rhythm.

"Marvin—Dr. Dark," Waldo2 says, "headed the Renaissance project at first—saw it through its infancy, before I realized what it was. But then, when I grasped the implications of the Fictionalizer, I knew that the person who possessed it would wield immense power—more than anyone else on the planet. Of course, Dark did too. He guessed rightly that I wanted him out of the picture."

"So he recruited me."

"Yes." Waldo2 is calm now, absorbed. "Apparently someone— Molotov is my guess—had caught his ear, and he grew convinced that you could help. So he gave you a few assignments to test your mettle. A mistake—you triggered alarms right away. We watched you via DEATH from the beginning."

"I see."

Waldo2's gaze wavers ... he looks about uncertainly. Waldo1 keeps his eyes on him.

"Anyhow, Gate came up with the idea of conning you into thinking Dark was trying to kill you. And I"—he studies Waldo1, throat working.

"I didn't think of the plan to kill your wife. But god help me, I approved it."

He wrings his hands. Waldo1 runs a forefinger along his gun's plastic barrel.

Waldo2 leans forward. Waldo1 scratches his ear.

Waldo2 is crying. "I'm so sorry … I know you can never forgive me. All I can do is apologize. Despite the wild rumors about me, I'd never committed any murders before. And I'd never approved any murders, not even tacitly. It goes against every value I have. I can't blame Gate. I was overcome by fear of you, and fear of Dark, and I did some monstrous things."

Waldo1 sobs. He rises and presses his water pistol between Waldo2's eyes. As if from above, he sees himself inserting the gun in his own mouth.

"You fuck! You fuck!" he shouts. He pulls the trigger.

Waldo2 doesn't blink as water runs down his nose and chin. He weeps freely while Waldo1 grins.

Waldo1 fires two more times. The squirts weaken. He keeps firing until almost no water is left.

Moaning, he pulls the gun back. "Why did you make me murder her!"

Waldo2 wipes away squirtgun water and tears. Waldo1 wipes snot from his nose and sits down.

"I knew from Molotov's file on you that you'd go after Dark," Waldo2 says. "Out of self-hatred if nothing else. I'd studied you a long time. And this plan had the advantage of … you know." Waldo2's face darkens. "We couldn't be sure how much you'd told her, or how much she'd sensed."

Waldo1 grits his teeth. Waldo2 tugs his right earlobe.

"And Marty?" Waldo1 says.

"As we'd planned, he heard noises upstairs and went to investigate. We guessed you wouldn't give him a chance to speak. You wouldn't have believed him anyway. One of Gate's men wrote the text message to your wife and planted your cell phone in his apartment."

Waldo1 points the squirtgun at Waldo2 again and pulls the trigger.

A trickle of water emerges. He curses and flings the PENIS away. It clatters across the floor and vanishes in the glare.

"Marty never knew a thing," Waldo2 tries to be reassuring. "We never talked to him. But at the time, we couldn't know whether you'd told him anything as well."

Waldo1 is following dully. "Then I'm killed at BioResearch."

"We let Dark know you were coming. The idea was that, if you killed him, you'd be shot trying to escape. If Dark killed you, he'd be arrested and killed in prison. Either way, everything would be taken care of."

"But you failed." Waldo1 seizes at a shred of triumph. "You didn't count on Molotov."

Waldo2 ponders this. "Actually I did—in a way. I'd been surveilling him too—the Duadine therapy made me suspicious. Then it struck me that he wasn't interested in keeping you stable. He was trying to—bring you out. So I had his office rigged with bugs and cameras. When I saw him show you those photos from the past, I knew I'd let it go on too long."

Waldo2 pauses, remembering. "I really was grateful to him. He was the only one who ever cared for me as a child. And my childhood was painful."

Waldo1 gnaws at his lip. Waldo2 shakes his head.

"I respected Molotov a lot," Waldo2 says. "I was interested in his research. But when I sensed he was about to expose me, it was clear we had to do something. Of course I couldn't tell Gate that. He'd learned too much about this project already. So I told him you'd informed Molotov about your activities, that the man had to go. And that whoever Gate sent should plant evidence leading to Dark in case you came there."

"Cleaning up."

"Yes, yes … but think of the consequences. We're dealing with a world-changing technology here. Literally. Of course, if I'd known about Molotov's association with Rebirth I'd have tripled our efforts."

Waldo1 shifts track. "Why tease me with the OR file. Why use a picture of yourself as a newborn for the block. Why use a Rebirth mantra for the check. And why use—HI DAD?"

"Believe me, brother." A sigh. "I didn't have a thing to do with OR. I never would have permitted that kind of security. In fact I tried to have it changed several times. But—*it*—repulsed me."

"Christ—what do you—"

"I mean," Waldo2 says, "the equations in there are incredibly advanced. I didn't invent the Fictionalizer—no one in my organization did."

Waldo1 knows what he's about to say.

"Joey invented the Fictionalizer, Waldo. Your son."

Waldo2 continues: "I couldn't believe it when it happened. It was not long after you wired Joey to DEATH. I was going over tax records and found what looked like garbled data. I sent for someone to look at it, but even as I waited it began to—change. The technician couldn't identify the problem, so he simply erased the garbled section … but when I looked the next morning it was back—and larger. I watched for about an hour … watched it take over the file like some kind of mold. It was disturbing—the organic way it changed, sending out creeping tentacles of data, pulling other data in … I sensed that no human at a console was doing this. So we threw up a security net and watched for several weeks.

"We destroyed it several times. But it always returned, usually larger—clearly it was hiding copies of itself in the network. And the more we tried to kill it, the more viruses infected the system, some of them catastrophic … it became clear they were intended as punishments. So we gave up and looked on.

"Eventually, one of our techs did more than that. He found a way to trace the file to its source. Over several weeks, we tracked it back, past decoys, encrypted sites, cul-de-sacs … through an incredibly intricate maze of systems and subsystems to your DEATH console—and the interface to Joey's brain.

"As we did this the entity in the DEATH network began posting early versions of the formula—rough drafts, so to speak. Each one seemed to build on the previous one, but none were complete. Joey arranged for the drafts to be buried well outside the Operation Renaissance file, so you never detected them—but we ran across them, in what seemed like an accident at the time. Looking back, I realize it wasn't an accident."

"Why would Joey do that?" Waldo1 wonders.

"I suspect he wanted to distract us but not you. In any case it took me some time to learn that Gate was experimenting with the drafts."

Waldo2 collects his thoughts.

"It's not so strange, really," he continues. "Joey had a very good reason to—give birth—to those equations."

"Christ."

Silence.

"Do you know," Waldo2 says quietly, "how lacerating, how crushing, how unspeakably excruciating it is to grow up an outcast? You may not"—he places a queer emphasis on the word *may*—"but I do. I know how Joey felt. And I'm convinced that he created the Fictionalizer because he wanted a change. He wanted to become—a normal boy."

Waldo1 sobs. Waldo2 sighs.

"Of course, the complexity, the parameters of a new physical body and personality and actions will depend on the complexity of the description—the text. But I suspect that with a complete enough suggestion one could arrive at a reasonable approximation of a human being ... at least a closer one than Joey was."

Waldo1 lurches forward. "But he died!"

"Don't be a fool. Whether he was alive or dead made no difference and he knew it. All he could hope was that whoever finally controlled the Fictionalizer would care enough to resurrect him."

Waldo1 thinks it through. "Joey saw the future."

"Yes. And even more than that, he may have had an ability to … *manipulate* events, create the future, or a bit of it at least. Who knows, maybe everything you and I have been doing over the past two months has been scripted in advance."

The shining face of Waldo2 comes closer and says: "Maybe all we've gone through is the angry, fevered, despairing lucid dream of a frightened child."

At this point Waldo1 can barely see his brother. In fact he could swear he's talking to himself.

What about Amy.

That was terrible. Tragic. I apologize from the bottom of my heart. My team allowed a trigger-happy younger agent to carry a PHALLUS, and he got excited. I fired him this morning. You have to understand that I don't have that many security men. Why would a corporate executive need a private army? I don't think I have more than twenty A-police nationwide.

What about the TV report I saw? What about the New York Times *article?*

I'm not sure what reports you're referring to, but I suspect you hallucinated at least parts of them. You're a dangerous paranoid schizophrenic psychotic, Waldo. Didn't you know that? You have at least two personalities—and the Duadine has made things much worse. Who knows how many identities are swarming around inside you now.

I've killed dozens of your men.

Impossible. If you really believe that, most of what you've experienced has been hallucinated. You've watched too many action/adventure movies. Please understand that I basically run a holding company. It's not an interesting job. We don't have many laser guns—maybe four. Then Gate had one. They're very hard to get. But it's true that you killed three of my employees—though one may have died due to friendly fire. Still, I'm annoyed about it. They were working men. Wives, kids, mortgages. Lives. One bowled in tournaments. Another tutored kids in math on the side. What do I say to the widows? That my bodyguards were cut apart by lasers?

I'm sorry. I am. But what about the lobby downstairs? It was crawling with A-cops. There were even more outside your building.

No ... they weren't there, Waldo. I didn't have any reason to create an armed camp. I think there were three men in the lobby, along with a security guard. I had a few men posted on the other main floors—48, 24, 3. But that's it. If I really had that many men in the lobby, you and your colleague would have been killed in the elevator, don't you think? I was watching the security cameras as you rose to the next floors. It was pretty strange to see you shooting your laser at nonexistent targets.

I don't know if you've thought about it, but a Glock 20's magazine holds fifteen bullets. If you've already chambered one bullet, that's sixteen. Yet in your gun battle at Cybersystems in Chicago you were spitting off automatic rounds like there was no tomorrow. Or so you thought. It reminds me of that Rambo movie that takes place in Vietnam. What's it called?

First Blood Part II.

Right. Anyhow, Rambo has a limitless amount of ammunition in that film. It's never explained. Which brings to mind ... did you or your supporters ever stop to buy more G20 ammo during your trip here?

I ... can't remember.

Hmm.

But Amy. She was fighting.

No. She appeared to be tolerating you, as I expect she always did. She seemed practiced in staying out of your way when you held a real gun. I don't think she fired a shot.

I don't believe you. What about Gate? He had a big squad.

It's true that Gate recruited some men and dressed them up as A-police. I suspect he bought SWAT uniforms at a surplus store and sewed A's on their backs. I had no control over it, and I didn't control his experiments either. But one of my techs gained access to his HR file. He didn't have that many security men. Maybe six.

Gate told me the OR file just protected some nonsense characters.

No. Those characters were the completed formula, and once you broke through, Gate tried to synthesize it.

Gate gave me the impression he'd been working on the Fictionalizer for some time.

It's true he'd been experimenting, but he made no real progress until December 29, when you cracked the final check in OR. By the time he kidnapped you, his synthesis team had been working on the completed formula for only 48 hours. In his haste to get a final product, Gate was ordering testing way too soon, and they were making mistakes.

Did they make a mistake with Molotov?

I don't know. I have a feeling they didn't.

But the protesters at Biotechnics in Colorado Springs—I thought they were trying to stop the use of humans in Fictionalizer experiments.

You misread that. Work on early drafts of the formula had begun only recently—within the past month or so—and as you know, it didn't all take place at Biotechnics. But Gate had a lot of black biochemical projects under way, and some of them used human subjects. Biotechnics was a center for this activity. The tests had been going on for years without my knowledge.

Why couldn't you control Gate?

Think about it. What do security chiefs do? They collect dirt on people. Gate held some compromising information about me—incidents from when I was younger and flush with material success. I couldn't just fire him. But things looked desperate. I couldn't let Gate gain control of the perfected Fictionalizer. I instructed Whitmore to send the final product directly to me, but I couldn't be sure he would. Who knows how much money Gate had spread around? Given Dr. Molotov's awful experience with the Fictionalizer, it seemed that Whitmore might have sent the formula to Gate as well. So I was pleased when you settled the matter.

You sent the message on the DEATH console? About getting rid of Gate?

Yes.

This is stupid. It's strange that you—Fish—couldn't do a better job dealing with me. Couldn't you have just given me a phone call? Or maybe a telepathic command?

My god. You think I'm Fish? Really? I'm not anything close to Fish.

Then who was resisting me? We were fighting psychic dragnets the whole way here—or so I was told.

That could be, but I wasn't doing it.

What about the Vermin? The black things? Where did they come from?

I suspect they're a dark aspect of your psyche that manifests itself under pressure. Something the hidden part or parts of your personality send to frighten and discourage the conscious part of you. And as for the vast, diabolical entity resisting you—the Bad Guy, the Evildoer, the Villain, the Mad Scientist—I suspect it's you.

What?

You're a complicated person, Waldo ... you, the anti-you ... Marvin Gomez's handler or handlers ... the Rebirth Executive Council ... I've done very little the entire time. It's true that I have some talents, but the best I've done lately is to read some minds. My abilities are minimal and failing.

But you repelled Rebirth agents. Drove them crazy ....

No. All I've ever desired is worldly power. I'm a businessman—a decent one, I like to think. But I'm not a paranormal warrior. The most I ever did to Rebirth was send out men to intercept their assassins. If people are going insane long-distance, someone else is doing it. And if I'm being protected long-distance, the same applies.

But—who is Fish, then?

C'mon, brother. You know who Fish is.

Waldo1 feels a throbbing between his eyes.

Even before we were born, I believe that you—or rather, the Fish hiding inside you—understood the opposition you'd encounter. Rebirth is an enemy to be reckoned with. So Fish decided to decoy them. It invented me to take them off the scent. It gave me a spectacular interdimensional entrance, a foreboding adolescence, a position of preeminence and power. It also threw a magnificent energy field around me—one I could never tap. And it defended me to create the illusion that I was capable of defending myself.

Meanwhile, Fish remained concealed in the body of another child —buried so deep that even the child was unaware of it. For that child, everything that occurred to him appeared to be a product of will or luck or chance. But in fact, Fish was behind it all, writing that child's history.

No.

Yes, brother. I suspected it for a long time. When I traced OR to Joey I grew convinced of it. But I couldn't bring myself not to pursue the Fictionalizer—it meant too much. I hoped you'd miscalculated somewhere, given me too much power. I bought the eyes and ears of every member of Rebirth I could—without, at the time, knowing you controlled the secret leadership—and used my telepathic abilities when possible. But I still feared you—and tried, foolishly, to destroy you. Now I wonder whether even my attack on you was part of your plan. Because you had everything planned.

It's terrible to realize that everything one does in one's life, every word, every action—one's physical appearance even—are preordained. But the moment you entered this room I knew, finally, that you had arranged every moment of our lives. I imagine you even arranged for that revelation.

But why would I make the whole thing so difficult? Why wouldn't I just produce the Fictionalizer and use it? Why would I make it so hard to get to this place? Why would I make so many innocent people die?

As I believe a friend of yours once said: "Even the darkest of fallen angels can suddenly turn into a creature of light." From a practical perspective, it's the best decoy imaginable—posing as an average, pitiful human battling a powerful twin. But really ... in the past day or so, beginning to despair of stopping you, and looking at the destruction you and I have wreaked ... I've been wondering—what's the point? Then it occurred to me: maybe you, deep down, were undecided—and fighting your own worst self or selves every step of the way.

Have you ever meditated on a crucifixion scene, Waldo? I believe you have. Almost every culture throughout history has revered a man-child torn apart on a cross. Jesus Christ is one of many examples. The cross is often associated with the pineal gland—the organ located between and just above the eyes. In any case, as I believe you also know, that man-child is often called the Big Man.

Stare at the figure long enough, and one understands that the Big Man never died for us—He took each and every one of us inside Him, swallowed and absorbed us, and the cross He struggles and shrieks on is the cross of our rage and longing, our sin and despair and endless yearning. Every bellow of rage, every murder, every atrocity, every hope, hunger and regret—each is another nail in the body of the Big Man. The Big Man is the sum total of human fear and desire—and for some reason beyond human understanding, He must navigate this Byzantine pathway to find peace.

You're aware, maybe, of a certain theory regarding Fish—that it isn't one thing but all things, that it isn't one person but all people, all entities throughout time and space. Like the characters in a novel, all facets of the personality of the Author. And I've been thinking—what if Fish has been killing off parts of itself? Tearing out diseased elements? Burning itself, purifying itself through violence, terror and torment, preparing itself for this meeting that may not—let's admit—be a meeting at all, in this room that may or may not have existed until Fish stepped through the door?

Who knows what twisted tracks the soul must take to find itself? What if Fish, finally humble, is imitating the Big Man—or indeed, has become Him?

A hand appeared through the glare … Waldo1 felt a *sizzle* between his eyes.

The hand opened … in the palm was a small white pill.

Waldo1 took the pill. The hand retreated into the light.

"Time for me to eat this," Waldo2 murmured.

Waldo1 nodded.

Waldo2 opened his mouth …. Waldo1 saw the smooth tube of the throat.

Waldo2's tongue unrolled. Waldo1 placed the pill in his mouth.

Waldo2 swallowed.

They waited. After a while Waldo2's eyelids began to flutter.

He leaned forward, closing his eyes.

"Now, brother," Waldo2 whispered. "Tell me what the world is to be."

Year 1, Day 63

Though Amutha and I are ostensibly rulers of the Interdimensional Federation, there's little to do at our palace here in Bora Bora. The universe does fine without us. The inhabitants are happy in their new forms, the former living and the former dead.

I sit on a veranda overlooking our beach. The sun hovers above the horizon. Somewhere, steel drums play.

I pass a hand before my face, watching trails of light follow my fingers.

Amutha emerges onto the veranda, dressed in a white cover-up over a blue bikini. She places a white rose in a jade green vase. Shading her eyes with a hand, she peers down the beach.

In the distance, Marty throws a Frisbee to Marvin and some former A-cops. Lounging on beach chairs, the former John1 (Alex) and the former John Prime (Peter) chat and sip drinks. Amy and others in the former Rebirth crew play volleyball, while others levitate two or three feet above their mandala mats.

Amutha glances back and points. "See."

A cement walkway leads down to the ocean. On it, Molotov is teaching Joey to ride a red bicycle.

Joey has inserted a sound maker in the back wheel: *clack clack clack*. Molotov staggers about in mock fatigue.

"Had your fill?" I shout.

Molotov swipes his black hair back while sucking at a cigar through a handsome set of teeth.

"Never! He's getting it!"

I set my piña colada down on a white metal table and press a button on a console beside me.

The sun begins to set.

Joey waves and leaps off his bike. He runs toward me, a handsome boy with sandy hair, just turned five.

The spitting image of his father, everyone says.

"Hi, dad!" he laughs.

Michael Schulze

Anna Maria Island
Hollywood
New York City
Boston
1981-2022

With thanks to the National Endowment for the Arts, ITT, and the Fulbright Program

Born and raised in the U.S. Midwest, *Michael Schulze* earned an MA in English and moved to Boston, where he played rock and roll in clubs. At this time he began expanding his first novel, *Love Song* (available on Kindle). Later he received grants from the National Endowment for the Arts and ITT (via the Fulbright program), both of which helped him write early drafts of *The Fictionalizer*. Schulze served for many years as Vice President of Editorial Services for the H.W. Wilson publishing company, where he managed about 200 people in New York and Dublin. He also helped launch the business magazine *World Tour*, served as Senior Editor for *Robb Report*, and taught many young writers.

The cover image for *The Fictionalizer* was created by *Scy Heidekamp* of Seyhan Lee, a Boston-based creative and production agency that uses artificial intelligence to create startling and powerful images and motion pictures for brands, musicians and other artists. The agency, which has won many prestigious design awards, was founded by *Gary Lee Koepke*, one of the top designers and creative directors in the world, and *Pinar Seyhan Demirdag*, a multidisciplinary artist and creative director who is an early adopter of A.I. visual technologies. Her works have been shown at and acquired by several international museums.

Artist and musician *Michael Thoresen*, who assisted in the design of the cover for *The Fictionalizer*, has collaborated with the author on various creative projects over the years, including the novel *Love Song*, designing the cover and creating the graphic portion of the book. Schulze, Koepke, and Thoresen also co-wrote songs for their musical adventures with the rock bands The Parapsychics (Kalamazoo) and The Bricks (Boston). Thoresen lives and works in Ann Arbor, Michigan. You can view his paintings and drawings on Instagram. @michaeljthoresen.

Michael Schulze

CPSIA information can be obtained
at www.ICGtesting.com
Printed in the USA
BVHW052329291122
652251BV00005B/20/J